AGED FOR ACRIMONY

(A Tuscan Vineyard Cozy Mystery—Book Six)

FIONA GRACE

Fiona Grace

Fiona Grace is author of the LACEY DOYLE COZY MYSTERY series, comprising nine books (and counting); of the TUSCAN VINEYARD COZY MYSTERY series, comprising six books (and counting); of the DUBIOUS WITCH COZY MYSTERY series, comprising three books (and counting); of the BEACHFRONT BAKERY COZY MYSTERY series, comprising six books (and counting); and of the CATS AND DOGS COZY MYSTERY series, comprising six books.

Fiona would love to hear from you, so please visit www.fionagraceauthor.com to receive free ebooks, hear the latest news, and stay in touch.

CHAPTER ONE

Summoned by the ringing phone, Olivia Glass rushed into her boss's office. Scooting around the desk, she sat hurriedly down—not in the visitor's seat where she was used to being, but in Marcello Vescovi's own comfortable and well-worn leather chair. With its generous size and high back, Marcello's chair felt slightly too big for her. So did her new role, although she was trying her best to grow into it.

When she'd been hired as sommelier last summer, she'd never dreamed that she'd end up being promoted to manage the whole of La Leggenda in Marcello's absence. He had recently embarked on an educational mentorship at a leading Chianti vineyard, and while he was away, he'd put Olivia in charge.

It had been a few weeks, and she'd managed to cope with everything that came her way. So far, at any rate.

Grabbing the trilling phone, she made sure to have a smile in her voice as she said, "*Salve!*"

She hoped the person on the other end of the line wasn't going to speak too fast. Although her language skills were improving, she still struggled with rapid-fire Italian.

"*Salve,* Olivia!"

Olivia was thrilled to recognize Elana's voice. She was one of her favorite customers, who owned a busy wine store in an exquisite village in the local area of Tuscany. Elana sold so many of La Leggenda's red wines that Olivia was convinced some of the villagers bathed in it.

"It's lovely to speak to you. What can I send you today?" she continued in slow, but she hoped accurate, Italian. She reached for the notepad and pen on the shiny mahogany desk, ready to write the order down.

"I need four cases of Miracolo red, four cases of the new Foculare blend, and four cases of the sangiovese, *grazie*," Elana said.

"What about a case of the vermentino white?" Olivia suggested, just in case she could further improve this already excellent order. After all, spring is around the corner."

1

Elana laughed. "You have sold me! We are soon likely to see a demand for lighter wines."

Pushing back her shoulder-length blond hair, Olivia scribbled down the items.

"How is Gucci?" When they last spoke, Elana had mentioned that she'd recently adopted a small brown pavement-special dog from the shelter near Florence.

"Gucci is too cute! He is such an adorable boy," Elana replied enthusiastically.

"I can't wait to see him," Olivia said, hoping she might be able to make the delivery personally, if there was time in the afternoon. Otherwise, Antonio would handle this local drop-off. "We will bring your wine before five p.m."

As she put the phone down, Olivia heard pounding feet from the tasting room.

She looked up, frowning as the footsteps grow louder. Someone was sprinting down the corridor in her direction. Either they were in urgent need of one of the restrooms at the end of the passage, or more worryingly, they were in urgent need of *her*.

Sure enough, a moment later, her assistant vintner, Jean-Pierre, skidded to a stop outside her open office door. The tall, tousle-haired Frenchman looked panicked. His eyes were wide and he was waving his arms frantically.

Clearly, there was an emergency.

"What is it?" Olivia leaped to her feet, filled with concern. For about the hundredth time since she'd been put in charge, she wished Marcello was around. Whatever this crisis was, it would rest on her shoulders to solve. If only she had more mileage under her belt! But she was only thirty-four, and had been working at La Leggenda for less than a year. Marcello was forty, and had a lifetime of experience, having grown up on the family-owned winery.

"Olivia, come quickly. We have a huge problem!" Flinging his arms as far apart as they would go, Jean-Pierre dramatically illustrated the size of the problem.

Racing from behind the desk, Olivia was hot on Jean-Pierre's heels as he hurtled back down the corridor. The small group of tourists seated at the polished wooden counter in the tasting room turned to stare in surprise. Olivia didn't have time to do more than give them a quick smile as she powered her way across the tiled floor and into the warm and welcoming lobby.

Her heart was pounding, and not just from the sudden exercise. How did Marcello always manage to stay so calm when unexpected disasters landed?

In the lobby, Jean-Pierre skidded to a halt.

"Here is our problem!" he announced breathlessly.

To Olivia's surprise, the young sommelier gestured toward the enormous statue that had been installed just a few weeks ago. The stone monstrosity featured a tall, muscular man, stark naked apart from a large bunch of strategically positioned grapes, which he clutched in his muscle-bound fingers.

The expensive eyesore was a blight in the otherwise tastefully decorated lobby. Unfortunately, it had been gifted to the winery by a grateful billionaire after he'd been a suspect in a murder and Olivia had helped to clear his name.

Olivia stared at the statue doubtfully.

"Well, I know it's a problem," she said, wondering why Jean-Pierre had only appreciated the full horror of the edifice at this late stage.

The team at La Leggenda didn't agree on much. With so many varied personalities, how could they? Marcello hardly ever saw eye to eye with his younger siblings, Nadia and Antonio. And if there was a decision to make, it was written into law that Gabriella, the restaurant manager, would take the opposite view to Olivia and argue it to the bitter end.

Despite their differences, every single person at La Leggenda had been unanimous that this statue, titled *The Love of Wine*, was an embarrassment of note. They'd agreed it must be moved to a remote corner of the winery sooner, rather than later.

The only problem was that the winery's customers had instantly fallen in love with it!

It had become the official selfie station within a day. Older tourists nodded approvingly at its size and grandeur. Younger customers took shots of themselves doing suggestive things with the grapes.

After seeing this, Olivia's marketing background had prompted her to place La Leggenda branding behind the statue. If the horrible thing had to remain in the lobby, it could at least bring them exposure when shared on social media.

"No, no. The problem is not the statue itself," Jean-Pierre elaborated.

"What is it, then?" Olivia asked curiously.

"Listen!" her assistant vintner whispered in theatrical tones.

Over the hum of voices from the tasting room, Olivia picked up a persistent buzzing sound. It seemed to emanate from nearby.

A few small flecks sped past her, heading busily outside.

As Olivia's shocked brain put two and two together, Jean-Pierre hissed out, "Bees!"

"Bees?" Olivia repeated, her mind reeling with disbelief. This was not one of the challenges she'd expected to face.

Now she could see more and more of the little flecks, whizzing in and out, dark spots against the bright light outside.

"A swarm of bees has arrived," Jean-Pierre elaborated, "and has made its home in the statue's... er... behind the grapes," he finished, blushing slightly.

"Behind the grapes?" Perplexed, Olivia moved closer, tilting her head as she peered behind the clump of stone grapes.

Loud giggling distracted her. Two teenage girls, walking into the winery with their parents, were pointing at her, sniggering helplessly with mirth. Olivia's improper actions had clearly tickled their adolescent funny bones.

Hastily she moved away, blushing even more than Jean-Pierre. But what she'd seen was enough. She had glimpsed a dark mass of insects nestled in that stony crevice.

For the hundred and first time, she wished Marcello was here.

"You had better go and attend to the guests. I'll figure out what to do," Olivia said.

Jean-Pierre sprinted into the tasting room and shimmied behind the counter.

"Welcome to La Leggenda," her young assistant greeted the new arrivals, placing tasting sheets in front of them with a flourish.

Olivia was proud of his calmness. Meanwhile, she was panicking inside. She couldn't allow any more guests to walk through the lobby. It was a danger zone. What if the bees swarmed again and somebody got stung?

She had to call a bee removal company as quickly as possible. And in the meantime she had to make sure that the guests stayed safe.

Were bees attracted to wine? With her eyes just about popping out of her head, Olivia imagined what would happen if the swarm headed into the tasting room to try the latest vintages! You didn't need much imagination to *know* that there would be at least one guest there with a serious allergy, she thought, feeling stressed.

4

Quickly, Olivia pulled the side doors closed, breathing a sigh of relief as the bees' route into the tasting room was blocked. Now, she had to make sure no guests entered the lobby. Taking a selfie next to the statue would be a dangerous move at this point.

She grabbed the mahogany table inside the lobby and dragged it across the wide entrance door. There! It blocked the space perfectly. Now, she needed to organize an alternative access point for guests to use. The only other possibility was the restaurant.

Feeling nervous, Olivia headed across the paved parking lot to break the bad news to Gabriella, who just happened to be her personal nemesis.

Gabriella was already peering inquiringly out of the restaurant doorway. Her tawny hair, knotted up in an artful bun, was so thoroughly sprayed it didn't move at all in the light breeze.

"What's going on? Why did you just close the doors to the lobby?" she asked.

Her tone was combative, implying she would never have done such a thing if *she* was in charge.

Gabriella had been outraged by the fact that Olivia had been chosen over her to manage the winery. She'd sulked for weeks after Marcello had made his decision, barely speaking to Olivia.

Now, Olivia knew she'd have to be as diplomatic as possible. She wished she could be honest with Gabriella, and confess to her that managing the winery, while a massive learning curve, also included bucket-loads of stress and punishing hours.

In fact, her long weekend off, which began tomorrow, would be the first time away she'd had since Marcello had left. She felt guilty about taking three whole days of leave, but it had to be done, because she was exhibiting her first batch of homemade wine at the upcoming Festa del Vino in Siena.

Appreciating the sensitivity of her relationship with Gabriella, Olivia made sure to be extra polite and respectful as she explained the current problem.

"There's a swarm of bees in the statue. Will it be all right with you if guests use the restaurant entrance until we can move them?"

"Bees?" Gabriella wrinkled her perfectly made-up nose incredulously, as if Olivia had somehow managed to attract this hazard.

Olivia nodded. "I'm going to print signage to redirect the guests now, and then try and find a bee removal company to take them away."

Gabriella thought about that for a minute, staring at Olivia disapprovingly.

Then she shrugged. "You can do so, but I think you will be very stupid," she announced.

Trying not to gape at her, Olivia bit back a snappish retort. Stupid? How could it be stupid to remove a swarm of bees that was a huge danger to visitors? Olivia felt steam coming out of her ears as she fumed over this insulting reply.

Then, managing to get control of her emotions, Olivia decided it would be better to ask what Gabriella meant. The words were deliberately rude, but that didn't mean she had to rise to the bait. Plus, there must be logic somewhere behind them.

This was a career challenge, she thought. She could either start a fight, or she could have a sensible conversation. The choice was hers.

"What do you think we should do instead?" she asked.

Gabriella shrugged. "It's obvious, isn't it? We should keep the bees. Just move them somewhere safe. After all, they have chosen us! And organic honey is one of the products at Castello di Verrazzano, where Marcello is doing his mentorship. I believe it's very popular with visitors. Now we can have some, too."

Olivia felt stunned by the elegance of this solution.

"That's brilliant!" she exclaimed. "Thank you, Gabriella!"

Gabriella's heavily mascaraed eyes widened. She tried to suppress a pleased smile, but couldn't.

"Don't mess it up," she said, regaining control of her usual pout. "If I had been in charge, I would offer to help. But I am not, and my oven is pinging."

She turned and marched into the kitchen.

Delighted that the bees would serve a constructive purpose, Olivia rushed into the tasting room to update Jean-Pierre.

"Guests must come and go through the restaurant. I'll put up signs now," she stage-whispered.

Jean-Pierre gave a quick nod before returning to the group he was serving, and Olivia speed-walked back to Marcello's office. Would he mind that she was going ahead and installing a hive without his permission? Should she call him and ask? Then she remembered that he had told her all decisions on the winery's running were in her hands.

"I have faith in your abilities, Olivia," he'd said. His words of praise had warmed her.

Now, she'd have to do her best to live up to his high opinion. Her mind was whirling with the logistics of this new project. Where would the best place be—or rather, bee—for the hive to make their home? Antonio was most familiar with the layout of the large, sprawling property. He should be able to suggest a secluded spot within La Leggenda's hilly two hundred acres that the colony would enjoy, she decided.

And a hive? They'd need some kind of wooden box to house them in. How would she get that at short notice? Olivia fretted, as she printed out the signs.

In a flash, she thought about the old wooden wine barrels, emptied and scrubbed clean, which were going to be repurposed as planters. A sawn-in-half barrel could make the perfect home for their new adopted insect family. Antonio could cut a hole in it, put a roof on, and place it on a stand or table. She was sure the bees would think this was luxury accommodations!

Olivia was starting to feel more and more excited as she searched through the local listings, looking for a company that could relocate the bees. Marcello would be so pleased to learn about this new venture, she thought. But she must be sure to credit Gabriella, who'd thought of it, and not take the glory for herself.

As Olivia reached again for the sleek black phone, she felt pleased that she was on top of things again, and not too badly put out by this unexpected event.

But then she saw movement in the doorway. Glancing up at the person standing there, Olivia felt her mouth fall open in horror. The phone clattered out of her hand and fell onto Marcello's leather-bound year planner.

On top of things? What a joke! She'd just made the most terrible, unforgivable mistake.

CHAPTER TWO

"Charlotte!" Olivia's voice was squeaky with shock. Her cheeks burned with confusion as she stared at her round-faced, russet-haired friend. Beaming back at her, Charlotte didn't look angry. But she should be, Olivia thought. What a dreadful mess-up she'd made. After looking forward to her friend's flying visit ever since Charlotte had told her about it, she'd clean forgotten about fetching her from the airport.

"It totally slipped my mind that you were arriving today," Olivia confessed in wobbly tones.

Charlotte wove her way nimbly around the desk and embraced Olivia in a huge bear hug.

Being nearly a head shorter than Olivia and a few pounds plumper, Charlotte was the most huggable friend Olivia knew. It was just one of her many awesome qualities, together with her huge heart, mischievous sense of humor—and, clearly, her ability to get herself to La Leggenda even when her friend forgot all about her, Olivia thought, feeling mortified all over again.

When Olivia reluctantly let go of her beloved bestie, she saw that Charlotte didn't seem angry, and was in fact laughing.

"You sent me a text first thing this morning saying 'See you tomorrow,'" she said.

"Yes, I did," Olivia admitted.

"Together with your descriptions of how frantic you've been, and the fact that your last two emails were sent after midnight Italian time, I realized that you had way too much on your mind to remember about an airport trip. And probably not enough time to do it anyway."

"I have been busy," Olivia admitted, sternly reminding herself that this was still no excuse.

"In any case, my reason for taking this trip was to write some Top Ten articles for one of the websites I manage," Charlotte reminded her teasingly. "That's why it's tax-deductible, remember? So I organized a rental car and headed off to one of the local towns, and I've already got all the content I need for 'Top Ten Gelato Flavors in Tuscany.'" She beamed.

"Are you sure?" Olivia frowned.

"Of course I'm sure. Absolute top of the list, number one without any doubt, is chocolate hazelnut. Closely followed by panna cotta and pear, lemon basil, café mocha, and blood orange."

"Panna cotta and pear sounds amazing," Olivia agreed, distracted from her own failings by these mouthwatering flavors.

"So, after my late gelato lunch, I'm now thirsty. I'm going to head back to your tasting room and meet Jean-Pierre, and taste some wine. And then when you're done, we can catch up properly."

"I won't be long," Olivia promised, relieved that Charlotte wasn't angry with her, and in fact that everything had worked out well. What a stroke of luck! She felt delighted that she'd have her best friend's company this evening at the farmhouse. Thank goodness she'd made up the spare room in a rush of excitement as soon as Charlotte had called to say she was planning to visit.

Charlotte headed for the tasting counter, and Olivia returned to her urgent Project Bee Relocation. She felt excited all over again that these surprise visitors, which had been the first of two unexpected arrivals that day, would hopefully form the foundation for La Leggenda's own hives.

*

It was late afternoon, with the beginnings of a brilliant, glowing sunset, when Olivia and Charlotte headed out into the estate to admire the new hive. Antonio had located it in a remote field, under a gnarled hazel tree, surrounded by wild lavender.

"I've never seen such pretty housing," Charlotte said, sounding impressed. "Never mind the exquisite venue, having them live in an old wine barrel is so appropriate. It looks so cozy and solid. I'm sure they'll like it better than the statue."

"They still look sleepy from the smoke, but the removal people said they'd be fine when they woke up," Olivia said. "I hope they love it here, and tell their friends."

She snapped a few photos on her phone and sent a quick message to Marcello.

"We had some unexpected visitors arrive at the winery. Gabriella had the brilliant idea to keep them on the estate so we can start producing honey. Look at the beautiful hive Antonio made. Otherwise, everything is well here. Hope you are having a great time—speak soon."

Pleased that she'd updated her boss on the successful start to their new venture, Olivia put her phone away.

"What kind of bees are they?" Charlotte asked.

"They're normal Italian bees. Gentle in behavior, and very easy to keep." Olivia giggled. "The beekeeper who removed them said the only problem with Italian bees is that they have a terrible sense of direction!"

"I bet they don't pull over and ask for help either," Charlotte snorted. "Oh, look, here's Erba."

Olivia's adopted goat had capered over to join them when they'd passed the goat dairy. She'd been distracted by a lush rosemary bush, but after sampling it, had caught up again.

Now, the small, orange-and-white goat pushed her head against Charlotte's leg, clearly delighted to have her old friend back again. Charlotte rubbed the goat's head lovingly.

"I'm sure Erba remembers me," she said.

"Of course she does. You are part of her family," Olivia said. "I often talk to her and tell her how her aunt in the USA is doing. Well, now that the bees are sorted out, shall we head home?"

"Do you think Erba would ride in my rental car?" Charlotte said as they turned to stroll down the hill and rejoin the pathway that led back to the winery.

Olivia sighed. "You would struggle to keep her out. She loves cars. Is there room for her in the back seat with your luggage?"

"Yes, it's all in the trunk. I decided to go for a roomier vehicle than Option One, which I took last time," Charlotte said, pointing to the slightly bigger Fiat parked near the winery's doors.

Olivia opened the back door and Erba sprang obediently inside.

"Wow!" Charlotte said.

Olivia couldn't help feeling a thrill of pride at her intelligent, self-trained goat.

Charlotte drove out of the winery and turned left, taking the short but scenic route to Olivia's farmhouse.

As they drove, Olivia felt as if she were looking with fresh eyes at the surrounding scenery. Early spring was a particularly beautiful time, she decided. Everything was lush and green after the winter rains, grass was growing wild, the sky looked washed clean, and trees that had been dramatically bare in the colder months were now sprouting bright green young leaves. The whole landscape was infused with a brilliant energy and hope. And so was she! As spring started to blossom, Olivia was reminded how happy she felt to have taken the huge leap into this exciting new life.

Perhaps it was living in the countryside that made her feel so connected to her environment, Olivia thought. After all, back in Chicago, her surroundings had been so urban that the closest she'd come to enjoying spring some years was noticing blossoms on the roadside trees.

"I've missed this place," Charlotte enthused. "It's so good to be back. I feel I have a natural affinity with this part of the world. Perhaps I should move here?"

Olivia's heart leaped. Imagine if her best friend came to Tuscany full time?

"You'd have to bring your adopted cat," she said.

"Bagheera would love it, too. He's an adaptable animal. He settled straight into the cattery yesterday."

Then, as they drove through the open, rusty gates of her farmhouse, Charlotte let out a shriek.

Olivia glanced sideways, wondering if Erba had tugged at a mouthful of her friend's hair. It was a very naughty trick she did occasionally to entertain herself. But Erba was perched obediently on the back seat. Charlotte was staring ahead with an amazed look in her wide, expressive eyes.

"Your farm! YOUR FARM!" Charlotte cried.

"What about it?" The Fiat's wheels scrunched onto the driveway, which Olivia had recently covered with neat pea gravel, as she craned her neck to see what the problem was. Was her house on fire? She was relieved to see it looked fine.

"I don't believe this. I need to take it all in."

Charlotte hit the brakes and, to Olivia's astonishment, jumped out. Olivia climbed out too, followed by Erba, who trotted ahead, enjoying the excitement.

Charlotte paced along the drive, gesturing expansively at the surroundings.

"This was a dump last time I came here. A dump! And now, look at it. You have beautifully trimmed grass. And flower beds lining the drive. Is that our grapevine plantation there? We put those seeds in the ground last summer, and now they're small plants. It doesn't seem possible."

Olivia felt a thrill of joy. How wonderful that her friend was seeing such a difference. Slogging along day after day, she barely noticed the

11

improvements that were slowly taking place. Thank goodness Danilo, her handsome new boyfriend who lived in the local area, had noted the jungle-like state of her garden, and had kindly offered to bring his ride-on lawnmower last weekend.

Danilo had spent the afternoon taming the grass which had gotten out of control after the nourishing rains. The result was so neat and pretty that Olivia had decided she needed to save up for her own ride-on mower. Although there was no way she would ever get around to mowing all of her twenty-acre farm, having smooth grass around her farmhouse made the old, stone building look even more beautiful.

She was seeing Danilo tomorrow night. They'd planned a restaurant outing. Olivia was counting the moments excitedly until that time. Thanks to their hectic schedules, she hadn't seen him since they'd enjoyed an early evening picnic on her lawn after he'd cut the grass. She was missing him!

"All right, let's go inside." Charlotte headed back to the car and drove it up to the farmhouse, parking it next to Olivia's Fiat, which was under the newly installed carport. Olivia walked to work whenever the weather allowed. Now that it was early spring, there were more days where this was possible.

Charlotte opened the trunk and hefted out her bags. Her friend was not a light traveler, Olivia remembered. Even though her stay was only a week, she had two huge bags, a carry-on, a laptop bag, and her gigantic purse.

They carted the luggage inside, and Charlotte stopped in her tracks all over again as she admired the hallway.

"That hall table is stunning! Look at that intricate carving around the top, and the tapered shape of those legs. I've never seen such a beautiful piece."

"Danilo made it." Olivia smiled, thinking of her talented, generous "ragazzo" with a rush of affection.

"And the art on the walls? You said these paintings are from local artists?"

"Yes."

"They're so colorful, and bring the place to life. Look at that landscape. Oh, here's your sweet little cat. Hello my girl, Pirate. You're looking so much fatter and shinier than the first time we saw you." Charlotte bent to stroke the black-and-white feline, who was meowing in a friendly way and sniffing at her bags.

Olivia felt a thrill of happiness. It was so wonderful to have her best friend here—really here, in her own renovated farmhouse.

"Now, I have been longing to see your mysterious map, the one you found in that secret storeroom."

Olivia made a face. "It's in the kitchen. I framed it."

"But I thought it had a hole in the middle."

"I framed it, hole and all."

Leading the way into her cozy farmhouse kitchen, Olivia gestured to the framed map on her kitchen wall. She'd mounted the yellowed, damaged page on a white background and placed it behind glass in a plain wooden frame.

It was certainly a talking point—as well as a frustrating reminder to her that although there were treasures on her farm, Olivia had no idea where they were hidden.

She remembered how excited she'd been when Danilo had found that ancient map in the secret storeroom located in her farm's forested hills. Even though the storeroom was empty, Olivia had believed the map would lead them to whatever was concealed elsewhere.

She could still remember the crushing disappointment when she'd realized it couldn't lead them anywhere.

Charlotte peered at the map, intrigued.

"It looks as if it was deliberately cut out, or ripped out. Not that it fell apart."

"I think so, too. I don't think it just disintegrated. Someone wanted to hide the location where—something—was buried. So they made a map, and then they cut out the important part of it."

"Fascinating," Charlotte murmured. "I can see a road on the edge of the paper."

"That's the road leading past my farm," Olivia confirmed.

"Well!" Charlotte said, spending another minute taking in the map. Just as Olivia had done, Charlotte gazed at it with narrowed eyes, as if she could magically decipher where X marked the spot, just by staring at the faint marks and lines around the gap. "I guess it's too big an area missing? Can't you search it piece by piece?"

Olivia shook her head. "It's enormous. The missing piece covers nearly half the farm. I'll have to hope I stumble across it one day, perhaps while planting more vines or another tree. And at least I have uncovered some interesting treasures already."

Even though she tried to sound resigned, Olivia was seething with frustration. How she wished there was a way to magically locate any hidden items.

Charlotte turned away from the map with a sigh. "On the bright side, I was fascinated to hear about the other treasures. Where are they now?" she asked.

"The ancient bottle fragments are being kept safe with Danilo's friend, who specializes in the area's history." Olivia still hoped that one day she might unearth a whole, undamaged bottle crafted from this rare and unique glass.

"And you found a full bottle of wine too, didn't you?"

"Yes. They think it's from the beginning of last century. It is still at the antiques store, having the label restored. I'll have to decide what to do with it when I get it back. Perhaps I can put it in a glass case and mount it in the dining room?"

"That sounds like a good idea," Charlotte agreed.

Returning to the hallway, they hauled the luggage upstairs and stowed it in Olivia's spare bedroom. Charlotte would be the first guest to stay there. Olivia was pleased her bestie would be able to enjoy the spacious room, which she had painted in warm cream, with yellow-and-lime-striped curtains, and a fluffy green rug on the floor. Charlotte could store her belongings in the large wooden wardrobe, which she had sanded and varnished until it shone.

And, because the evenings were still chilly, she was sure Charlotte would appreciate the radiator under the window, which was now in perfect working order, like the rest of the house's heating.

"Before it gets too dark, I need to see your barn," Charlotte said. "And try your wine! You mentioned that you're launching it at a festival?"

Leading the way downstairs, Olivia's happiness was replaced by a chill of nerves.

"I am. I think it might have been a bad decision, though," she explained, opening the front door and heading along the pathway which was now cobbled.

"Why's that?" Charlotte demanded.

"I didn't know at the time, but this festival is very famous, and it's huge. It's an international event that's attended by hordes of well-established wineries and elite visitors. I assumed it would be a small, local show. Probably because I wanted it to be," Olivia sighed.

She opened the tall wooden doors and switched on the lights she'd recently installed. She loved how the lanterns she'd positioned along the wall gave the barn a mysterious Gothic charm. Plus, when a bulb blew, Olivia could replace it while standing on a simple chair. She wasn't going to have to risk her life teetering on an enormous ladder to access the barn's high ceiling.

One day, she dreamed of hosting public wine tastings within this atmospheric barn. But for now, there was an even more important tasting—Charlotte's verdict on her wine.

"I remember that ice wine we had so well, even though it was years ago. How amazing to be trying the same type of wine in this gorgeous place," Charlotte enthused.

"Mine won't be as good. It's just a beginner's wine," Olivia warned.

She headed over to the big oak barrel which now housed her total harvest. Thinking back, she couldn't believe what a journey it had been. Harvesting the wild vines in a panic, doing everything on the fly, feeling stressed and disorganized. Somehow, her wine hadn't spoiled and hadn't been ruined.

Danilo had tasted it a few weeks ago and had liked it. But Charlotte had tasted a good ice wine before, so she had a higher standard to compare it with.

Olivia took two glasses from the shelf and opened the tap at the bottom of the barrel. It gave her a sick feeling to think that tomorrow she'd be emptying this barrel and bottling every drop of the contents.

She poured two tasting portions, pleased by how the wine glowed lively ruby red in the barn's muted light.

"It looks the part," Charlotte said thoughtfully.

"It's the taste that will count," Olivia said, feeling her stomach twist again.

She thought her wine had a magnificent aroma, and the time spent in oak had enhanced it, giving it a smooth, complex richness. Sipping, she thought it tasted exactly the way it should. Not overly sweet, but fresh, and bursting with fruity flavor.

Anxiously, she watched as Charlotte sipped.

Olivia felt her heart plummet as her friend frowned, then grimaced.

She put her empty glass down and stared sorrowfully at Olivia.

"It's not quite right," she said. "I can't put my finger on it, but there's something wrong with it."

Olivia felt the bottom fall out of her world as she stared in horror at her friend's frowning face.

CHAPTER THREE

"What's wrong with the wine? Can we fix it?" Olivia asked, feeling as if there wasn't nearly enough air in the barn for her needs.

"Let me taste again," Charlotte said. "Can you give me a bigger portion this time?"

Quickly, Olivia refilled the glass, giving her a very generous amount of ice wine so that Charlotte could pinpoint the problems with her first-ever vintage.

Feeling dizzy with stress, she leaned against the barn's cool stone wall while Charlotte sipped, and then drained, her glass.

"I'm almost sure I have the answer now," Charlotte declared.

"Is it going to be something we can adjust?" Olivia asked. "Should we add sugar?" At this stage, she knew that was a terrible idea. But she was willing to do anything to make it right! Visions of people publicly criticizing her wine at the festival swam through her mind in horrific technicolor.

"One more glass and I'll tell you," Charlotte said solemnly.

Olivia let out a shaky breath. Why wasn't Charlotte able to tell her already? Was it going to be that difficult to make it right?

She took the glass from her friend, but as she did, she saw that Charlotte's lips were twitching in an odd way.

Was the wine far too sour? Olivia wondered in a panic. Then she remembered where she'd seen that expression before. It was what Charlotte always did when she was desperately trying to smother a bellow of laughter.

"Just one more glass," her friend repeated, but now, glancing closely, Olivia saw her eyes were bugging out of her head with suppressed emotion.

"Are you sure you don't want two more glasses?" Olivia challenged her sternly.

Sure enough, Charlotte let out a huge snort of mirth.

"Olivia, it's brilliant! It's absolutely delicious. It's so good I had to resort to devious tactics to sneak another taste. I was trying to hold out for two more but I just couldn't. Your face was too funny."

Olivia felt her knees sag in relief. Actually, Charlotte's tactics had been hilarious. To her astonishment, a giggle escaped.

"I'm glad you find it drinkable," she said.

"It's better than the ice wine we had at that fancy restaurant. How are you going to price it?"

They headed out of the barn. Erba was already hovering eagerly at the door. Given the chance, Olivia knew that her wine-loving goat would find a way into the barrel and the following morning, she'd arrive to find it opened and empty with her goat's head peeking out the top. She made sure Erba was safely outside before closing up.

"I am still thinking about how to price it. Being a dessert wine, I decided it should be sold in smaller bottles. Sweet wines and port wines are traditionally sold in half-liter bottles, unlike normal wine, which is sold in the bigger, 750-milliliter bottles. I looked at the stock available and chose very pretty and distinctive half-liter bottles, narrow and tall, in dark brown glass."

"That sounds perfect. When are you picking them up?"

"I was planning to pick them up tomorrow sometime. The shop is in Siena, but I still need to send through the label artwork so that they can get everything ready."

Olivia opened the fridge and took out a bottle of the La Leggenda rosé which she had blended. She felt thrilled she and her friend could enjoy it chilled, with dinner.

She poured the wine and handed Charlotte her glass. But Charlotte was deep in thought, seeming distracted.

"Siena is where the festival is taking place, right?"

"That's right." Olivia sipped her wine.

"Let's go and explore the city tomorrow. I've always wanted to see Siena. We can check out where the festival is happening so we know where to go, and then see the sights. I'm sure we'll be too busy on the day, and too tired afterward, to do the tourist thing, so tomorrow's the only time. We could have lunch at the Piazzo del Campo. Have you been there yet?"

Olivia felt a surge of excitement at the thought of seeing the famous Piazzo, as well as the magnificent Duomo of Siena, which was supposed to be one of the most beautiful cathedrals in the world. Siena had been on her to-do list for ages! She'd planned a visit there with Danilo a while ago, but a weekend of torrential rain had put paid to their plans.

"It's been on my to-do list also. It would be fabulous to see it properly, but I don't know if there'll be time tomorrow. I need to prepare for this festival." Excitement was quickly dampened by guilt at the thought of enjoying herself when so much pressure lay ahead.

"Come on," Charlotte coaxed. "A fun day out will clear your mind and leave you freshly energized for the show. We deserve it!"

Even though she had butterflies of nervousness every time she thought about Festa del Vino, Olivia had to admit Charlotte was right. They did deserve a day of fun.

"As long as we set time aside in the afternoon to bottle my wine. We don't want to run late on that," she conceded.

"Absolutely. I'll draw up an agenda for us. With any luck, I can also get a website piece out of it. "Top Ten Sights in Siena!"

While Charlotte got her laptop out and started planning their day, Olivia opened her own computer. She had to complete her wine label. The bottling company needed it first thing tomorrow, and she was all out of inspiration.

While Charlotte hummed happily to herself as she clicked through tourism sites, Olivia frowned down at her own screen, preoccupied with the difficulty of choosing the right visual.

She had created an online mood board to help her, filled with photos, screen shots and key words. There were even a few lines from the works of the famous Florence-born poet and philosopher, Dante.

> *"Nel mezzo del cammin di nostra vita*
> *mi ritrovai per una selva oscura,*
> *ché la diritta via era smarrita."*

Roughly translated, this quote from Dante's Inferno read, *"Midway along the journey of our life, I woke to find myself in a dark wood, for I had wandered off from the straight path."*

To Olivia, that summarized the state of shock she felt at her sudden career change. She still wondered sometimes if she'd been mad to impulsively follow her dreams, and turn her back on her ordinary, if stressful, life.

Staring at the mood board, she felt transported back to her advertising agency days at JCreative in Chicago. With a wry smile, she knew that James, her ex-boss, would have forced her and her team to sit in a meeting until the perfect wine label was found, even if it took till midnight!

Olivia hoped this process would be quicker, because she wanted to enjoy a relaxed dinner with Charlotte.

Her first inspiration had been a pretty vine leaf. Simple, natural, and detailed, the line drawing of the leaf filled the label. Though Olivia loved the simplicity and that this design was something different, she worried it was too plain, and not personal enough.

Clicking through to the next design, Olivia found she was having second thoughts about it. She'd been proud of the fresh, fun collage of wineglasses, grapes, plates, and bottles that made up this label. Now, though, she thought it looked too garish and on the cheap side.

That left her third and final option, and looking at it again, Olivia decided it was the perfect choice. She'd stylized a photo of her farm's rusty gates, hanging askew off their gateposts, with her vines and farmhouse in the distance beyond. Using one of her design programs, she'd created a realistic-looking line drawing of the scene.

It was the one to use, Olivia decided. It was original, eye-catching, and personal and seemed to invite the viewer in. One day, if visitors came to her farm, they would recognize the label—and it meant she didn't have to upgrade her gate anytime soon as it was part of her brand identity. What a win-win.

The name was more of a challenge.

"What's the sigh for?" Charlotte inquired, looking up from her own laptop.

"I'm battling with the brand name for my wine. I need something that isn't just for the ice wine, but for every wine I might make in the future. It's a really important decision because the name needs to be meaningful, but must sell the wine, and I have writer's block!"

Charlotte rubbed her chin thoughtfully.

"What's the main aim of the name? Have you decided on that?" she quizzed.

"I want people to know I'm an American, making wine in Italy. That it's become my new home country but it's not quite yet my new home," she said.

"Hmm. You want to go in the personal direction, something like Olivia's Farm? Glass Winery?" Charlotte suggested.

"I thought of using Glass as a play on words but I'm not sure enough people would understand it, seeing I'm not at all well known. I think you would have to be a famous personality for that one to work. So I binned that idea," Olivia said sadly.

"Any other ones?"

Olivia scanned through her disappointingly brief shortlist.

"I thought about 'Chicago to Collina'—Collina being the closest village to my farm. I liked the idea but it's long. And again, I don't know if it stands out enough. There are plenty of wineries in the surrounding area with Collina in their name."

"You basically need to say that you're an American in Italy, but using short words." Charlotte nodded. "Maybe just say so directly."

"Italian Americano? That gives it an Italian feel," Olivia pondered aloud.

"But it's long. You said you wanted a shorter name. Why not combine the words?" Charlotte suggested. "Italicano?"

"Italicano," Olivia repeated, feeling elated. "I love it. It's perfect. Catchy, short, memorable, and there's a story behind it. You're a genius!"

She added the word to the top of her label. In a curvy, delicate script it playfully partnered with the rickety open gates and scenery beyond.

Sighing with relief, Olivia realized she had her label. It was done, and it looked beautiful. Quickly, she saved it and emailed it to the bottling company.

While as proud of it as she could be, she wasn't convinced that this attractive label and clever, catchy name would be enough to market her unknown wine at this prestigious festival. The more Olivia thought about this upcoming event, the more nervous she became. She feared she'd been far too optimistic when she'd booked the small but expensive stall, and that the event would prove to be a disastrous waste of money.

In fact, she was dreading the festival.

CHAPTER FOUR

"Hello? *Ciao?*"

Narrowing her eyes against the morning sun, Olivia leaned against her Fiat, concentrating hard on her phone call. She'd dialed La Leggenda's direct restaurant number and was speaking to one of the waiters.

"Is Gabriella there?" she asked.

A moment later, Gabriella's piercing tones shrilled out of the phone.

"*Ciao.* At this hour of the morning, I am guessing the caller is you, Olivia?"

Olivia blushed, feeling as if she'd been caught out.

"I wanted to make sure everything was okay. Do you need me to come by and spend some time there, just to set up for the day?"

Anxiously, she stared over at the farmhouse, where Charlotte, her jacket slung over her shoulders, was saying goodbye to Pirate and Erba.

Gabriella huffed out a loud, impatient sigh.

"Olivia, you are taking three days of leave. Do you know the word? Leave! The winery will be fine. Do we have wine left, Paolo?" she called teasingly. "Oh no, we are all out. So I guess we will just close up and go home." Gabriella cackled wickedly. "Wait, Paolo has found some. A few thousand bottles, I believe, so we have plenty to offer guests. The tasting room is still standing. Jean-Pierre is at work already. Even your bees are well. So, please, stay away for the long weekend. There is no need to call again," she concluded, in tones that implied if Olivia did call again for a random reason, she would receive an earful.

"I'm glad to hear it. Thank you," Olivia said, reminding herself not to be a control freak and to have faith. She didn't want to come across as a micromanaging tyrant. This was her chance to prove she could trust her team to manage things in her absence.

"Let's go," she called to Charlotte.

They climbed into Olivia's car and headed out of the gate, taking the main road that would lead them to Siena.

As they drove, Olivia heard her phone ping.

Automatically, she jumped, thinking of her winery responsibilities. She knew Gabriella had literally just told her everything was under control, but even so she couldn't help herself.

"Would you mind checking that?" she asked Charlotte.

"Sure." Grabbing her phone, Charlotte scrolled through. She paused for a while and then said, "It's an incoming email. Uh-oh."

"What is it?" Olivia gripped the wheel, feeling nervous.

"You're in trouble with the authorities."

"What?" Olivia nearly drove off the road as she stared at Charlotte in alarm. Her friend didn't look like she was joking at all.

"It's an important notification from Visa Control."

Thank goodness the light ahead on the main road was red and there was the usual morning snarl-up of traffic. Quickly, Olivia braked.

"Visa Control? Let me read it. Hopefully, it's just that I need to renew my stay again."

Charlotte handed her the phone and Olivia scanned the message hurriedly. She realized immediately that this was not a simple reminder, but an urgent prompt for further action.

"*Signora Glass. You are urgently required to attend to an official matter of importance,*" the scary email began.

Then it became even more terrifying. Scanning the content with widening eyes, Olivia read that she could no longer apply for another three-month visa as she had been doing. Signora had exceeded the maximum number of renewals, the official wording informed her sternly. The email implied that she was lucky not to have been thrown out of Italy already thanks to her irresponsible actions.

"They're telling me that if I want to stay in Italy, I have to apply for a long-stay visa," Olivia said, feeling jittery.

"Is that difficult?" Charlotte asked in concern.

"It sounds complicated," Olivia said, scrolling further and goggling at the long list of requirements for approval. "It seems I now have to apply for an Italian residence permit. And that means providing a whole mountain of information."

"Like what?"

"Top of the list is proof of health insurance and bank statements. They might throw me out immediately if they see my bank statements. What if they think I'm too poor to reside here?"

Charlotte snorted. "You have a job. I'm sure proof of employment is part of the requirements?"

"Yes, it is. But so is filling in several long, complicated forms. They haven't even attached them, but sent a link to where I must look for them. What if I get them wrong? Italy is terrible when it comes to red tape. I could be sent back to the States if I forget to fill in one of the compulsory fields." She had learned from her limited experience that Italians loved bureaucracy, but that its outcomes were puzzling and often unpredictable. And she was hopeless with forms. Hopeless!

From behind her, a horn blared, signaling that a driver was impatiently waiting for her to crawl forward the three yards that traffic allowed. Olivia closed the gap and then returned to her perusal of this awful email.

"Oh no!" she exclaimed, reading the worst part of all.

"Now what?" Charlotte's eyebrows were just about hitting her hairline.

"They need details of my next of kin."

Charlotte grimaced in sympathy. She knew Olivia's mother well enough that nothing more needed to be said about *that*.

At that moment, the light changed, and Olivia continued driving. She felt cold with horror about her mother's reaction if the authorities contacted her to check the information. Her mother would probably tell Visa Control that the application was a terrible mistake. She was convinced that Olivia's obsession with living in Italy and her goal to be a winemaker was simply a passing phase. She stubbornly refused to accept that Olivia was determined to make her dreams reality.

Every week, Olivia received a breezy email from Mrs. Glass, filled with links to available apartments in her neighborhood, marketing jobs, and even dating agencies in Chicago. This despite Olivia having told her mother *four times* that she was now in a relationship with Danilo.

It would be so much easier if she could just hunker down and keep renewing her three-month visa. Why did she have to be forced into this scary new journey, with its potential for failure and disaster?

"My goodness, it's green here. You know, I remember Tuscany being very dry and golden when I left," Charlotte remarked. Olivia was glad of the distraction from her worried thoughts. Smiling, she glanced in the direction where her friend was looking.

"This time of year is the greenest I've seen it, too. And that's one of my favorite views, because it literally changes every week," Olivia agreed, seeing that Charlotte was transfixed by the road leading to their local town of Collina.

The ruined castle on the outskirts of the village was lit by the morning sun, the stone glowing in a warm and magical way so that the crumbling battlements looked scenic, rather than threatening. It was like a jewel set in a brilliant green backdrop, Olivia thought, giving her inner poet free rein.

They weren't going into the village. Instead, they swung left, in the direction of the *strada nazionale*. Olivia was pleased that she'd picked up on how to drive like a local. The secret seemed to be: go fast! Idling along and taking in the spellbinding vistas ramped up the average Italian's blood pressure to dangerous levels.

For that reason, Olivia was glad she was in the driver's seat and could focus firmly on the road, allowing Charlotte the fun of taking in the passing scenery. Even if it flashed by at speed.

*

Luckily, there was a broken down truck in the valley approaching Siena. The chaos, accompanied by blaring horns from surrounding drivers, meant that everyone slowed to a crawl. It gave her a chance to take in this majestic hilltop city.

Olivia stared up at the checkerboard of roofs and turrets, with a tall spire reaching high into the deep blue sky. This city, nestled atop a green hill, looked to be made of gold. Or maybe copper, she decided, taking in the mellow glow of the ancient buildings.

The Etruscans, who had built many of the historic cities in Tuscany, had chosen high-lying sites because they were easy to defend, Olivia remembered. It had the added advantage that the cities looked imposing and magnificent on the approach, and also that the lucky residents enjoyed stunning views out over the rolling countryside.

"So, before we start doing the tourist thing, where's your bottling shop?" Charlotte asked.

Olivia glanced down at her satnav. "It's on the city's outskirts. We should reach it in five minutes. I see the festival hall is close by, around the corner and along the main road, so we know where it is now."

Heading into a part of Siena that was clearly built in medieval times, Olivia kept her full attention on the narrow road, winding its way between high walls. Squeezing through the gaps with inches to spare, she was relieved when Charlotte shouted, "I see it!"

There was an even tinier turning which led to a shoebox-sized parking lot. Olivia squeezed the Fiat into the only available gap. She climbed out feeling excited and positive. Here she was, about to buy bottles for her first-ever batch of wine.

She headed into the store and stopped immediately, staring in admiration at the ranks of stacked bottles. There were glass containers of all shapes and sizes, neatly arranged on shelves, gleaming in the brightly lit space.

"*Buon giorno,*" the attendant greeted them.

"I've come to pick up an order," Olivia said, gazing around. She was second-guessing her choices. Should she have chosen a brighter shade? she wondered, transfixed by a deep, glowing green bottle near the door.

"Ah, is this the Italicano order?" The woman smiled, clearly picking up on Olivia's accent. "A lovely label. Your bottles are ready."

She went into the back room, which Olivia guessed must be far larger than the compact shop, and returned with the first crate holding twelve slim, amber, dessert-wine bottles. Olivia was glad that they looked securely packaged in their cardboard home, with a corrugated sleeve for extra protection around each bottle.

Lifting one out, she caught her breath. It was beautiful! The color of the glass was unusual and striking. The label looked stunning—artistic and evocative with a touch of mystery. In marketing terms, she was reassured that she'd done the best job she could. But in winemaking terms, it was the contents inside that would make or break her reputation.

"Stunning," Charlotte confirmed approvingly.

Olivia had chosen the best quality screw-top lids for her wine. These were cheaper and easier for her home setup than corks, and would provide the perfect seal for her already matured wine. She'd also bought a heat sealer so that she could secure the lids fast and correctly. The store attendant added this to her order.

"One hundred bottles and a pack of lids. Let me help you carry the crates," the attendant offered.

"Thank you," Olivia said, picking up the first box.

"I see you have made a Tuscan ice wine. How unique. I have never heard of that being produced here before," the attendant praised.

Olivia glowed with pleasure at the compliment. "It's a shame we can't just drop them off at the festival now," she joked as she packed the first lot of crates inside, glad that she had a good-sized trunk.

"Are you going to sell them there?" the friendly woman asked.

"Yes, we are. We've booked a stall to launch Olivia's brand new small winery." Charlotte beamed.

"Is the festival going to be busy, do you know?" Olivia asked anxiously.

"It's always busy, yes. Many visitors are in town for the event," the attendant said, but she sounded more reserved than Olivia had expected her to.

"Is it a good place to launch a new wine?" Olivia asked anxiously, closing the trunk. The attendant didn't reply immediately but seemed thoughtful as they headed back inside for her to pay.

She frowned as she took the credit card. "To be truthful with you, not in recent years. A while back, under the previous management, there were many small kiosks and home wineries. It was fun and friendly, and there was always something new to discover. However, since then, it has become bigger and much more corporate. Small newcomers and home wineries have been mostly discouraged, and those who have exhibited have complained they did not get a good audience and were not well treated. I am surprised you were even given a stall there."

"Really?" Olivia said. She was hyperventilating so badly the room was swimming around her. This was awful news.

"Don't worry. A few have made the same mistake, but learned from it, and there is another solution. You can book space at the monthly Food and Wine Fair which runs throughout the summer months. It is held in one of Siena's public parks," the woman reassured her. "I will send you the information on it."

"Thank you," Olivia said faintly.

Reading the consternation in her friend's expression, Charlotte hustled her out of the door, grabbing the receipt as she left.

"Don't panic," Charlotte gabbled at her as Olivia slumped into the driver's seat. "That's just one person's opinion."

"Just the opinion of the one person who supplies bottles to the majority of smaller wineries? She knows what she's talking about."

"She might have a vested interest in this local fair," Charlotte argued in a firm voice. "She sounds like she must benefit from it somehow. Perhaps she runs it."

"This stall was so expensive! I'll be too broke to exhibit anywhere else, plus it will mean more time away from work. I can't take one weekend off every month to sell my wine, when weekends are the busiest times at La Leggenda," Olivia lamented.

As they headed out of the parking lot, she was literally seething with anxiety.

"We're going to fail," she jittered, starting the car and immediately stalling in her panic.

Charlotte squeezed her arm supportively.

"You will not fail! Your wine is awesome and it's something new. People will love it. I'm sure that woman has a lot of friends who make bad wine. She seemed the type, talking about all those home winemakers. Bad wine doesn't sell, right?"

"I've messed up," Olivia insisted, feeling fraught.

Charlotte tapped the dashboard musingly. "Is La Leggenda exhibiting?"

"No, they're not. Marcello said they'd decided to give events a miss in the first half of this year, with him being away on the mentorship. Also, La Leggenda won gold in all four competition categories a few years ago but he said they've stopped entering that competition now."

"Competition? There's a competition at the festival? Why didn't you say so before now? Are you entering?"

Olivia stared at her friend as if she'd started babbling in Cantonese.

"Of course not. What chance would I have?"

Charlotte rolled her eyes. Then she pointed her finger at Olivia and waggled it firmly.

"You. Are. Going. To. Enter."

"But I—"

Olivia didn't get a chance to protest against the unstoppable force that was Charlotte.

"I will personally organize it first thing tomorrow when we get to the show. If there's a fee, I'll pay it," she steamrollered on.

Olivia stared at her friend, aghast. As if participating in this newcomer-unfriendly show wasn't bad enough, her well-meaning bestie was now going to ensure that a panel of critical judges tore her wine, and her remaining shreds of confidence, apart.

She felt as if she'd been thrown to the wolves!

CHAPTER FIVE

"Entering the wine competition is a done deal. No more buts. And no more fretting," Charlotte said sternly.

"What do you mean, no more fretting?" Olivia protested. "I need to set the whole day aside for it. I have such a long list of worries I don't know where to start."

Charlotte sighed. "Right now, we have Siena to explore. We have to leave here while it's still light, because we need to get back home and bottle your wine. And then you're seeing Danilo and I'm heading out to meet my friend for dinner. After that, and only after that, you may agonize. Right?"

Olivia sighed. "Right," she agreed. Much as she wanted to go home and pace the barn in despair, Charlotte's argument was logical. Worrying would only burn her out and achieve no purpose. After giving a dramatic shrug of acquiescence, she shoehorned the car out of the tiny parking space, and they headed into the city.

"Turn right here, then left." With unerring precision, Charlotte directed her to the public parking lot closest to their first sight of the day.

They climbed out, and Charlotte paused, staring admiringly at a uniformed police officer walking his beat along the paved sidewalk.

"You know, there's something about the Italian police," she admitted. "Aren't they just devastatingly attractive? Tall, dark, and well-built. And clearly fine, upstanding men, custodians of the city. Ready to protect and serve!"

Feeling better, Olivia grinned. Charlotte was irrepressible, she decided.

After giving a last, longing look in the officer's direction, her friend marched purposefully down the street, with Olivia striding beside her.

"Now, if my map is correct, we should have the first of our sights ahead—the Duomo of Siena. Don't peek! You can already see the top of it from here, so look the other way until we're past this building."

As they rounded the corner, the magnificent Gothic Romanesque cathedral stood in front of them. Olivia stopped in her tracks, gawping at the massive, intricately decorated structure. With its finely carved stone frontage, including triple archways with an enormous round window above them, and a regal tower, it was the most stunning building she'd seen in Italy.

"Can you believe the amount of work this must have taken? Isn't it exquisite?" She thought it looked more like a fairytale castle than a cathedral. And the workmanship, crafted from pale filigree stone, made her think of the fanciest wedding cake she'd ever seen.

"Imagine cutting a slice of it." Charlotte echoed her thoughts. "But seriously, the detail is incredible."

Olivia was entranced as she snapped photo after photo, pleased that the stonework looked just as fascinating when immortalized on her phone. It had been a while since she'd posted any travel shots on social media. What fun she would have showing off this cathedral to her friends back in the States.

They headed toward the building, although Olivia found herself stopping every few steps to take in a new feature she hadn't noticed before. The triangular facades above the enormous archways and towers were filled with colorful mosaics depicting religious scenes. And it seemed like every remaining square foot of space had been allocated its own miniature statue, decorative carving, or stone bust.

What a feast for the senses, Olivia decided, feeling happy as she admired it one more time.

Entering the enormous space, she stared around her in awe. The high, vaulted ceiling featured huge archways that crisscrossed far above. The walls were covered in narrow stripes of black and white marble, for an unusual and highly dramatic effect.

"From my reading, I believe that the stripes were chosen to pay homage to the Sienese coat of arms," Charlotte said.

"And look at the stars!" In between the vaulted arches, Olivia saw to her amazement the dark blue ceiling was studded with constellations of gleaming golden stars.

"The cathedral itself was designed and built in the early to mid-1200s," Charlotte said softly as they paced through the enormous interior. "I believe the artwork inside was created and added to over the next few centuries. You can see why it took time, looking at the amount of detail."

Olivia felt fortunate all over again to be living in a country where so many ancient treasures had been created and preserved, a record of some of humanity's most glorious accomplishments over the centuries.

That gave her an uneasy pang as she remembered she'd only be living here if her new visa was approved. But putting her misgivings aside, she focused on the incredible workmanship within this treasure-filled interior. Even the shiny floor had roped-off areas that featured stunning mosaics. The balconies were created as lively frescoes, and the tall pulpit was an ornate, carved work of art.

Each of the many statues and figurines along the walls were described in loving detail, and the altar was the splendid centerpiece. Dancing angels clad in rose gold surrounded a massive, framed mosaic of the gold-crowned Madonna and child.

It was astonishing, she decided. This treasure trove of historical art was a destination she would remember forever.

"We can't stay here too long, as time is limited," Charlotte reminded her. Reluctantly, Olivia tore her gaze away from the altar.

"Where to next?"

"Next is the Piazza del Campo. But don't think for a moment we're going to have an easy time, once there. We have to earn our glass of wine in the sunshine," Charlotte said sternly.

Wondering what Charlotte was talking about, Olivia followed her curiously out of the Duomo. They headed down Via dei Pellegrini, a famous road name that Olivia recognized from reading books set in the area. The narrow road was thronged with tourists and lined with inviting-looking shops. She caught her breath as they reached its end, and took in the magnificent Piazza del Campo.

"It's so huge," Olivia said incredulously as she gazed around the massive space. She'd expected it to be a modestly sized square, but this was vast. The paved expanse, surrounded by historic buildings, was shell shaped and stretched for hundreds of yards. Surprised, Olivia realized it was truly a blank canvas, without any benches or other features. Tourists were walking, standing, or even sitting on the neat brick paving. They looked tiny and insignificant in the enormous square.

"It was originally a field, before they paved it over. Campo means 'field' in Italian, as I'm sure you know," Charlotte said as Olivia nodded. Now the square's name made sense.

A huge tower located next to the square cast a long, dark shadow across the vast expanse.

"That is where we are heading next," Charlotte said, indicating the tall tower with a flourish.

"Inside?" Staring at her friend incredulously, Olivia started to realize what she meant. "Up? To the top?"

"That's correct," Charlotte said, sounding pleased. "Climbing the Torre del Mangia is going to be item one on my list of Top Ten Calorie Burners in Tuscany!"

"But it's enormous," Olivia said, gazing in trepidation at the tower, which seemed to be growing in height with every step she took toward it.

"Over one hundred meters in height, yes."

"Can't we take the climb as read?" Olivia tried, but was silenced by Charlotte's stern frown.

"The views are magnificent," her friend insisted, in tones that allowed for no argument.

After checking in and purchasing their tickets, the attendant allowed them to step into the tower's shady interior. Sure enough, the flight of stairs did look practically vertical. Charlotte seemed energized by the challenge.

"Come on. Wine won't wait forever. Let's conquer this climb. It will earn us extra pizza points. Or gelato points. In fact, I have an idea."

"You do?" Olivia asked. Charlotte's idea could be anything. What on earth was her crazy friend going to suggest?

"Before we climb, we each make a wish. It can be whatever we like. Any aim or goal we have in life, big or small. And if we reach the top, then our wish will come true."

"That's a great idea. In that case, I wish—" Olivia began, thinking of the festival ahead and how important it was for it to be a success.

But Charlotte put a finger to her lips.

"Shh," she said. "You don't tell me, I don't tell you. Only if and when it comes true, do we reveal it."

"All right," Olivia said.

As they set foot on the first stair, Olivia found herself filled with curiosity. What was Charlotte's wish going to be and why was her friend keeping it such a secret?

CHAPTER SIX

Gasping for breath, Olivia forced her quivering legs to step up the final, five-hundred-and-fifth, stair of the Torre del Mangia. She'd managed the torturous climb, and felt a sense of triumph at having reached the top.

Might this mean her wish would come true? Would her wine's launch at Festa del Vino be successful, despite the scary and negative things she'd heard about the venue? Olivia hoped that through her own determined efforts, it might be so! At least by conquering the tower, she'd proved she wouldn't give up easily.

What a workout. As she leaned against the sturdy stone wall, she felt a flash of sympathy for the bell ringers. They must have had to climb up here numerous times a day. What quads of steel they must have possessed.

"This beautiful yet far too tall structure is known in English as the Tower of the Eater," Charlotte informed her in breathless tones, scrolling through her phone.

"Why? Is it because you work up such an appetite climbing it?" Olivia asked curiously.

Charlotte shook her head, tossing her hair back from her now-shiny face.

"Apparently it's a nickname given to the first bell ringer, Giovanni di Balduccio. It says here he was called 'Profit Eater' for his spendthrift tendencies. Or gluttonous tendencies. The text is not sure which," she hazarded.

Olivia craned her neck to read.

"How interesting. I am sure the poor man was wrongly accused. Most probably he was just starving the whole time from burning so many calories. No wonder he needed a lot of food."

"I agree." Charlotte nodded. "I think, through common sense and reasoning, we've solved an ancient mystery. Now, let's see if this view is worth it."

Following her on aching legs, Olivia headed to one of the doorways in the round tower, which led out onto a railed balcony.

She gasped in amazement. This view encompassed what seemed like the whole of Tuscany. Far below them was the square, which she now saw featured a small, turquoise fountain on one side. The people dotted on the paving far below looked like ants.

"Oops!" Charlotte clutched at the rail. "Vertigo moment. I'd forgotten what looking straight down does to me."

Grabbing her friend's arm supportively, Olivia caught her breath at how the city of Siena was showcased in detailed splendor below. Their dizzying vantage point meant that they saw farther still, over the distant hills that were still cloaked in mist. The hilly landscape was highlighted in variegated shades of green. She picked up the dark, shadowed forests, the bright lime glow of young crop plantations, and the distinctive stripes of vines just starting to bloom in their spring splendor. She wished she'd brought binoculars. She was sure that if she knew the right direction to point them, she could have checked on La Leggenda without even bothering Gabriella!

This had been so worth the climb, she decided. As usual, Charlotte was right.

"And now, we return to the piazza," Charlotte said.

They headed down the winding staircase, with Olivia feeling glad that this return trip was a lot easier on the legs. As she walked, she imagined that she was following in the footsteps of the original bell ringer. If she'd been him, she would have found an easier way to get down the stairs. Olivia giggled to herself as she wondered if sliding down on a tray would work. Then she started wondering if he could have set up a rope and pulley system to get him up the tower more easily.

She didn't have time to ponder the logistics of this idea in depth before they reached the bottom and staggered out of the tower.

"Now, we can choose a bistro and quench our thirst. Perhaps we need food, too," Charlotte suggested.

"Where shall we go?" Olivia asked. There appeared to be a multitude of bistros, bars, restaurants, and shops surrounding this amazing space.

"How about we follow the tower's shadow?" Charlotte pointed. "We choose the place closest to where it leads us."

Nodding in approval, Olivia set off across the piazza, walking along the dark line of the shadow and then purposefully following the same direction when she left its shade. Reaching the other side was a surprisingly long walk.

"Can you believe the entire piazza is packed when they hold the famous annual horse race, the Palio di Siena?" Charlotte said.

Olivia stared around her, trying to imagine a crowd so huge that it would fill this enormous space. And horses, galloping round the outside? That sounded crazy, even by wild Italian standards.

"I don't know if I'd be brave enough to watch," she confessed. "What if one of the horses slipped and fell?"

Charlotte nodded. "I researched that. Apparently, for the Palio, they put sand along the route. So it's like a normal racetrack for the horses, and probably a nice, soft landing for the riders who fall off. As it's a bareback race, I'm sure there are many of those."

Olivia decided she might have to come back for it, after all. It sounded full of thrills.

Finally, their route across the piazza led them to the far side, and she was delighted to see a tiny bistro directly in the line they were walking. This would be the perfect place for her and Charlotte to rest their tired legs and watch the world go by.

They sat down, and the waiter brought menus with a smile.

Olivia was tempted to enjoy a big glass of wine, but mindful of her get-together with Danilo that evening, she decided to pace herself with a bellini mocktail. She'd had this before and loved it. Served on ice in a tall glass, it consisted of sparkling white grape juice with a dash of apricot concentrate, along with some colorful sliced fruit.

Charlotte, not pacing herself at all, went for a Birra Moretti lager.

"I crave beer when I'm hot and tired," she explained.

Relaxing under the shady umbrella, Olivia gazed at the tourists dotted around the piazza, taking photos of the square, the tower, and each other. She loved sightseeing in Italy. How amazing was it to live in a country where she knew she would never run out of incredible places to discover?

With a flourish, the barman brought their drinks and placed a small basket of grissini in front of them, together with a bowl of olive tapenade.

Olivia dunked her breadstick in the bowl of dark, rich tapenade, enjoying the crunchy snack, studded with sesame seeds and salt crystals. The bread was the perfect complement to the tapenade, with its intense flavor of salty black olives and sumptuous oil.

Sipping her cool, refreshing drink, she felt invigorated. When she'd sat down she'd been happy never to get up again. Now, she couldn't help glancing at the surrounding shops. Perhaps she should take a stroll past them, she decided. Not to buy anything, of course, but simply to feast her eyes on the variety of wares for sale.

One of the bonuses of being a tourist in the same country you lived in, she decided, was that you could shop as much as you wanted without worrying about how you would get all your loot on the plane. She could stow her purchases into the car and take them home, to enjoy there and then.

With a contented sigh, she put down her glass.

"Shall we wander around the shops?" she said and Charlotte nodded eagerly before draining her beer.

Olivia felt a moment of guilt, knowing that the expense of bottling her wine and booking her stall had just about maxed her card to its limit. But as she started walking, she saw she was passing store after store selling the most incredible leather goods. Siena specialized in it, she realized. And she desperately needed a new purse. Her old one was falling to bits.

Her eye was caught by a beautiful, roomy purse in soft blue leather, displayed outside a tiny kiosk. Moving closer as if inexorably drawn to it, Olivia ran her hands over the smooth, quality leather. She sighed. This purse was stylish, perfect for her needs, and would be a useful and necessary part of her life. With only the slightest quiver of guilt, she paid for the exquisite item.

She handed over her credit card, and as the smiling attendant packaged up her order, she noticed an embossed belt made from dark brown leather on a neighboring display.

This belt was perfect for Danilo, Olivia thought happily, feeling only the tiniest jolt of worry as she handed her card over again. How lovely it would be to give Danilo such a special gift when they saw each other later.

Although the purse and the gift were surely essentials, the same could not be said for the large ceramic serving plate that immediately caught her eye in the next-door store. Moving closer to take in the detail, Olivia admired the large, glazed plate which was creamy white, with a decorative border of bright green grapevine leaves and deep purple grapes. Although not strictly necessary, the plate would be ideal for setting out antipasti at home. And she had nothing as pretty. She could use it whenever Danilo came around for dinner, Olivia told herself firmly. This was, in fact, an equally important purchase.

She felt a glow of satisfaction as the attendant packaged up the plate for her.

Looking around for Charlotte, she saw her friend had also been lured by the wonders of Siena's retail offerings. She was picking out a light, stylish jacket in soft, ocher leather. Quickly, she slipped it on, hooking her russet hair out of the way.

"How does it look?" she asked Olivia. "It's really comfortable."

"It looks like it was made for you," Olivia had to reply truthfully, even though she worried her friend's credit card was also taking too much punishment.

Laden down with their purchases, they wandered to a nearby kiosk that offered a colorful selection of pastries and chocolates. This was not a healthy outing, Olivia decided, staring at the treats hungrily. She found herself unable to resist a luscious-looking cannoli, its baked shell filled with sweetened ricotta cheese, chocolate chips, and glace cherries.

"Do you want one?" she asked Charlotte, hoping her friend would agree.

"I think we each need one. My treat," Charlotte said, pointing to the gorgeously filled showstoppers as she took out her wallet.

With their sugary creations in hand, they headed to one of the nearby bar tables to munch them on the run.

Olivia bit into the delicious pastry, promising herself that tonight, when she went out with Danilo, she would stick to salad. Even though she knew that was a resolution she was certain to break.

The cannoli, though tasty, was surprisingly small. It was finished in only a few bites. Wiping her fingers with the napkin, Olivia acknowledged that this calorie-filled tidbit had unfortunately not touched sides.

"Well, if that was starters, what's for main course?" Charlotte turned back to the cake counter. Following her, Olivia weakened again when she saw the slices of panforte displayed behind the counter. The first few times she'd tried it, she hadn't known what to make of this sumptuous cake, packed with fruit and nuts and dusted with powdered sugar. It had felt too overpowering. But as she had discovered, its rich flavor and dense texture was addictive, and it had become one of her favorites.

At least it contained fruit, she told herself with a sigh. It wasn't empty calories as long as there was fruit inside, was it?

"Shall we share a slice?" she asked her friend and fellow spendthrift.

Olivia watched expressions chase themselves over Charlotte's face. The first response was: *Are you crazy? I need a whole one all to myself.* It was followed by: *Although, how much am I going to end up eating tonight and will it spoil my dinner?* The third one: *But they look so tasty!*

Giggling inwardly, Olivia realized she could read her friend perfectly. She understood every stage of her dilemma, and she hadn't even said a word.

Grimacing, Charlotte capitulated. "I could eat a whole one. You know it and I know it. But I'll settle for sharing."

This time, Olivia paid for the cake and they returned to their bar table where they dug into their slice. This was definitely a more substantial choice, Olivia decided, staring happily at the growing crowds thronging the piazza as she wolfed the tasty forkfuls down. Watching these visitors, she enjoyed picking up the bursts of foreign languages, and English in a medley of accents, as the clusters of people passed by. It was fun to guess where all of them were from, and to be able to pick out the locals, weaving in a businesslike way through the dawdling groups and not ogling the magnificent tower and stately buildings that surrounded the piazza.

She couldn't help feeling fortunate all over again that she was actually a local. If she chose to, she could return to this scenic square to enjoy cakes and people-watching every time she had a day off. It was a comforting thought.

By the time she and Charlotte were done, there wasn't a crumb left. They stared at each other guiltily. This had been a cake binge of note.

"If you don't say anything about this, I won't," Charlotte muttered, dabbing her mouth with a bright green serviette.

"The less said, the better," Olivia agreed, feeling utterly contented. Traveling with Charlotte was always such fun, even though excessive. What a day they'd had. She felt sad to have to leave this spacious, sunny square, its bustling ambience dominated by the stately presence of the tower. Today had felt as if they were on a mini vacation.

But all vacations had to come to an end. Putting down her fork, Olivia knew that their fun outing was over. It was time to get back to the harsh, real world and prepare for the challenge of the festival, which now loomed scarily ahead of her.

CHAPTER SEVEN

For the fourth time, Olivia staggered up to her barn clutching a crate of empty half-liter wine bottles. Puffing tiredly, she placed the crate on top of the stack that she and Charlotte had carried there.

Then she unlocked and pulled open the heavy doors, turning on the lights because the late afternoon had become cloudy and was getting dark.

She felt a sense of disbelief that they were about to bottle—actually bottle—her first-ever ice wine. She couldn't believe she'd managed to get this far with her small harvest. Now, it felt as if she was about to launch herself off a precipice, while wearing a flimsy and inadequate set of wings.

"Let's get this job done," she said bravely to Charlotte, glad that her friend was with her at such a pivotal moment.

They carried the crates into the barn, the golden glow from the lanterns on the walls cutting through the gloom, and set about the task.

Each bottle had to be filled directly from the barrel, before being closed and heat-sealed. Olivia took the first bottle and opened the tap. As the light ruby liquid poured inside, her stomach clenched with nerves. Might someone buy this actual bottle tomorrow? Surely, there was a small chance, since she'd won her bet with fate, and climbed every step of the way up the Torre del Mangia.

She filled the small glass bottle and then passed it to Charlotte, who screwed on the lid and secured it efficiently with the sealing machine.

They stood for a moment, admiring their handiwork.

"Our first full bottle of wine! It looks so professional. That label is lovely. I wonder where it will end up," Charlotte said.

Olivia sighed. "Probably back here, if we're unlucky."

"The first ten we bottle could be valuable collector's items one day. Should you not number them?" Charlotte asked.

"Won't it spoil the label?" Olivia frowned.

"If people don't like it, there will be ninety others to choose from," Charlotte argued reasonably.

"All right. Let's set the first ten aside, and we can write on them afterwards."

It did sound like a fun idea, Olivia thought. She felt glad Charlotte was here. Her friend always had great ideas, even if they were sometimes crazy.

Olivia was surprised by how easily she was able to get into a rhythm. The first four bottles seemed to take forever. But by bottle number five, she realized she was developing muscle memory. Number six was easier still. By the time she reached bottle number seven, Olivia started feeling as if she was a human wine bottling machine. She knew exactly what to do, how to tilt the bottle, how long to wait, and when to close the tap. She passed it to Charlotte without even looking, as if she was in a proper assembly line.

Bottle eight was the same, and so was nine, although Olivia's arms were starting to get tired.

When she passed bottle ten to Charlotte, instead of feeling her friend grasp the bottle, she encountered a warm, furry, and inquiring nose.

Olivia squeaked in surprise. She spun around to find out what on earth was happening.

Erba was waiting to help, looking expectantly at her, with her forelegs propped on the table that Charlotte had been using.

"Erba!" Olivia exclaimed.

"Oh, no." Charlotte rushed back to the bottling station from the corner of the barn. "I stepped away for a moment to stack the wine in the crate. How did she get in? I didn't even see her. She's so stealthy."

Olivia started to feel bad. "Perhaps we should give her some to taste. After all, this barn was her home for months. And she's been so invested in the process."

"I agree. Do we have a saucer here?"

"No, but we have a coffee cup." Olivia had brought it down on one of her morning inspections and forgotten to take it back. "Erba can drink out of a coffee cup if you tilt it for her."

She rinsed the cup out with some bottled water. Then, turning the tap on, she half-filled the cup with wine.

"I'll give it to her," Charlotte said. "Outside is best, I think?"

She headed to the door, with Erba trotting eagerly after her, and Olivia returned to her assembly line of filling bottles. With the additional pressure of getting everything wrapped up before her goat became thirsty again, she went back to work at top speed.

*

An hour and a half later, Olivia felt a sense of disbelief as she took the ninety-ninth bottle from the cardboard crate. They'd filled them all, and the wine was almost finished. Charlotte had to tilt the rapidly emptying barrel.

The hundredth one was filled only halfway before the wine ran out altogether. So they would be able to take ninety-nine to the festival.

Olivia climbed to her feet, stretching out from her cramped position by the barrel. Looking at the neat row of filled crates by the door, she thought they looked intimidating. She couldn't imagine selling any. If she brought ninety-eight back with her, she'd consider it a well-spent weekend!

Olivia and Charlotte lugged the now-heavier crates of bottles back to the Fiat and packed them in, keeping aside the very first crate they'd filled. These were going to be the specially marked bottles. Olivia hurried to the farmhouse and took a black marker pen from the kitchen.

She wrote a big, bold number on each of the ten bottles' labels, and initialed the back with a scribble.

"There we go." Charlotte smiled delightedly. "Sealed and signed. I'm going to jump in the shower now and head out. I'll be back much later. Say hi to Danilo for me."

As Charlotte rushed upstairs, Olivia headed to her laptop. There was one task she had to complete, and that was to decide on her wine's pricing.

She was going to be showcasing her wine among top, established brands. The correct price would be critical. Too high, and she wouldn't sell any, she decided. If her pricing was reasonable and competitive, then a few people might be willing to buy.

Feeling unsure all over again, Olivia opened up the document she'd created to display the price. She'd made a decorative border for the page and had written underneath:

"New Launch from Italicano Vineyard: Tuscany's First Ice Wine."

Five euros per bottle was as low as she could go, she decided. That was roughly six US dollars a bottle. She hoped it would be acceptable to the visitors at Festa del Vino. She needed to sell some of her stock, but if she priced it any lower, she'd be selling at a loss.

Olivia printed out several of the sheets, just in case she needed extra, and placed them in a folder. Then she rushed upstairs to get ready, excited that she'd be seeing Danilo in just a few minutes.

She showered and changed in record-breaking time, deciding to wear the bright turquoise top that Danilo always complimented her on, together with a pair of dark blue jeans and her worn but comfortable ankle-length boots.

After tugging a brush through her hair and misting on some hairspray, Olivia freshened up her eyeliner and lipstick. Then she raced downstairs again as she saw the gleam of headlights in the driveway.

Quickly, she spritzed on some perfume, realizing a moment later she'd probably overdone the gorgeous floral Idillio scent that had been a gift from Danilo. Oh, well, if she was swathed in a cloud of the stuff, at least he'd know how much she loved it!

She pulled open the front door, and there he was, smiling warmly at her. His dark eyes were sparkling, and his favorite, well-worn leather jacket was slung over his broad shoulders.

Olivia was about to fling herself into his arms for a welcome hug when a small but unmissable detail drew her eyes.

He had pink in his hair.

"Oh my goodness!" she exclaimed, remembering that Danilo had always joked about having pink hair as his worst fear. "Were you tied down? Blindfolded?" Olivia laughed loudly. "You look so cute. Like My Little Pony. I hope you asked for your money back."

Too late, she realized that Danilo wasn't laughing with her. Instead, he was glancing uneasily over his shoulder at the young woman who Olivia hadn't seen, because she'd been bending to stroke Pirate.

Her face flamed as she realized she recognized this attractive, dark-haired young lady. This was Danilo's niece!

His *hairdresser* niece.

The one who used him as her model to practice, and who'd clearly just put the pink in. And here was she, shooting her mouth off about him looking like a little pony and how he should demand a refund.

She could see the family resemblance in the young woman's strong features and high cheekbones, with the same dark, intense eyes, although Danilo's were usually sparkling with humor and hers were not.

What a terrible impression her comments must have made. Olivia wished the ground could swallow her up. Why hadn't Danilo told her that he was bringing his niece along? If she'd been warned, she would have chosen different words to comment on his pink hair, ones that had no chance of being unintentionally hurtful.

No second chance at a good first impression, she lamented inwardly, wishing she could rewind time.

"I am pleased to introduce my niece, Francesca," Danilo said, sounding awkward and apologetic. "Francesca, this is Olivia, my girlfriend."

Fearing it was too little, too late, Olivia tried for a warm welcome.

"It's so lovely to meet you, Francesca. Danilo has told me so much about you. He and I have an in-joke about his hair. I always tease him."

"Pleased to meet you," Francesca said coolly, extending a slim-fingered hand.

Danilo put his arm around Olivia and gave her a warm hug and kiss hello. His fond greeting made her feel even worse, because Danilo was so amazing, so thoughtful and caring, and at this important moment she'd let him down.

Although, if Olivia had to name one drawback her wonderful boyfriend possessed, she had to admit he shared the famously Italian quality of being somewhat disorganized.

Perhaps that was it. Danilo, a carpenter and cabinet maker, would have been rushing to meet job deadlines, and rushed out without remembering to call ahead.

"I gave Francesca a ride from work. Her motor scooter is being serviced today, and wasn't ready in time," Danilo explained, confirming Olivia's theory that this had been a last-minute arrangement.

"Do you want to come out to dinner with us, Francesca?" Olivia invited. It was the last thing she wanted, but at least the invitation would be a friendly gesture.

"What a good idea!" Danilo exclaimed, looking delighted.

Olivia sensed that Francesca would rather have said no, but was now unable to decline without seeming rude.

"That would be lovely," she said.

"Please, come in. Would you like a drink before we go?" Olivia said, realizing that it was rude to keep everyone waiting on the doorstep in the dark, breezy evening.

They trooped into the kitchen, closely followed by Pirate, who seemed to be Francesca's new number one fan, and was meowing at her heels.

"I thought we could head out to Pronto. It's a new restaurant in the same village as the jewelry store." Danilo glanced at the bracelet on

Olivia's wrist with a smile. He'd gifted her the braided gold piece, set with sapphires, a few weeks ago.

"This bracelet is so beautiful." Olivia smiled at the young girl. "I believe you helped choose it?"

"Yes, I did," Francesca replied, but she still sounded reserved. Olivia started fretting inwardly. Was there going to be a way to get through to her? What if that careless comment about Danilo's hair, meant only as a joke, had ruined things forever?

"The restaurant looks like fun. It serves modern Italian dishes with creative ingredients," Danilo continued as Olivia poured a glass of sparkling water for herself and Francesca. Danilo's traditional pre-dinner drink was a San Pellegrino Aranciata—the less-sweet Italian version of Fanta. She poured it into a tumbler for him and added lots of ice.

"You must choose a filling dish tonight, Olivia. You will need lots of energy to get through your long day at the wine show tomorrow," he teased.

Olivia laughed nervously. If she'd been alone with Danilo, this would have been the perfect moment to unload all her worries about the festival. In fact she'd been looking forward to sharing how scared she felt and getting his input. Danilo was always supportive and positive, with words of calm advice.

Now, she didn't want to say anything negative in case it might further prejudice her chances of becoming friends with Francesca.

Since she didn't reply, an awkward silence descended after his words.

"I'll grab my purse," Olivia said, remembering that her stunning new bag was still in the bedroom. So was the leather belt she'd bought for Danilo earlier that day. She decided to bring it with her and give it to him at the restaurant.

Heading upstairs, she felt relieved at the chance to break this uneasy moment. But as she hurried away, she realized that the situation was worse than she had thought.

She overheard Francesca say to Danilo, in a soft, astonished voice, "Why didn't you tell me your new girlfriend was American? I thought you said you were serious about her!"

CHAPTER EIGHT

Olivia's throat felt dry as she hustled downstairs, purse in hand. She wished she could fake a sudden headache and cancel the dinner, which promised to be fraught with further tension. How on earth was she going to convince Francesca that she didn't plan on leaving the country anytime soon?

Especially with her visa worries. Those forms!

She pasted on a wide, fake smile as she reached the kitchen.

"If everyone's finished, shall we go? I can't wait to experience this restaurant, and I'm longing for a big glass of wine."

Olivia hoped that wasn't too much honesty.

"So am I," Francesca said meaningfully.

Well, even though they weren't friends and had gotten off to a rocky start, at least Olivia knew that Francesca felt just as stressed, and was just as much in need of a relaxing drink.

"Are you close to completing your hairdressing studies?" Olivia asked as they headed outside and climbed into the car. She hoped some light conversation along the way would atone for her terrible faux-pas earlier.

"Yes. I still need more practical experience, but have passed all my modules."

"With distinction," Danilo said proudly. "Francesca has already been offered a place at a top salon in Florence."

"I am considering it, but might also prefer to work more locally, in one of the nearby towns," Francesca explained. "I love living in this area. My dream is to buy one of the apartments next to the ruined castle."

"Oh, wow! That's one of my dreams, too!" Olivia agreed as Danilo accelerated onto the main road. The minute she'd seen those gorgeous apartments she'd imagined how incredible it would be to live there.

"Really?" Francesca sounded suspicious. "I thought your dream was to own your wine farm."

Confusion descended on Olivia. Despite her best intentions, she'd messed up, and Francesca had taken her words too literally. It had eroded her trust instead of building a friendship. Olivia could have smacked herself for not thinking before speaking.

"I—I mean, it's a sub-dream. What I was trying to say was if I had two lives to live, the second one would definitely be in one of those apartments," she stammered.

Danilo reached over and gave her knee a supportive squeeze. Olivia gave his hand an apologetic squeeze back. Clearly, he'd picked up on the tension between his two passengers, and how Olivia was putting her feet more firmly in her mouth with every word she uttered.

"Here we are," he said, sounding relieved.

He nimbly wedged the car into the last available space outside the bustling small restaurant, with a row of sparkling lights around the door. They scrambled out and hustled through the misty rain, into the warmth of the buzzing interior. As Danilo spoke to the maître-d', changing their table for two to a table for three, Olivia breathed in the mouthwatering aroma of garlic and cheese. Was there anything more delicious than walking into a restaurant in Italy? she wondered briefly, as the waiter showed them to their seats.

It was only when they sat down, and she found herself staring awkwardly at Francesca across the table, that unease filtered back.

"When did you come to Italy?" Francesca asked.

Pleased that she'd initiated conversation, Olivia replied enthusiastically. "Last summer. I suddenly decided to quit my job in the States and joined my friend Charlotte on an impulse vacation in a Tuscan villa. Then we visited La Leggenda and I saw they were looking for an assistant sommelier, so I applied on the spur of the moment and got the job."

"Really?" Francesca said. She seemed interested and Olivia felt encouraged as she continued.

"Then I went for a walk and saw this farm for sale. I figured out that if I sold my apartment in Chicago, I could just about afford it. So I took the plunge. I've always wanted to grow wine. The land is not ideally suited to being a wine farm but years ago, it was a very successful one."

Danilo had ordered a deliciously fragrant local vermentino—a white wine, in celebration of spring. Olivia clinked glasses with him and took a large gulp of the wine, hoping it would calm her nerves. She felt as if she were walking a tightrope.

Then, as she saw Francesca's dubious expression and replayed what she'd said, she realized that she'd already fallen off the tightrope. She'd made herself sound like someone who did everything on a whim. Absolutely every action she'd described to Danilo's favorite niece had been taken with seemingly no forethought. Horrified, she knew Francesca must now be convinced she was an unreliable person, who might decide tomorrow that winemaking wasn't for her, and take off back to the States to do something completely different.

Anxiety flared inside her as she realized what problems her quest for cheery conversation had created.

The fact that she'd endured almost a decade in the same unspeakable job with the same awful, domineering boss—setting a company record, in fact—while only moving house once during that entire time to an apartment two blocks away, was something she couldn't explain now. It would feel like she was trying to justify her sudden flood of irresponsible actions.

Olivia now realized she'd been like a champagne bottle! She'd had a whole heap of pent up energy for changing her life. She hadn't used any of it for years and years. She'd been so busy trying to get ahead at the ad agency without being fired, and to please her mother who wanted her to be a "career woman, established home owner, and pillar of the community, with an investment portfolio."

I mean, really, Olivia thought, cringing over how hard she'd tried to achieve her mother's lofty ideals for her future. Not that she'd managed much of it, having always been too broke for the investment portfolio. And probably, having a stand-up screaming fight in a local restaurant when breaking up with her cheating boyfriend hadn't been the best route to becoming a pillar of the community.

She'd done what other people wanted her to do for so long that when the cork had popped, all the changes had foamed out. Now, she was back to her normal, boring self. She loved where she was now and didn't want to change ever again.

The waiter was hovering and Olivia scanned the menu.

"I'll have the pesto-filled ravioli with spinach, artichokes, capers, and sun-dried tomatoes," she said.

"I'll have the pumpkin and prosciutto pizza," Danilo said.

"Wait a minute. I need time to decide." Francesca was clearly agonizing over her choice. As a fellow food lover, Olivia felt her pain. Having only one decision when you wanted to eat everything on the menu was the equivalent of torture. As she watched poor Francesca hungrily devouring the page with her eyes, Olivia wished they could become friends. They obviously had so many qualities in common.

At least this gave her a chance to have a quick chat to Danilo.

Rummaging in her purse, she handed him the gift bag with the leather belt she'd bought.

"I bought it in a store overlooking the Piazza del Campo. Charlotte and I went to fetch my wine bottles and decided to do some sightseeing."

Danilo's face lit up as he admired the belt. "It is beautiful. Thank you." He slid his arm around her. "Are you excited for tomorrow?"

"I'm terrified," Olivia murmured. "The festival seems much bigger than I thought, and not very friendly to newcomers. The bottling shop owner told us."

Danilo's eyes widened. "Is that so? I feel bad now because I advised you to enter. I visited it a few years ago and it was very friendly. There were many small wineries as well as larger exhibitors and it was great fun. I have heard the management changed, but did not know it had changed beyond that. But you will succeed whatever it takes. You are so fiery and determined. I know you will impress the guests and that everyone will love your wine."

His encouraging words, combined with the strong warmth of his arm around her, made Olivia feel both better and worse. She appreciated the moral support, but it would be even more heart-rending if she had to burst Danilo's bubble after the show ended, and tell him she'd failed. That would be unthinkable.

She had to succeed, Olivia resolved. Whatever it took, she had to live up to Danilo's high opinion of her!

Francesca had finally decided, and gave the waiter her choice.

"I'll have the brown butter lobster and spinach pizza," she said.

"That sounds wonderful," Olivia quickly said. "I was also tempted by it. My mother said from the time I was small, I loved spinach, which she found quite unusual."

"Does your mother live in America?" Francesca asked.

Emboldened by having drunk half a glass of wine far too quickly, and by Danilo fondly rubbing her back, Olivia found herself conversing more freely than she'd meant to.

"Yes, she does. She's always lived there and is quite proud of never having left the country." She sighed. "She says that the States is so big it has everything—deserts, beaches, mountains, snow. So there's no need to travel anywhere else. Which is true enough, I guess, but it doesn't explain why the only place she ever goes on vacation is Key West in Florida!"

Danilo laughed. Francesca gave a hint of a smile. Hoping she could forge a connection with her through humor, Olivia soldiered on.

"She's obsessed with the idea that I will come back to the States one day. She keeps on sending me information on housing and jobs." Olivia snorted.

Francesca was looking more serious and with a sudden stab of insight, Olivia realized her attempt at a joke had given entirely the wrong result. Francesca hadn't understood the jokiness in her words. Rather, she'd picked up that Olivia's mother—the family matriarch—was summoning her home.

There was simply no way to redeem the evening, Olivia decided. From this point, she was only going to open her mouth to eat and drink, because every word she spoke was causing damage.

The only good that could possibly come out of this agonizing dinner date was that by comparison, the show tomorrow was certain to be a breeze. There was no way it could be more of a disaster than this restaurant meal.

Or could it?

Olivia wondered, with a frisson of worry, what would happen if another metaphoric champagne cork had popped, and all her bad luck was foaming out at once.

CHAPTER NINE

The next morning, just as the sun was rising, Olivia pulled into the parking at Festa del Vino. She felt breathless with nerves. She'd spent the whole drive stressing about the show and wondering whether any of the wine she'd packed so carefully in her trunk would sell.

Charlotte, much more sensibly, had spent the time snoring in the passenger seat. As Olivia stopped in the crammed basement area, Charlotte opened her eyes suddenly and smothered a yawn.

"I think I might have dozed off for a moment," she admitted. "Jet lag, probably. So, how do we get all this wine up to the first floor? Is there an elevator anywhere? We need a dolly."

Looking at the steep flights of stairs that led to the upper level, Olivia hoped there was an elevator.

In the crowded, cramped, and damp-smelling basement, everyone else seemed to know where to go. People were streaming purposefully up the stairs. She didn't notice anyone heading toward an elevator, or see any signs for one.

"*Scusi!*" She hurried to ask a passerby. This man already had his exhibitor tag on a lanyard around his neck. Olivia still needed to get hers. "*Ascensore?*" she asked, luckily remembering the Italian word. "Where is the elevator?"

"*Ascensore?*" he repeated, and laughed, as if this was the funniest thing he'd heard all day. "No!" He shrugged dramatically, with a sweeping arm gesture to indicate the complete absence of elevators in this small basement.

"But…" Olivia felt shocked. "How do we take the crates up to the hall?" she asked.

"Ah. You should have come here yesterday. That was set-up day, when we were able to park outside the venue and use the dollies to transport. Today, we cannot park outside the venue or bring in dollies, as the public will be arriving soon." He nodded in a satisfied way before striding off.

"Why did nobody tell me?" Olivia said in a small voice. The confirmation email she'd received hadn't mentioned that at all. Clearly all the other exhibitors knew, and she couldn't help remembering the words of the bottling-store woman, that this venue wasn't friendly toward small newcomers.

She was starting to see why.

The stairs were long and steep, and based on how far around she'd had to drive, Olivia guessed it would then be a lengthy walk to the exhibition hall itself.

"Well, it's lucky we didn't do anything stupid yesterday, like climbing to the top of the tallest tower in Siena," she muttered to herself. Her legs were already burning as she hefted the first of the eight heavy wine cases out of her trunk.

Olivia limped up the steep stairs with Charlotte puffing behind her. It was even busier up top. Exhibitors were thronging into the hall through a fancy entrance archway that had clearly been set up for the occasion, and was twined with fake vine leaves.

With her buttocks aching, Olivia tried to go through, but she was stopped by an officious-looking young attendant.

"Where is your exhibitor tag?" the woman asked.

That was a good question.

"Where do we get it from?" Now her arms were starting to ache, too!

"From the temporary show office. Yesterday, it was at this point. Today, it's moved to the far corner of the basement."

Olivia stared at her in despair. That was all the way back again.

"Can we leave these here?" she asked, but there was an arrogant voice from behind her.

"Please can you not block the entrance? Some of us are in a hurry."

The speaker was a tall man with swept-back dark hair and an expression as condescending as his voice. Glancing at his name tag, Olivia noted that this was Fugo from Siena Associated Wines.

"Why did you not set up yesterday?" another man asked. He was wearing a gray suit that made him look ready for the office boardroom, and sounded just as impatient.

"I didn't know we were supposed to," Olivia replied honestly to the frowning Sergio from Buonconvento Vineyards.

"Is this your first time at the show?" a woman asked curiously. She had the same hairstyle as Gabriella, the type that used a whole can of spray to affix it in place. Her name was Helena from Montepulciano Cellars, Olivia saw.

"Yes, our first time," Olivia replied. "We're a small, new winery."

Now Helena was frowning, too. "I thought they were not allowing smaller, new wineries in any longer, as they lower the standard of the event."

Oh dear, Olivia thought. This really wasn't a friendly venue.

"I believe there was a cancellation from another exhibitor," the assistant explained, checking her list. "You can leave the boxes here if you are quick," she relented.

Gratefully putting down the heavy crates, Olivia and Charlotte scarpered back down the long, steep stairs and headed over to the far corner of the parking lot. There, they were reluctantly served by a harassed-looking woman.

"Did you not get your tags yesterday?" She asked the obvious and unnecessary question while searching through an old-fashioned filing box until she located their paperwork.

"I'm so sorry," Olivia said.

As well as being unfriendly to newcomers, she was starting to suspect that this show was also not efficiently run. But there was no point in complaining, she told herself. She was here now, and would have to make the best of it. And it was a proud moment when she put the lanyard around her neck with the tag that stated: *Olivia Glass—Italicano Winery*.

When Charlotte had her tag in place, they headed back up the staircase, to find that the attendant was being screamed at by a tall, scary-looking woman perched on platform heels, with a mass of dark, wavy hair cascading around her shoulders.

"What is this?" the tall woman shrieked. "These boxes are in the way!" She stabbed a crimson-nailed finger in the direction of Olivia's ice wine, which they had placed neatly alongside the wall before going downstairs. "I told you to keep this area uncluttered. Why are you not doing your job? Remove them instantly. I don't care where. Take them downstairs and dump them outside with the rest of the trash!"

"They're mine. I'm so sorry. We went downstairs to get our tags," Olivia said, feeling terrible for the poor attendant.

The woman spun around and glared at Olivia. To her alarm, Olivia saw that she had a gleaming silver name tag that stated, "Cadenza Cachero: Show Organizer."

"Take them away!" As Olivia headed over to pick up her crate, Cadenza turned back to the luckless assistant and continued berating her. "This is the third time you have allowed exhibitors to do what they want. What kind of show do you think this is? I am going to fire you if it happens again. You are useless!"

Olivia felt her hackles rise. What right did this woman have to publicly humiliate her poor assistant? No wonder this show was so unfriendly and so badly run, she thought, realizing exactly where this attitude stemmed from.

She had a sudden flashback to the days when she was a lowly junior at JCreative, and had been screamed at in front of clients, unfairly blamed for the boss's errors, and had been forced to suck it up. She'd made a promise to herself back then that she would never, ever stay quiet if she saw this happening to someone else.

It was time to make good on her promise, Olivia resolved.

"No, no, no," Charlotte hissed, grabbing her arm as she realized what her friend was up to, but it was too late. Filled with righteous wrath, Olivia faced up to the unpleasant organizer.

"Ms. Cachero, if you run this show, then you should remember the exhibitors are the customers. *Your* customers!" she said in what she hoped was a polite but firm voice although even she could hear it was sharp with anger. "So far, I've paid a lot of money to be here and it's been a disorganized nightmare. I haven't received any good service as yet except from this kind attendant, who was the first person to show us that she cared, and help us get our stall set up in time."

Despite her best intentions, she'd ended up speaking louder than she meant to. A few exhibitors, passing by, were glancing curiously at her. Now committed, Olivia continued.

"Also, it reflects badly on the entire event when someone in charge insults their staff in public. Don't do it. It is the worst kind of corporate bullying and I won't stand to see it!"

The woman's hawk-nosed face had grown furious. Seeing this, Charlotte tugged harder at Olivia's arm.

"Well, it's good to have gotten that off your chest," Charlotte said in loud, pleading tones. "Perhaps there'll be an official survey we can complete after the show and give our feedback. In the meantime let's get our stall ready."

Reluctantly, Olivia turned away as the woman marched off, practically leaving a cloud of sulfurous smoke in her wake.

"I had more to say," Olivia told Charlotte as they hefted the crates through the hall. "I wanted to tell her to discipline in private, praise in public. That was drilled into me at the first advertising agency where I worked as an intern."

"I bet James didn't do it," Charlotte said, reminding Olivia of her ex-boss.

Olivia snorted. "Never."

"Did you ever confront him about it?"

"How could I? I was on the receiving end, the same as that poor assistant. That's why I feel so strongly about it now."

As she staggered through the hall with her heavy crate, Olivia couldn't help noticing that the stands she was passing looked like miniature wineries, only fancier. They were decked out to the nines with wooden shelving, standard lamps, oaken casks, artificial vine leaves, and real live potted plants, together with state-of-the-art furniture. One stand even had a small statue of a cherub at its vine-swathed entrance. The effect was completed by subtle yet powerful branding.

Olivia didn't have any branding at all. There hadn't been time, and she'd only decided on her label and name two days ago.

"These are looking very sophisticated." Charlotte echoed her thoughts in a wary voice.

Olivia realized she'd been mistaken to think this would be more like a local fair. Instead, it was corporate and upmarket.

Finally, they reached stand number C23, their allotted space for the next two days. Putting down her wine with a sigh of relief, Olivia stared doubtfully at the stall.

It was very small. The smallest size had been the only one still available, and in any case she wouldn't have been able to afford anything larger, but she hadn't realized how insignificant it was compared to all the others. It was slotted in like an afterthought, at the end of a row of three enormous stalls. Their neighbor, Siena Olive Oils Incorporated, had topiary bushes positioned around their entrance, which practically obscured Olivia's stall.

They were hidden away and almost invisible, their tiny cubicle dwarfed by the other giants. And although it was not yet opening time, Olivia had already fought with the organizer.

This was not an auspicious start and, to Olivia's concern, she didn't see things getting any better. Would they sell even one bottle of ice wine? she wondered, with desperation clenching her stomach.

CHAPTER TEN

Finally, just ten minutes before Festa del Vino opened to the public, their stall was ready. Olivia stood, staring dubiously at the neatly stacked crates while she massaged her aching arms.

She didn't want to think about the chore of carrying them all back again. If she had to give the wine away, it would be easier than doing this in reverse tomorrow.

Even with the wine in place and the pricing displayed, her setup looked bare and underdressed. Since the charges for hiring furniture had been exorbitant, she'd gone for what she thought was a tasteful yet affordable solution—a long table at the back to stack her wine, and a bar table at the front for people to taste it.

Now she was realizing this was laughably inadequate. Her A4-sized posters proclaiming *"Italicano Wineries: Tuscany's First Ice Wine"* looked silly compared to the door-sized banners of the big wineries. She'd thought everyone would have smaller kiosks and hadn't been prepared for their overpowering size.

Olivia had ordered a bulk pack of eco-friendly bamboo cups for people to taste from. She'd thought that was very clever, but now she saw everyone else had actual glassware set out, with mini dishwashers installed in their back rooms.

Her phone rang, distracting her from her gloomy contemplation. Seeing it was Jean-Pierre on the line, she answered quickly. All she needed now was a crisis at the winery!

"Olivia!" Jean-Pierre was speaking in a hissed whisper. "I thought I should call you urgently, even though I know you are busy. I think Gabriella is planning something bad."

"What?" Olivia squeaked out. "Why? What's happening there?"

"I saw her sneak out of the building just now. She looked suspicious, so I watched her. She was pretending to go to her car, but then she ran past it and took the side path up the hill. She's going in the direction of the new beehive!"

Olivia felt appalled by this information. What was Gabriella going to do? Anxiety surged inside her as she thought about the nefarious motives the restaurateur might have. Surely she wouldn't damage the hive just to make Olivia look bad? For the past couple of days, Olivia had thought their relationship might actually be improving. Now, it seemed that Gabriella was still out to get her, just the same as always.

"Jean-Pierre, can you follow her?" Olivia asked. She was feeling so tense she began pacing through the hall as she spoke. There was no need for her to whisper, but all the same she found herself hissing conspiratorially into the phone.

"I can. I will have to be careful, though. If she sees me, she will be very angry."

"Yes, please be careful." Olivia could imagine the drama that would erupt if Gabriella noticed the tall assistant sneaking in her footsteps. "Just see what she's up to."

"I shall observe and report," Jean-Pierre confirmed in an excited mutter.

Disconnecting the call, Olivia bit her lip. Gabriella's shenanigans were adding to an overly large burden of worry. Her pacing had taken her almost all the way to the expo's entrance, and she needed to get back to her stall in a hurry.

Putting her phone back in her purse, Olivia headed back through the hall, taking a look at everyone else's superb efforts along the way, even though she knew it would make her feel even worse.

Helena from Montepulciano Cellars was busy arranging crystal goblets on top of a massive wine barrel at her empire of a stall. She glanced at Olivia, and then stared beyond her at her humble little setup.

She raised an eyebrow and sniggered to herself, before muttering something to the assistant next to her, who was setting out porcelain snack bowls filled with grissini. He looked and sniggered, too.

Olivia glanced toward her stall, feeling like she was Miss Cheap and Nasty of the show. The space looked incomplete, as if waiting to be filled with magnificent oaken barrels and fake climbing grapevines.

It wasn't like she hadn't had dreams, Olivia fumed. Of course she had. She was in marketing, after all. But, with Marcello being away and having to run the winery, she'd had no spare time, and also zero budget. The stand had been diabolically expensive! Booking it had been a punishing blow to her credit card. Now she was wishing she had backed out.

A few of the other exhibitors were strolling around the hall. Her face burned as she saw them stare in surprise at her stand, and then either sneer or snigger, depending on who they were.

"I'm not feeling good about this," she muttered to Charlotte, who was prowling alongside her, eyeing their opposition with a narrowed gaze while checking her watch.

"There are only a few minutes till opening time. I'm sure the crowds will want to taste every wine on show. Trust me, your stall will be buzzing in no time," Charlotte said confidently.

Olivia wasn't so sure. As the seconds ticked down, she had that nasty feeling in her stomach again.

A suave-looking, streaky-haired man who Olivia had seen putting the finishing touches to a stall near the entrance strolled past and hesitated.

"*Ciao*," he greeted them, looking down his aquiline nose. "What is this you are selling? Where is my friend Giacomo? He was supposed to be in this spot."

"I don't know where he is. There was a cancellation, so maybe he couldn't attend," Olivia said. Deciding to press ahead with her sales pitch, she continued. "This is Tuscany's first ice wine, and we're launching it today,"

"Ice wine?"

Olivia nodded, feeling proud all over again even though her stomach was doing flip-flops of nervousness. She glanced at his exhibitor tag to see his name. "Would you like to try some, Signor Rocco Sorrento?"

The man stared at the bamboo cup she was offering him with an expression of horror.

"Wine in *that*? I think not!" He shrugged dramatically. "This festival is to celebrate the top local wineries. Regular customers come here year after year, to visit the places they know and love and to try their new launches. You have chosen the wrong venue to come and peddle your little bottles. Nobody here will want to buy such a wine, made by an American."

He let out a sneering laugh. Then his phone rang, and answering it hurriedly, he hustled back to his exquisite-looking stall.

Olivia felt as if her world had ended. She exchanged a horrified glance with Charlotte. What if he was right, and her wine ended up being ignored by visitors in favor of the established, traditional wineries?

"I'm sure he's just trying to intimidate you," Charlotte ventured. "Probably, he's jealous. In any case, we have two full days to prove him wrong."

Olivia bit her lip. Or for him to be proven right, she thought disconsolately.

At that moment, the music stopped and there was a loud crackle.

"The show is now open!" the loudspeaker rang out. Olivia recognized the piercing tones of Cadenza, the organizer. "The thirtieth annual Siena Wine Festival welcomes visitors. *Buon giorno* and enjoy your experience here today."

A stream of well-dressed visitors flocked inside. Eagerly holding her breath, Olivia waited for some of them—or even one of them—to approach her stand.

She held her breath expectantly, but then let it out again as she saw the crowd part and form small tributaries, trickling over to all the major stands. Above the strains of light classical music over the loudspeakers, Olivia could hear the convivial cries of "*Salve!*" and "*Ciao!*" as regular visitors headed to their favorite established wineries.

Those new to the show were gravitating toward the most exquisite stalls, lured by their magnificent frontages, with cries of appreciation as they took in the sumptuous décor.

At last, there were some visitors heading her way. Olivia stepped forward, relief surging inside her, ready with a welcoming smile. How should she introduce her wine? she wondered. This was a busy show and she needed to get to the point. Perhaps a bold announcement would work best. "Try Tuscany's first ice wine!"

But at the last moment, the group veered to the right. Without even glancing at her, they headed directly for the neighboring olive oil stall.

Olivia's smile wavered and then vanished. She wished the floor could swallow her up. This was excruciating.

"Should we just take our wine and go home now?" she muttered to Charlotte, watching the throngs of visitors detour for a visit to the olive oil, and then stream past her stall without as much as a glance in her direction.

Although the fox-faced Rocco was very busy greeting visitors, Olivia noted how he glanced in their direction from time to time, with a superior smile and a dismissive toss of his head.

"Now, now." Charlotte patted her arm. Olivia thought she sounded way too cheerful for this tragic moment. Way too cheerful. "I've been thinking how to solve our problem. And I have decided we need a draw card for our stall."

"A draw card? Our *wine* is supposed to be the draw card!" Olivia protested. They hadn't even had the chance to open the first of the three bottles she'd set aside for tasting. With any luck, Erba would drink them.

"No, we need something more visual. I noticed, as we headed in, that they have a 'Schools of the Winelands' kiosk outside the hall. There are arts and crafts and stuff there, and they had items for sale. I'll go and pick up something to make the stall a little more noticeable."

"All right. If you think it will help. Thank you," Olivia said gratefully.

Charlotte headed out of the hall in a purposeful way. She must have a plan up her sleeve, Olivia decided. Perhaps she'd seen a mini wine barrel, or a tasteful wooden bookshelf. Something that would delight the visitors, and align them better with the ambience of the others.

In any case, it wasn't like she felt short of manpower with her friend gone. The only contribution they were making to this day so far was consuming a little of the oxygen within this spacious hall.

She watched a few more well-dressed patrons stroll by. Business was being done here, that was for sure. Staring enviously around at the other stalls, Olivia saw credit cards being swiped, forms filled in, bunches of euros changing hands. People were tasting, enjoying, conversing. One man in a Pierre Cardin suit took a sip of a wine, then got on his cell phone and started shouting enthusiastically, waving his arms in delight.

If only that could have been her wine, Olivia thought desperately.

Then a blaze of color caught her eye.

She turned, reeling back as she saw Charlotte pushing her way through the crowds.

Olivia's jaw dropped as her friend approached.

She was carrying a huge, bulky item almost as tall as her. Luckily, for its size, it was light in weight, being constructed mainly from polystyrene and nylon.

The item was a shocking pink unicorn, leaping over a garishly colored rainbow that had indigo missing. Olivia doubted that the creator was familiar with the anatomy of horses. In fact, it looked more like a luridly colored rhinoceros. The horn seemed to have been constructed entirely of glitter, the rest of which was strewn over the unicorn's body.

Coarse, brightly colored wefts of nylon hair in purple, electric blue, and silver comprised the animal's mane and tail.

"Well!" Olivia exclaimed.

Her stall was already a laughingstock, and she didn't think the morning could get any worse. Somehow, though, Charlotte had achieved the impossible.

"I noticed this as we came in," Charlotte said proudly. "It was in an 'Arts and Crafts of Wineland Schools' competition. See the sticker there on its backside? The work was for sale, and proceeds go toward each school's art department. So it's supporting a good cause as well."

She propped the unicorn against the bar table. Its sparkling horn jutted high into the air.

"And that was the winner?" Olivia asked in amazement. She thought the school's art department needed all the help it could get. Perhaps a teacher, for a start.

"The winner? Oh, no, it wasn't the winner," Charlotte explained helpfully. "It wasn't even placed. I saw it right at the back, and think it must have been an also-ran. But I was looking for something bright and cheerful, and thought it fit the bill."

"Cheerful," Olivia echoed.

She glanced at Rocco's stand. He was staring in astonishment at their unicorn, laughing openly at her.

She closed her eyes. The unicorn's awkward, garish form stayed on her vision in vivid purple. It had been imprinted there. There was no way of erasing this horror that Charlotte had brought, to trash her new winery's reputation forevermore.

"I'm really not sure this is the right solution," Olivia tried, deciding to approach this diplomatically. She didn't want to hurt Charlotte's feelings by grabbing the unicorn and marching straight out with it again.

"There's nothing else we can do. The problem is that among all the other stands, people aren't seeing yours. They're walking past and missing you. We have to snag their attention for them to try your wine."

"Can't we go among the crowds and hand out samples?"

"Nope. It's against the rules. You have to stay within the stand's boundaries and may not approach visitors. They'll kick you out of the show. So you need an attention grabber."

"But—" Olivia tried. She should have known better than to try and stop Charlotte in full flow.

"You see, you're too personally involved to think clearly in this matter," Charlotte continued, wagging her finger in a chiding way. "It's because it's your wine. Your baby! You're too emotional. If you were wearing your marketing hat, and not your wine-mom hat, you would have probably thought of this for yourself already."

Olivia considered her words.

What harm could it do? she concluded, staring around at the knots of well-dressed visitors that were thronging elsewhere, while her stall remained as bleak and bare as the Sahara Desert. Unless they could get a breakthrough, they would continue to be ignored. She wasn't convinced that even this unicorn would be enough to save her.

Although, the colorful décor item was starting to attract attention. Visitors were pointing, smiling and laughing as if entertained by the stall's unusual look. A few people stepped closer to read the unicorn's label and then glance curiously at her wine's description. She felt suddenly hopeful that this might, in fact, start luring in the crowds.

"Can I taste?" an elegantly coiffed woman asked in French-accented tones.

Olivia nearly fell over in amazement. The moment she'd been waiting for and dreaming of had arrived. A real, live customer was finally standing in front of her and had asked to sample her wine.

Suddenly the hall seemed lighter and brighter, and the day full of promise.

"Of course!" Olivia poured her first-ever tasting portion, beaming with delight as Charlotte looked on proudly.

The woman looked down at it with a disappointed frown. "Ah, it is red wine. I am looking for white wine." She sipped it curiously and her frown disappeared. "It is very nice, all the same. Very tasty." She put the bamboo container down and headed off.

Olivia sighed. In Tuscany, notable for their magnificent red wines, she'd managed to attract the only white wine lover at the show. Still, at least their stall was now exerting a small gravitational pull on visitors. The laws of average dictated that the next visitor would surely be a red wine fan.

But the next visitor was a serious-looking young woman who stared at Olivia in surprise, before standing back from the stall and taking a photo of the unicorn. Immediately afterward, she got on her phone and started speaking rapidly while pointing to their stall.

Her behavior was making Olivia nervous. She feared that by bringing in the unicorn, she'd infringed a show regulation without meaning to. What would happen now? she wondered, as the woman hurried off without even having asked to try any wine. Would the bad-tempered organizer march over to their stand and demand they remove it?

She suspected she was setting herself up for public humiliation in a new and different way. And then, a loud bellow jolted her from her thoughts.

CHAPTER ELEVEN

Looking up, Olivia saw a large, bearded man standing on the far side of the hall, pointing vigorously at their stall.

He yelled again, and then headed toward them at a lumbering half-run. He didn't look like show security, Olivia thought, but perhaps it was worse. Could he be Cadenza's right-hand man?

His presence attracted attention. Heads turned in surprise as he thudded past.

The large man was followed by a buxom, cheerful woman holding the arm of a bright-eyed, gray-haired senior. Behind her was a small knot of others who were clearly from the same party.

"It is Liora's unicorn!" the man announced in booming tones that resounded over the hum of voices and background music. More visitors looked around curiously.

"The unicorn of peace! She made it in crafts," the dark-haired woman added. Though higher in pitch, her voice was as loud as her husband's. "Her teacher just called to say it was at this stall. How wonderful to see it displayed."

She pulled out her phone and started taking photos. The large man was on his phone as well. From what she could make out, he seemed to be calling other friends.

"Oh, you are so kind." The grandmother squeezed Olivia's hand. "Our young Liora was so proud of her creation, and could not understand why it did not win a prize. But now it has won something even more important—a place in this festival."

"What wine are you selling?" one of the women in the party asked.

Olivia was too stunned by surprise and relief to say a word. Thankfully, Charlotte was less blindsided by events. She'd already gotten busy pouring some tasting portions.

"Tuscany's first ice wine," she informed the large party, handing out the bamboo cups.

Olivia's heart swelled at the appreciative comments that Liora's family made.

"It is wonderful. Such a different taste. Better than a dessert wine," the father stated.

"So well made. A superior wine." his wife nodded.

"I love the bottle. Italicano? Because you are Americano, no?"

Blushing with delight, Olivia conceded that the grandmother was right.

"How much is it? We are going to buy some!" the father announced.

"It's—" Olivia began, but she was interrupted by Charlotte.

"Fifteen euros a bottle." Her friend smiled, pointing at the printed paper Olivia had made.

Charlotte had changed it, Olivia realized with a twist of her stomach. Her price had been five euros. She had agonized over whether it might be too high, and had thought she'd be lucky to get some sales. But at some stage while Olivia's back was turned, Charlotte had neatly drawn a 1 in front of the 5.

At a loss for words, Olivia found herself gasping in horror. But it quickly changed to amazement as the father drew out his wallet.

"We will take four," he said, handing over three crisp twenty-euro notes.

"Four. Thank you so much for your business." Finding her voice again, Olivia tissue-wrapped the four bottles, placing them carefully in the father's canvas shopping bag. She felt stunned by how her luck had turned. Her first four sales—at a far higher price than she'd dared to advertise.

She handwrote an invoice for the cash sale and added it to the bag.

The activity had attracted attention. Noticing the group clustered around their small stall, others were now heading their way. Suddenly, Olivia found herself impossibly busy.

She was inundated by a flood of visitors wanting to taste. In fact, she couldn't keep up. She felt proud to be able to repeat her summary of the wine, not just once, but over and over again.

"It's Tuscany's first ice wine. I tasted it in America, and decided to make it here after the wild vines on my farm froze during a hard frost."

"What a story," a bejeweled, wealthy-looking woman with a German accent praised her, impressed. "Two bottles, please."

No sooner had she packed the wine up than more people converged. She didn't even have time to tell her ice wine's story to the two new guests who were impatiently waiting to taste.

She glanced at Charlotte, hoping her friend could help out, but Charlotte was frantically packing up another wine order at the back.

"This is delicious," the man in the business suit said to the glamorous older woman as they sipped.

"It is so refreshing. I'm taking a bottle back to Brazil for my daughter. She loves ports and dessert wines," the glamorous woman said.

"I'll take two bottles," the business-suited man said, putting down his eco-friendly tasting cup. "And I need your card. Here's mine. We are based in the United Kingdom, and distribute rare and boutique wines throughout Europe. Let's talk soon."

As Olivia rushed to the back of the stall to tissue-wrap the new orders for these two guests who seemed to be striking up a friendship over her wine, she saw that Charlotte was removing an empty crate. That must mean they'd sold twelve wines already.

"I'll stash the cash in my purse," Charlotte stage-whispered, transferring their crumpled euro notes and coins to her large wallet, and hiding the purse away behind a panel in the tiny back portion of their stand. "Oops, got to go. Here comes another group."

Olivia's head was whirling. She felt totally confused that the new cluster of people heading into the hall were making a bee-line for her stall, pointing at the unicorn and nodding.

As the incoming visitors swept past Rocco's sophisticated stall without even a glance in his direction, she saw the opposition winemaker fold his arms and stare at her with a hard, sour expression. She didn't have time to do more than give him an apologetic wave.

"Photos, photos, please! You two ladies, on either side of the unicorn. Hold a wine bottle each!" the leader of the group directed Olivia and Charlotte. "There. Magnifico! So wonderful to have support for the young artists of our wineland schools. For years, we have hoped to see this."

Olivia didn't know what was going to give in first, the smile pasted on her face, or her arm holding out the bottle, which was starting to ache as the group snapped away. Finally, they were ready to taste.

"Impressive. What a novel and interesting wine," the man at the front of the group said appreciatively. "How much is it?"

"Twenty-five euros a bottle for this very exclusive and limited-edition vintage." Charlotte smiled sweetly as Olivia spun around in alarm. Her friend was engaged in an upward price war with herself. She'd substituted another of Olivia's posters and redrawn this one with a 2 in front of the 5.

The group didn't blink at the price.

"How unique. May I have one bottle, please?" the man at the front said.

"I would like two," the woman behind him stated.

"We also have limited-edition items, suitable for collectors or investors." Charlotte smiled—with a hint of steel in the expression, Olivia noted. "Our first ten bottles of this unique vintage have been specially numbered and signed."

"I want one," a woman at the back of the group said. "I would like number three, please. It is my lucky number. How much is this?"

Olivia looked down at the floor, not daring to speak as Charlotte stated calmly, "Fifty euros for the limited-editions."

"Number three is mine!" Eagerly, the woman handed over the money and Olivia had to scramble among the crates to find the bottles she'd labeled. Never did she think when she had written the number on this wine that it would be selling for fifty euros. On its own. She'd wondered if she'd make fifty euros in total.

"Enjoy it." She handed it over, after wrapping it up carefully.

"What a special bottle." The woman smiled. "We will keep it as a memento of your exciting new vineyard."

"Can I have number eight, please?" another of the group asked, and Olivia had to scramble all over again.

*

An hour later, when the flow of crowds finally thinned, Olivia noticed that a woman in trendy, ripped jeans, carrying a large camera, had arrived and was waiting patiently near her stall.

"*Buon giorno*," she said. "I am Marisa, from the *Siena News*. I am covering the show. It is nice to see new arrivals here. For a few years it has felt very much the same. Your wine is causing quite a sensation, I see. And you are displaying school artwork, too."

"I'm thrilled that our stall has had some interest at this very prestigious festival," Olivia said, as Marisa scribbled down some notes. "I feel honored to be a part of such a popular event and for my wines to be displayed among such top-quality vineyards." Hopefully if she said nice things about the other exhibitors, they might start liking her better, Olivia thought.

"How did you learn winemaking?"

"I am working as sommelier at La Leggenda," Olivia said, pleased to be able to mention her employer's name.

"And this wine? This is your own?"

"I bought a farm which turned out to have been a vineyard many years ago. There were a large number of grapevines scattered around the farm, growing wild. By the time I harvested the grapes, there was a cold snap and they had frozen, so I decided to make an ice wine."

"And are you planning on staying in Italy?" the reporter asked.

Olivia felt a pang of anxiety. If she could, she would.

"When I arrived here, I didn't know I would fall in love with the country as much as I have," she explained. "I can't imagine living anywhere else. It's the most magical place. I feel so lucky to have a farm and I hope I will have the chance to farm it and grow more wine, for many years to come."

As she spoke the words, she wished that Danilo's niece could be there to hear them. If only Francesca would believe how passionately she felt about Italy, and how committed she was to her new career as a winemaker.

"What a story," the reporter enthused.

She took Olivia's photo, as well as some close-ups of the wine, and accepted one of Olivia's new business cards.

Olivia felt thrilled by her first-ever press interview. Imagine if her wine made it into the local media. What an honor that would be.

The reporter hurried away, and Olivia saw to her consternation that another group of visitors were making their way to her stand. There was no respite today. She wished she'd had a cup of coffee before the show opened.

With the mention of La Leggenda, she'd been reminded that there would surely be some friendly faces at this festival. Olivia made a note to look out for her friends and neighbors.

But, as she searched the crowds hoping to pick up someone familiar, she frowned.

The lean, balding man approaching her reminded her of someone. It took her a split second to work out whom.

The angle at which he jutted his jaw, that swaggering walk, even the way he tossed back the trailing end of the cashmere scarf he wore.

If it hadn't been for the fact this man had such a deep suntan that he looked as if he'd just spent a year on a Greek fishing trawler, Olivia would have sworn that this was her ex-boss, James.

Who knew that James had an Italian doppelganger? Olivia wondered in amazement.

Then, as the man saw Olivia, recognition lit up his face.

67

Olivia recoiled in horror as he strode determinedly over. Charlotte was grimacing at her anxiously, clearly anticipating a problem.

This was no doppelganger. It was James! The last person on earth she ever wanted to see again had just arrived at her stall.

CHAPTER TWELVE

"Well, this is a shock," James announced to Olivia and the world at large. "I can't believe I've bumped into you here. You're looking wonderful, Olivia. Very well indeed. Have you put on some weight?"

Olivia seethed inwardly. She remembered James had always been the master of the insult disguised as a compliment—it was so much second nature to him that he probably didn't even realize he was doing it.

"What a surprise to see you, James," she replied politely.

She scooted over to the side of the stand, because the bar table was crowded. Charlotte was pouring tasting portions for three different groups, who all looked eager, and as if they might want to buy.

"I didn't realize you were doing events work now. Isn't that a bit below your pay grade, so to speak? Or do they make a career of it here in Italy, the same as the waiters?"

Realization dawned. James thought she was working as a for-hire helper at this stall. He'd forgotten anything she'd told him about how she'd ended up in Italy. It was time to update him.

"Actually, this is my stall. And my winery. I've just started it, on the farm I bought. This is my first small batch of wine," she explained.

James looked blank with shock. Clearly, he was struggling to reassign Olivia into a different folder from the "Ex-Employee and Total Loser" one he'd pigeonholed her into.

"Well! Well, this is unexpected. What a career change. So this is your new venture, is it? I see you've made a clean break from marketing," he said, staring in puzzlement at her bare-basics, minimalistic setup.

"What about you?" Olivia asked, changing the subject from this thorny issue, to the more perplexing topic of his appearance here. "Are you on vacation?"

She wouldn't have thought a wine festival was James's thing. Never mind that, she wouldn't have thought a vacation was James's thing. The only time he went anywhere was for work.

Suddenly, light dawned.

"Oh, of course," she said. "I hadn't put two and two together. You obviously have a client here?" She looked around the bustling stalls again, wondering which one was James's client. Most likely, the biggest and most expensive, she guessed.

It suddenly occurred to Olivia that James was taking a long time to answer this relatively easy question. In fact, he was looking discombobulated, shifting his feet and running a hand over his gelled hair, and even glancing down at his shiny leather shoes.

"Actually, I'm taking a career sabbatical," he explained.

"A what?" Olivia asked, perplexed.

With more and more visitors milling around their stall, she and James were ending up wedged into the back corner.

"Coming through! Seventy-five euros for this collector's item," Charlotte called, reaching between them for special wine bottle number nine.

James leaned out of the way for her.

"Are you okay?" she hissed to Olivia. "Wave if you need rescuing!"

When Charlotte had taken the bottle, James leaned back to Olivia again, speaking in low, confidential tones.

"You know, the problem was that Valley Wines was my biggest account, which is why I put you in charge of it. I always admired your caliber, Olivia."

Olivia stared at James, mystified. She was receiving more praise from him now than she had in the decade she'd worked for JCreative.

"Yes?" she asked carefully.

"But after that FDA raid, when all the shortcuts and banned ingredients that Valley Wine had been using were made public—well, it ended up having a slight backlash for my business. Other clients jumped ship. What a fickle bunch!" James grimaced angrily.

"I'm sorry to hear that," Olivia sympathized.

"Luckily I was in the process of merging with another leading agency, so we had plenty of additional business flowing in. But then, the owner of the other agency—a very difficult man—said that he couldn't work with me a moment longer. Can you believe it?"

"Surely not," Olivia said, trying not to let her voice give away that she could, actually, believe it very easily.

"He insisted on buying me out. That left me with a wad of spare cash, but nothing to do with my time. It was rather unusual," James remembered. "I took a long vacation, and spent some time on

Copacabana Beach in Rio, and Bondi Beach in Sydney, soaking up the sun. Then I started traveling around Europe, to decide on a new career direction."

"What is that?" Olivia asked curiously.

"I found myself entranced by the wine culture here. The vineyards, the brands. So many great products and stories. It made me remember that Valley Wines was my most successful account ever. And that if I wanted to have a new success, I shouldn't just do the marketing. I should take charge of the whole process. I don't want to be some rich import-exporter's marketing lackey this time. Lesson learned, you know? I want to be the import-exporter myself."

"So you're here looking for brands?" What a career leap that was, Olivia thought in amazement.

"I am!" James nodded proudly. "I'm looking for the right wine, and the right winemaker."

"What are your requirements?" Olivia asked.

"A cheap, humble, yet drinkable wine. Made by a winery owner who's prepared to sign a sole mandate with me that gives me absolute authority over how to market it, and doesn't expect too much money in their own pocket. Not greedy, is what I'm saying. Someone compliant, yet reliable. An individual who has a history with me would be better still. And, Olivia, I think I may have found exactly the right person."

"That's wonderful," Olivia said.

A moment later, her brain caught up and she realized what he meant.

He wanted to go into business with *her*?

If Olivia hadn't been wedged in the corner of her stall, she would have wobbled on her feet with shock. As it was, she clutched at the wall for support.

James gave her that narrowed, catlike smile that made Olivia think of a leopard about to pounce.

"Well, obviously you'll need to look for a winery big enough to meet your demand for bulk supply," Olivia countered hurriedly, but James was ready with a dismissive wave of his hand.

"It's all in the name, right? Once we have the name, we can source the wine. It doesn't all have to be produced on site."

Of course not, Olivia realized in growing concern, given the trash, fake wine that Valley Wine had been. Why would James have changed his spots? She knew how his mind worked. He was thinking of doing the same again, and using her.

This put her in a very difficult situation.

Of course the answer was going to be no. That was non-negotiable. But if she gave James an outright refusal, she knew what he would do. He would throw a massive temper tantrum. He'd shout and scream. It would destroy the ambience of her stall and distract her buyers. Having James act out would severely impact upon her wine sales.

Her best bet was to tactfully tell him she would think about it, while making it clear how privileged and honored she was to be asked.

"I am privileged and honored to be asked," Olivia began, in a voice ringing with fake enthusiasm. "What a wonderful proposal. I can't actually believe you are considering me!"

Hoping to get him away from center stage, and into a safe area where it wouldn't matter if he threw a tantrum, Olivia tried her best to edge out of her own stall. But the press of crowds made it impossible. There was no way of escaping him.

"James, your business acumen is extraordinary. I will definitely consider your offer. Let's talk after the show."

James wagged his finger at her in a reproving way and shook his head.

"Uh-uh, Olivia. What's that word 'consider' you are using? Not a word I expected to hear from you. This must be decided now. You should not need to give it any thought. It's simple."

He raised his left eyebrow at her in that same fake-friendly way she'd seen him do a hundred times in the boardroom, where a refusal from the client had always resulted in eight levels of hell being unleashed.

At that moment, she was saved by Charlotte grabbing her shoulder.

"Olivia! We need you in front!"

At first, Olivia thought her friend was staging a crisis to break up the uncomfortable pow-wow with her horrible ex-boss. But her next words showed that the crisis was real. "Come quickly. The judges have arrived to assess your wine."

Olivia felt a stab of terror. She'd forgotten all about the competition. Now, she remembered that Charlotte had said she was going to enter her wine for it.

"I have to go, James."

Pushing her way to the front of the stand, she saw the panel of three judges standing in the middle of the crowd, who'd parted respectfully to give them space. They had their backs turned and were discussing something together.

What would these leading experts think of her wine? Olivia's stomach twisted with nerves.

At that moment, the judge in the center of the trio, who had been filling in some details on her clipboard, turned around and Olivia felt herself go pale with horror.

She recognized this woman. She was Cadenza Cachero, the bad-tempered organizer of Festa del Vino. The same person Olivia had loudly criticized at the show's entrance just a couple of short hours ago.

CHAPTER THIRTEEN

Cadenza Cachero tossed back her mass of wavy, jet-black hair and placed a crimson-nailed hand on her skinny hip. She glared at Olivia before staring disdainfully at her minimalist stall.

Olivia saw she now wore two tags around her neck. The second one read: *Festa del Vino Annual Wine Competition: Head Judge.*

"You are in the competition?" Cadenza asked in tones of disbelief.

"You are head judge?" Olivia asked in a wobbly voice that sounded equally incredulous. She exchanged a glance with Charlotte, and saw her friend looked just as astounded.

Pulling herself together, Olivia realized it was up to her to mend the situation, even though she feared it was too late to smooth things over with this scary femme fatale.

"Thank you so much for giving of your time and expertise. I'm so excited to be part of this competition. It was a last-minute decision to enter. I hope we did everything right?" Olivia asked, trying for a warm smile even though it felt forced.

"Unfortunately, last-minute decisions do not always work out well, as your stall's décor clearly proves," Cadenza reprimanded her icily. "Still, let us judge. Come, Alexander and Aldi."

Only then did Olivia look at the two judges flanking Cadenza.

To her astonishment, she recognized the taller man, with his wavy gray hair and rugged, noble features.

He was Alexander Schwarz, winemaking expert and leading critic. This icon in the world of wine had visited La Leggenda in late summer and given Olivia some valuable tuition. They'd become good friends. Alexander had even helped her solve a murder. How wonderful to see him here. Olivia felt delighted, if nervous, that she would receive an opinion on her wine from someone she knew to be a world-renowned expert.

She knew that this fair-minded guru would never allow his judging to be influenced by a past friendship, but even so she felt encouraged when he raised a bushy eyebrow at her and gave her a quick, warm smile.

At least she had one friend in this otherwise inhospitable crowd. Scanning the watching faces, she saw that James had retreated, but was hovering near the stall, watching the judging with interest. Olivia remembered that he didn't normally have a long attention span. With any luck, if the judging took some time, he would have moved on to find another potential target among the wine sellers.

"Pass me a glass." Cadenza clicked her fingers. As if by magic, a gleaming crystal tasting goblet materialized.

"Give one to the other judges."

She stepped aside. Only then did Olivia see the much shorter, stressed-looking young assistant who was carrying a tray of glasses and a huge folder of papers.

Another assistant wheeled up a gleaming steel cart, atop which was a large copper spittoon, a plate of crackers, and bottles of water.

"Entry number forty. A Tuscan ice wine?" Cadenza asked, checking her clipboard.

"That's right," Olivia agreed enthusiastically. "I made it—"

"Ice wine. Thank you."

Cadenza held up a stern hand. Olivia got the message. She was not supposed to speak.

She waited expectantly as the first judge, Aldi, stepped forward and tried the wine. He took a long time over it, first holding up the glass to take in the color, then swirling and thoughtfully smelling the wine. Finally, he tasted, holding the wine in his mouth for a long time before turning to the spittoon.

Olivia couldn't bear the suspense. Would this wine tasting expert give any of his feelings away? Or would she have to wait until the actual results were announced to find out if he'd liked it or hated it?

She became aware of a repetitive background noise. Charlotte was drumming her fingers nervously on the table. Her friend stopped instantly when Cadenza glanced her way, and laced her fingers together.

Then they all waited in tense silence for the judge to step away from the spittoon.

Staring anxiously at him as he turned, Olivia felt her heart leap. The expression of surprised joy on his face was unmistakable. A massive beam spread over his broad features and he nodded several times as he jotted notes on his clipboard.

Then her friend Alexander stepped forward and accepted his tasting portion. Olivia felt even more nervous now watching him swirl, smell, and finally taste her wine. Her palms were damp and her heart was jumping into her mouth. She knew how strict, yet fair, Alexander was. There was no way he would show any favoritism. Olivia's wine would be judged the same as all the others.

She could hardly breathe as she saw the same expression of incredulous delight on his face, too!

Reaching for the clipboard, Alexander started scribbling notes.

Cadenza stared at her co-judges sourly, as if she'd hoped Olivia's wine might be a non-contender.

"Fill my glass," she said.

She smelled the wine carefully and Olivia decided she looked miffed. Perhaps she'd hoped to find immediate fault with it and hadn't. Well, that had to be good news, right?

Cadenza tasted her wine. Then she went into a huddle with the other judges.

The huddle lasted quite a while. Olivia wished she could hear what was being said, because there seemed to be an argument brewing. Cadenza was insisting on something, stamping her platform-sandaled foot emphatically. The other two judges were shaking their heads.

"No!" Alexander shouted. "You cannot do that!"

After another minute of furious discussion, Cadenza beckoned her over. She looked quietly satisfied. Both Alexander and Aldi, in contrast, appeared mutinous.

"We agree your wine is excellent," the woman told her. "Outstanding, in fact. It is high quality, and well made. We have noted that the bouquet is fresh, floral, and appealing, and the balance of oak is perfect. Key flavors include intense cherry and strawberry notes, and there is a smooth, slightly sweet, and pleasing finish. It is an exciting, innovative addition to Tuscany's offering."

"Thank you," Olivia gasped. She'd never expected such praise. This was beyond her wildest dreams.

"However," the judge continued, in tones that snapped Olivia off her happy cloud and straight back to grim reality. "We have a problem."

"Oh dear! What's that?" Now her heart was in her mouth all over again. Had she somehow made a terrible mistake in spite of all the praise they'd given it?

"We have no category for this wine, as it is new to our area's portfolio."

"Oh, of course." Light dawned. Given that it was Tuscany's first ice wine, it was logical there would be no category for it. Olivia didn't feel disappointed. She guessed that was par for the course when making something new. And in any case, their words of praise had been enough.

But it seemed there was dissension in the judging ranks.

"We could include it in the Best New Wine category. There are no restrictions on type of wine there," Alexander growled, and Aldi nodded vociferously.

Cadenza ignored them.

"It is a great pity. Perhaps next year we can include a category you will be eligible for." She paused. "Although, our show is already very much prebooked for next year. You will only be able to exhibit again if there is space available," she added in meaningful tones.

She turned and swept away, creating a minor pandemonium as her assistants scrambled to organize themselves, the wheeled cart, and the other two judges, to follow in her wake.

Olivia was trembling all over.

What an outcome. She'd never expected that they would love her wine. That was the most important fact. Their words of praise felt engraved in her mind and she knew she would remember them forever.

"That's a shame about the categories," Charlotte commented sourly. "If you ask me, that head judge was making up her rules on the fly. I'm not sure it's legitimate. I think you should complain and say it isn't fair."

Olivia shrugged. "Who is there to complain to? Cadenza seems to fill all the roles. In any case, I don't mind at all. I wasn't expecting to get such amazing critiques, and from top experts, too. Plus, there's no point in winning a prize when most probably, we will have sold almost all the wine by the end of the show. So we wouldn't even get to put a pretty badge onto the bottle saying 'Highly Commended at Festa Del Vino.'"

Placing her hands on her hips, Charlotte gave Olivia an exasperated stare.

"Although you are my best friend and usually very intelligent, at this moment you're missing the point. The point is that this woman doesn't like you, hates your stall, and hinted strongly that you couldn't come back next year. So it won't matter how good your wine is, or what category you enter," she warned.

Olivia considered the logic. With a chill, she realized that her friend was right. Though Cadenza had clearly loved her wine, it hadn't made the judge like her any better. And she seemed to wield absolute power on every decision-making front.

"What can I do?" Olivia asked, beginning to panic. This show had been such an unexpected success. She had to come back.

"I'm not sure apologizing now will work. Too little, too late? Perhaps a written apology?" Charlotte mused, but she still didn't sound positive.

"I know! I have the perfect solution. I'll gift her a bottle of my wine. That will prove my good intentions, and hopefully it'll increase my chances of being allowed to come back next year."

"That sounds workable. You'd better hurry and do it now, while they're all still together. I'll see to sales here."

Grabbing a bottle of her ice wine, Olivia threaded her way through the crowds in the direction the judges had gone.

She hoped that her last-ditch attempt to smooth things over with Cadenza would work. If it didn't, this would be her one and only appearance at Festa del Vino. Worse still, this well-connected woman might go out of her way to make sure that other doors slammed shut in Olivia's face.

CHAPTER FOURTEEN

The judges had crossed the exhibition floor before Olivia managed to catch up. It was slow work pushing through the press of people and she kept losing sight of the group.

Finally, through a gap in the crowds, she saw they were going in the direction of a raised stage. There, banners announced: *"20ᵗʰ Annual Festa del Vino Wine Awards Ceremony."*

"Wait!" Olivia called breathlessly. "Cadenza! Please may I speak to you for a moment?"

Finally, Alexander heard her shouts and took Cadenza's arm.

Once again, Olivia stood face to face with this cantankerous woman. Cadenza frowned impatiently at her, and Olivia knew that this was make-or-break time for her future at this show.

"I wanted to thank you again for the judging. As a newcomer, it's been such a valuable experience, and I've learned what I need to do in order to achieve the high standards that you set. I hope I'll have the chance to come back next year. In the meantime I wanted to give you a gift, and wondered if you would accept a bottle of my first-vintage ice wine."

Olivia wished that she could have shared her carefully worded apology with the whole group, but the hall was too noisy. Still, at least Cadenza had heard. Would it be enough?

Cadenza paused for a moment. Then her angry expression softened slightly as she looked at the wine. Olivia felt a surge of relief. Clearly, free stuff paved the way to this difficult woman's heart.

"I will accept your bottle," she said in firm tones.

"Oh, thank you, I'm so grateful," Olivia gushed, feeling heady relief that she hopefully wouldn't be banned from the show.

"I did not say, however, that you would be welcome here next year," Cadenza said sternly, bursting Olivia's bubble as soon as it had formed. "Your display has lowered the tone of the festival. I will always give priority to my loyal repeat customers. We must prepare to announce the results now," Cadenza said to Alexander, raising her voice as she turned away. Still holding Olivia's wine, she strode away, followed by her retinue.

"But—but don't you think new blood is important?" Olivia said to herself in a small voice, feeling crestfallen. Despondently, she weaved her way back through the press of crowds. Despite her best efforts, this might be her only appearance at the show and she'd just have to try to make the best of it.

As she neared her stall, she saw to her alarm that in her absence, Charlotte had capitalized on the judges' positive comments.

She'd raised the price to forty-five euros—forty-five! Olivia read the notice in horrified amazement. But the expense wasn't putting off the crowds, who seemed mesmerized by Charlotte's sales pitch.

"Praised by the judges!" she announced to the clustering visitors. "It would have won gold except it's so unique there wasn't even a category for it. Taste Tuscany's first ever, groundbreaking, industry leading ice wine that's the most memorable product at this entire show. Only forty-five euros for the first-ever limited-edition vintage. Trust me, very soon this label will be famous. Plus, we're the only winery supporting local schools!" Beaming at the crowd, she displayed one of the tall, slender ice wine bottles.

"Nice to see a winery supporting schools," she heard one of the onlookers say. "We've been waiting for this for years."

Charlotte passed around the tasting portions, which were met with appreciative murmurs.

Olivia would never have dared to hike the prices so high. But the weird thing was, the higher the price went, the more people believed that the wine was good.

She felt incredibly thankful that her friend was there to help. Charlotte had always been a hustler of note, Olivia remembered. Back at the school fair held in their junior year, she'd managed the Spin and Win kiosk along the same principles, and it had been the biggest money-taker at the event. Olivia and the rest of the team had basked in the reflected glory and the principal's praise. It was reassuring to see that, since those days, her skills had only improved. Raising the prices as the day went along had been a genius move. Olivia would never have thought of that—or gotten away with it if she had.

Quickly, she squeezed in the side of the stall to help her friend package up the bottles.

"You're a superstar. Thank you so much for everything you're doing, and on your vacation, too," Olivia praised her.

"We're on the last crate, and it's nearly finished." Beaming in satisfaction, Charlotte pointed to the one remaining crate which she'd carried out from the back. "Your reputation is growing. I've had a few people come along and say they've heard of this new ice wine and must have a bottle. A couple of people have asked for business cards and given me theirs. Useful connections. Import-export agents and international distributors."

Olivia couldn't believe it. Her wine had almost sold out, with people asking for it and interest from business people. It had been astonishingly successful.

"How many bottles for you?" Charlotte smiled at an approaching customer.

"Three, please."

"It just so happens we have exactly three left. Here you go."

"What about the numbered bottles?" Olivia asked.

"All sold out but one," Charlotte told her in a satisfied murmur. "Number six is the only one left."

Charlotte handed the tissue-wrapped bottles to the customer, and helped her stow them safely in her carrier bag.

At that moment, Olivia saw an anxious-looking man approach. His shirt was creased and his mussed, flyaway hair made Olivia wonder if he'd brushed it with a balloon.

"You are the vintner making the ice wine?" he asked.

"Yes, that's right," Olivia said. Quickly, she glanced at his tag. Giacomo was his name.

"I need a bottle! I want to know how you made it."

Pleased to be able to give him the abbreviated version of her wine's story, Olivia smiled. "Well, it was accidental. I waited too long before harvesting any of the wild vines on my farm, and a hard frost set in. I thought the grapes were ruined, but then remembered that I'd once had a wonderful ice wine in a restaurant. So I decided I would try and make the same wine here using frozen grapes. It was an intensive process, but since my harvest wasn't big, I managed to do it correctly. It was really just making the best of things, but I was lucky and it worked out well."

"I see, I see," the man said. He dug in his pants pocket and pulled out a battered wallet. "The wine, please."

"We only have one of the specially numbered bottles left," Olivia said, thinking that she wouldn't charge this man the premium rate, as he looked like he'd had a bad day.

She turned round to the stand where the single bottle waited. Except it wasn't there.

Confused, Olivia glanced at Charlotte, who was wrapping it in tissue paper. Then Charlotte handed it to the woman she'd been dealing with while Olivia had been explaining about her ice wine.

"Oh," Olivia said. "I'm so very sorry, Giacomo. The last bottle just got sold."

Giacomo's eyebrows raised in an expression of disbelief.

"That is not possible. I needed a bottle!"

"No," the man behind him said. "*I* needed a bottle!"

Startled, Olivia saw there was now a queue for the wine she no longer had. The tall man behind Giacomo, whose name tag read "Fernando," looked even angrier that supply was unavailable.

"If you had accepted credit cards, I could have bought earlier," Fernando said. "You told me I had to go and draw cash. Why did you not have this facility?"

"I'm really sorry. I'll accept cards next year. I had no idea we'd sell out so fast," Olivia explained to both of them.

Her apology fell on stony ground. With an angry snort, Giacomo turned on his heel and marched away from her stand. Fernando stomped irritably past, casting a jealous glance at the package which the final customer was carrying triumphantly away.

Quickly, Charlotte took down the pricing notice. She turned it over and wrote on the back in large letters, "SOLD OUT,"

"There you go. It's official. I guess if our wine is finished, we can close up shop for the day?" she said, picking up the last empty box. She carried it out of the stall and put it in a recycling can.

"I guess we close up for the festival. There's no point in being open tomorrow without anything to sell," Olivia said when she came back. "I'm definitely taking this unicorn home. It brought us so much good luck. It can live in the barn."

Olivia picked up the glittery unicorn, suddenly aware how bare the stall looked with no wine on the back table, and all the posters removed.

"Maybe we should find Cadenza and tell her we've sold out. They might want to take down our stall completely, rather than having it stand empty? It won't look good having an abandoned stall in the show. I want to keep on her right side."

Charlotte considered, tapping her fingers on the bar table.

"True. We don't want to be rude, and do want to make sure she's happy. Best to tell her."

"If you put the unicorn in the car, I'll go and find Cadenza. Then maybe we can get a bite to eat somewhere before heading home?"

"Good idea. Let's meet at the entrance in ten minutes," Charlotte agreed.

With their plans finalized, they headed in different directions. Crossing the expo floor, Olivia saw that people were beginning to prepare for closing time. Wine racks were being unloaded, cash boxes were being surreptitiously stowed away. Strolling past in a haze of tired contentment, she wondered how everyone else had done and whether their day had been as successful.

With a jolt, Olivia saw James ahead of her. He hadn't noticed her and was talking to another stall holder. Quickly she changed her route to avoid him and went the long way around, skirting the outside edge of the hall.

Where were the admin offices? Staring at the overhead signs, she saw the one she was looking for. *Ufficio Amministrativo.*

She headed down a corridor and, to her surprise, found herself climbing a short stairway to a raised stage that now had the curtains drawn. Getting her bearings, she realized she was heading onto the awards stage. A look at the now-stacked signage confirmed to her that this was where the wine awards had recently been given out. Olivia hadn't even heard who the winners were. She'd been too busy selling wine to do so much as glance in that direction.

Now, the stage was empty and with the curtains closed, it was much darker than the brightly lit hall. Olivia found herself treading carefully in the gloom.

There was a smell in the air she recognized—the aroma of spilled wine.

Her foot brushed against something that skittered away. To her surprise, Olivia realized it was a shard of glass.

There had been breakage here and nobody had yet cleaned up. Olivia thought that was odd. Had someone dropped a bottle during the awards? She shivered. This abandoned stage area was giving her the creeps.

Where was the organizer's office?

As her eyes adjusted to the gloom she noticed a narrow side passage that led behind the stage. So the admin offices were somewhere behind here? She guessed in a historic hall in central Siena, you had to use whatever nooks, crannies, and back rooms were available.

As she headed backstage, she picked up that the smell of wine was stronger. In fact, she could see the spillage. Jagged fragments of glass and a dark stain spread over the tiled floor. There was nobody around to clean it up.

"This feels strange," Olivia told herself, deciding then and there that she didn't want to come back the next day. There wasn't a soul in sight, only a pile of tarpaulins in the corner. Ahead was a doorway that must lead to the office.

Tiptoeing toward the door, minding her step around the glass, Olivia glanced again at the tarpaulins and saw what looked like a platform shoe sticking out of the pile.

She gasped, her heart banging in her chest. Fumbling in her pocket for her phone, she took it out and turned on the flashlight.

Olivia let out a horrified shriek.

It wasn't tarpaulins at all!

Slumped in the corner of the backstage area was the motionless form of Cadenza Cachero, show organizer and head judge.

"Oh, no!" Olivia whispered. The room seemed to spin around her and the flashlight beam wobbled wildly. "No, no, no. What has happened here?"

She wanted to turn and run, but with a huge effort of will, she stopped herself. As the first person to stumble across this terrible scene, she had to be responsible.

Stepping over the pool of wine, Olivia crouched down next to the woman. She was hyperventilating with anxiety. In contrast, Cadenza didn't appear to be breathing at all and was completely still.

With trembling fingers, she grasped the woman's wrist. It felt cool and she could pick up no hint of a pulse.

It was then that she realized the most terrible fact of all.

A shard of glass glowed in her flashlight beam, and she noticed it had part of a wine-stained label on it.

Without a doubt, Olivia recognized it. This broken bottle was her own   ice   wine.

CHAPTER FIFTEEN

Olivia scrambled to her unsteady feet and backed away from the horrific sight. She hustled around the corner, returning to the now-closed stage. Goosebumps prickled up and down her spine.

Her wine had been smashed in splinters near Cadenza's body. How had that happened? she agonized.

Shaking her head in confusion, she reminded herself she had to manage this terrible situation. What should she do first?

Call the police, Olivia decided, wishing she could call Marcello instead.

Quickly, she dialed the emergency number.

"I need to report a death," she said breathlessly, using English because in the shock of the moment, she didn't feel up to describing this scene in Italian.

"What has occurred, signora?" the officer on the other end of the line asked.

"I'm at the wine festival. Festa del Vino in Siena. Cadenza Cachero, the organizer, has died. I've just found her body. It's behind the stage, on the way to the organizer's offices."

"At the festival?" The officer sounded surprised. She heard the crackle of a walkie-talkie in the background and guessed he was already contacting his team. But he wasn't finished with her yet.

"How did you discover this?"

"I was looking for her to ask her about our stall."

"And you are?"

"Olivia Glass. I'm one of the exhibitors," Olivia said, worrying as she spoke her own name that she was incriminating herself. She hoped that the police would find this death was due to natural causes, except it didn't look like it. The smashed bottle spoke of a fight or struggle.

How was she attracting these disasters? she wondered briefly. She knew that Italy was a country where hot-blooded passion ruled the day but why, oh why, did people have to kill each other when she was around?

And why, oh why, had her ice wine ended up at the scene?

Olivia's eyes widened as she realized that the bottle itself could have been used as a weapon!

"Please, stay where you are until the police arrive. They are on their way and will be there in a couple of minutes. Do not touch anything," the officer warned.

Well, it was too late for that. The ice wine bottle would be covered in her fingerprints, Olivia realized, with a frisson of worry.

She heard approaching footsteps behind her and spun around.

A woman was hurrying toward her, holding a microphone in her hand. Olivia recognized her vaguely. She thought she'd seen her doing something official in the exhibition's lobby area.

"Is there someone in the offices?" she asked impatiently. "This needs new batteries, or a replacement. It is refusing to work. Is Cadenza there? She said she would assist, and she has not." She brandished the microphone impatiently.

"Wait," Olivia said, twitching all over with tension. "Please don't go backstage."

"We have to announce the show's closing. We are running late already," the woman explained impatiently, fiddling with the switch.

"The only problem is that Cadenza is dead," Olivia said in a pleading whisper.

"What?" the woman cried, looking appalled. "Cadenza is dead? You are telling me she has died?"

With a shock, Olivia realized that the stupid microphone had suddenly started working. The woman's horrified words boomed around the exhibition hall.

"Please, turn it off," she beseeched.

"Where is she? Is she behind the stage here? Why are you not letting me see?" The woman pushed past Olivia even though she did her best to grab at her arm.

She took one look at the gruesome scene and let out a shriek. This, again, resounded around the entire show.

"Oh, *mio Dio*! What has happened? What have you done to her?"

Grasping her arm more firmly, Olivia managed to wrestle the microphone away and turn it off, before handing it back and leading the woman out of the gloomy backstage area. This situation was spiraling way out of control. She had to stay calm and try to contain the damage.

"The police will be here in a minute," she said breathlessly.

But, thanks to the unwitting announcement that the woman had made, Olivia saw to her alarm that other people were arriving sooner.

Exhibitors were streaming down the corridor, their faces filled with worry. To her dismay, she recognized some of them.

"What has happened? Has there been a crime?" Helena from Montepulciano Cellars called.

"Will the show continue tomorrow?" Rocco Sorrento shouted. "I need to know whether to bring in more stock!"

"The show had better continue after what we have paid to be here," Fugo from Siena Associated Wines said threateningly.

"Are you the vintner who made that ice wine everyone's talking about?" someone else called, and the growing group looked at Olivia with more interest.

Olivia felt at her wits' end. This was a nightmare scenario. Three people were already on their phones, making calls. And a fourth had his phone pointed at her. He was taking her photo! This was a level of fame, or rather notoriety, she'd never wanted to achieve.

"Can we see where it happened?" Helena asked. Immediately, there was a buzz of support for this idea.

"Yes, we need to look," Fugo agreed.

"We must check. Perhaps she is just resting," Rocco insisted.

"I agree. Why are we taking this Americano's word for it?" somebody else threatened.

The crowd pushed closer. Olivia sensed animosity was building. She glanced to her right. At least her new microphone-holding friend could confirm her story.

To her horror, she found she was alone. Somewhere in the mayhem, the woman had disappeared. She was on her own, and now had to try and hold back a clearly aggressive crowd.

"Please don't pass," she said, stepping into the narrowest part of the passage and squaring her shoulders.

At that moment, she heard the crackle of walkie-talkies and a loud, authoritative man's voice shouted, "Clear the way!"

Never had Olivia imagined that her main emotion upon the arrival of the police would be relief, but that was how she felt as the group of officers trooped toward her.

"Move aside. Move aside, *grazie*."

Curiously, she eyeballed the lead detective swaggering through the crowds. He looked as if he spent more time pushing weights than combing through crime scenes. Bulky, toned arms protruded from the tight, short sleeves of his white golf shirt. His mirrored shades were pushed up onto his close-cropped dark hair, and his tanned jaw jutted purposefully.

People moved respectfully aside for the muscular investigator, who sashayed through to the accompaniment of admiring glances from many of the onlookers. Clearly, his bronzed, toned presence had soothed the fires of anxiety that Olivia had set.

Behind him followed his team, comprising another plainclothes detective, lean and intelligent-looking, as well as a uniformed police officer.

Once the lead detective reached her, he turned and faced the crowd. Many people already had their cameras out, snapping eagerly at the eye-candy that this tragic situation had so opportunely provided.

"Stay back, please, while we investigate."

Realizing she was going to be in the photos as well, Olivia ducked away, but the movement attracted the detective's attention.

"Ah," he said, distracted from his moment of fame. "Are you Olivia Glass, the woman who made the emergency call?"

"Yes, I am," Olivia replied apologetically.

"I am Detective Giorgio Barrazzi. As from this moment, I am in charge of this case."

The detective drew himself up to his full six-foot-one height and squared his jaw. Olivia was sure she saw a couple of women in the crowd faint.

"Lead me to the scene," he commanded.

"It's here," Olivia said, heading reluctantly behind the stage once more to face the disturbing sight.

The crowd stayed back, efficiently contained by the uniformed officer, but the other detective followed Olivia into the gloomy area.

"The coroner's van has arrived," he told Barrazzi. "They are on their way into the hall."

"Good. Let us photograph the scene, Artoro."

By "us," Barrazzi clearly meant "you." Olivia sidled out of the way, pressing her back against the wall as Artoro stepped over the broken glass. He efficiently checked Cadenza's pulse, before photographing the scene from many different angles.

Olivia hoped he might be able to give an instant opinion on Cadenza's death, but it didn't seem to be so conveniently simple. A moment later, she found herself in Barrazzi's crosshairs again.

"You found the body?" he asked sternly.

"Yes, I did," Olivia admitted. She wished she hadn't innocently walked behind the stage at that moment. Why had she been the one to stumble upon this sight? Thinking back, she guessed Cadenza's death must have been recent. The show was busy. Someone would have gone to the organizer's office sooner, rather than later. If she hadn't found the body, the woman holding the microphone would have.

"Why did you come to this backstage area?"

"I'm an exhibitor. We sold out of wine this afternoon, and I wanted to ask the organizer if she wanted to dismantle our stand. I found her here."

"So this deceased woman is the organizer?" Barrazzi sounded confused.

"She has a card around her neck saying 'Head Judge,'" Artoro called.

"She's the organizer and head judge," Olivia said.

She hoped that after this simple explanation, she would be off the hook. But at that moment, Artoro spoke again.

"The deceased woman has a visible mark on her temple. A deep abrasion, possibly even a fracture," Artoro called.

Barrazzi's gaze went from her slumped body, to the smashed bottle of wine, back to the body, and then to Olivia.

"We must put two and two together, Artoro. There is a valuable piece of evidence here. Bag the bottle fragments, and we will take them in for fingerprinting. Can you read the label?"

"I can. It says *'Italicano Winery—Special Vintage Ice Wine.'*"

Now, Barrazzi's gaze rested calculatingly on Olivia's name tag.

"Olivia Glass—Italicano Winery? You are the maker of this wine?"

This was getting worse and worse, Olivia fretted.

"I am," she admitted.

"Do you know how this bottle ended up here? Backstage, smashed, and probably used as a weapon?" Barrazzi sounded stern.

There was nothing for it but to tell the whole truth. It was better that Barrazzi heard it from her, than from one of the hundred exhibitors waiting eagerly in the corridor to give him their version, which would probably be even worse.

"I gave her the bottle to thank her for judging my wine."

"So she judged your wine?"

"Yes."

"What was her opinion on it?" Barrazzi asked carefully.

"She liked it, but said it didn't qualify for any of the categories so it couldn't win a prize," Olivia admitted.

Just as she'd feared, Barrazzi pounced on this tidbit of information with a suspicious frown on his chiseled face.

"You must have been angry about that?"

"No, I wasn't." Olivia shook her head firmly.

"There was an entry fee?"

"Yes, it was quite expensive." Realizing this was a bad argument, Olivia continued hurriedly. "My friend paid it."

"So when were the winners announced?"

"Just now, I believe."

"And after they were announced, you came here to find the judge?"

"No, no," Olivia protested. "I'd sold out of wine. We did really well today. I didn't care about the competition."

She stared pleadingly at Barrazzi, who seemed to relent slightly.

"We will need to interview you again. What is your phone number, and do you have identification on you?"

Olivia gave the detective her phone number and handed over her passport. He paged through the document.

"You are here on a visitor's visa? I see it expires in a week," he observed. "Are you not a resident here?"

Why was he picking up on completely irrelevant angles? Olivia fretted.

"I'm busy applying for my residency, and the year-long visa," she explained.

"You have left it very late," Barrazzi said in disapproving tones.

"I've been really busy." Olivia spread her arms and tried for an innocent smile.

"You realize that your visa will be denied if you have a criminal record? Even being arrested on suspicion could affect the success of your application," Barrazzi warned.

Olivia felt as if she'd landed in a waking nightmare! Was he trying to scare her? If so, his tactics were working. She was scared. Was he trying to encourage her to confess—either to the crime, or to give up more information? She couldn't do that because she hadn't committed the crime and had no clue who else could have done it.

"I'm innocent," she protested.

"We will be investigating this as a matter of urgency. For the time being, you are under suspicion," the detective emphasized. "You may not leave town."

"I can't leave town? But I have to go home tonight, to my farm near Collina," Olivia protested. "I have to feed my cat and goat. And soak my feet in mustard bath salts!"

"Check into a hotel," the detective ordered, showing absolutely no sympathy whatsoever for Olivia's predicament.

At that moment, two medics wheeling a stretcher arrived and Olivia retreated hurriedly. As she headed out, she hoped that the coroner might somehow find important evidence to clear her beyond any doubt.

In the meantime, she was in a dire situation.

Her biggest problem, Olivia quickly realized, was that everyone thought she was guilty. As she headed through the waiting crowds, she noticed that every onlooker was watching her. Conversation fell silent as she passed, and the whispers intensified behind her.

"Why did they let her go?" she heard one young woman ask curiously.

"You should have heard her fighting with Cadenza this morning," another said.

"Someone needs to tell the police about that," his partner whispered in tones just loud enough for Olivia to overhear.

Spinning around in concern, she saw him look away with a smug smile.

She needed to get out of here. In a panic, Olivia pushed her way past the waiting exhibitors, knowing that each and every one suspected her of this crime. Leaving in a hurry only confirmed her guilt in their eyes.

By the time she'd run the gamut of the crowd, Olivia was feeling frazzled. She was certain her visa would be declined, and that she'd end up spending the night in jail after Barrazzi had heard all the tidbits of information from the eager-to-gossip crowd.

CHAPTER SIXTEEN

Olivia headed back into the now-emptying exhibition hall and to her relief, saw Charlotte hurrying across the tiled floor.

"What's happened?" she asked. "They closed the doors for a while and I couldn't get back in. Then I saw a whole bunch of police arriving."

"There's been a murder," Olivia updated her friend in a quivering voice.

"Here?" Charlotte sounded incredulous. "Who?"

"Cadenza."

"No!" Charlotte clapped a hand over her mouth and then removed it to exclaim, "*Her?*"

"It looks like she was hit over the head. With my wine, which was smashed all over the floor. And I found her body when I went to ask her about the stall, so the police suspect me now."

Charlotte clapped her other hand over her mouth and stared at Olivia in shock.

"This is terrible. I can't believe it. Are you okay?" She enfolded Olivia in her warm, cuddly embrace and hugged her tightly.

With her face mashed into Charlotte's thick, red-streaked hair, Olivia started to feel better.

"I'm okay, I think. But I can't leave town. The police detective told me to find a hotel."

"We can work with that. It's not a train wreck," Charlotte said thoughtfully. "They haven't told me not to leave town, so I'll head back home and feed your animals. You can book us in somewhere in the meantime. There's bound to be a few places within walking distance. You need a change of clothes, I'm sure? Pajamas? Toiletries? Toothbrush? I'll bring back a bag for you."

"What if Pirate's lonely?" Olivia asked forlornly.

Charlotte snorted. "Pirate's a strong, independent woman. Plus, you've been working such long days at the winery that she won't even notice you're gone for a few more hours. In any case, you need to prepare your animals for when you really do head off on a romantic vacation with Danilo and you have to get a pet feeder in."

Overwhelmed by Charlotte's rational words, Olivia could do no more than nod in agreement. She was grateful beyond words that her friend was here, even though she felt bad that Charlotte was now embroiled in this situation too.

How could she make it up to her bestie? she wondered. Well, for a start, she could calm down, Olivia resolved.

"You're an absolute star. When you get back, dinner's my treat. In the meantime, I'll go hunting for a good spot," she said, forcing herself to sound calm and sensible.

With a satisfied nod, Charlotte hurried away in the direction of the basement. But, as she headed to the exit door, Olivia felt stressed to the nines all over again.

What a rollercoaster ride today had been. She'd thought she'd managed to overcome the odds stacked against her and make her name as a new player in the wine market.

Thanks to the murder, all that people would remember was that the show organizer had been bashed over the head and killed with a bottle of her ice wine! They were all talking about her, but in the completely wrong way.

Worse still, her visa was now in jeopardy thanks to the horrific timing of this disaster. How could such a terrible thing have happened?

Trailing out of the hall, Olivia couldn't help picking up yet more murmurs from passersby. For once, she wished she didn't understand Italian so well as a group headed past her, talking animatedly. They were all discussing her. The Americano, whose ice wine had been found smashed near the organizer's body.

"I have just heard from the police that because of this, the festival may not open tomorrow," one of the group said in anxious tones as she passed by.

Olivia stopped, trying to overhear more details, but the speaker had hurried away. Unfortunately, looking back attracted other unwanted attention.

"Hey! Olivia!"

Her heart plummeted even further as she saw James eagerly swaggering in her direction.

"Have you thought about my offer?" he yelled, attracting more curious and suspicious glances.

James, who didn't speak Italian, clearly had no idea that Olivia was implicated in this nefarious crime. She wished she could warn him that most probably, everyone who overheard him now thought he was a hit man.

"I've been a bit busy," she said faintly as James strutted toward her, his legs looking like chopsticks in his faded skinny jeans.

"I would have thought you'd have considered my proposal as a matter of urgency," he said, sounding the way he had back at JCreative when Olivia had asked for a deadline extension.

"I am considering it. But I am on my way to a meeting that might have a great outcome for us." Olivia gave him a hideously fake, conspiratorial wink as she voiced her terrible lie. "I'll catch up with you tomorrow. Gotta run!"

Even that might not have been enough to stall James, but at that moment his own phone rang. Seizing the moment, Olivia rushed out of the hall, taking the ground-floor exit that led onto the streets of Siena.

Marching along in the darkening evening, Olivia resolved to find the closest possible hotel and hunker down. Luckily, she had a wad of cash in her pocket which would pay for the accommodations.

The first hotel Olivia tried, closest to the venue, had a sign outside saying "No Vacancies." Reaching a crossroads, she decided to turn uphill. She found herself climbing a narrow, cobbled road closely lined with scenic buildings. She gazed at the wrought-iron balconies and colorful window-boxes, feeling soothed by the simple beauty of these homes.

A signboard pointing the way to Hotel Siena Vista encouraged her to keep going. This tiny lane didn't even seem accessible to vehicles. Taking in the quaintness of this scenic corner of Siena, Olivia felt better and more hopeful.

A hundred yards further on, at the top of the hill, was Hotel Siena Vista. Heading inside, Olivia hoped that they would have space.

"Is there anything available?" she asked, looking around the small lobby which was gorgeously decorated with a bright array of painted ceramic plates on the wall.

"We can help you. We have one twin-bedded room available on the top floor," the receptionist informed her.

"I'll take it," Olivia said, feeling relieved.

The porter was standing by, but since she had no luggage, there was nothing for him to do except escort her to the shoebox-sized elevator.

Heading up to the third floor, Olivia was delighted when she found Room 304. It was a luxurious, beautifully furnished room with a massive window that gave a panoramic view over the countryside north of Siena.

Looking out over the dusky evening sky and sparkling lights of the city below made her feel more hopeful about her admittedly grim situation. Even though she was in a world of trouble and shouldn't have felt hungry at all given her serious predicament, Olivia realized she was, in fact, starving. She quickly researched dinner venues, discovering that there was a pasta and seafood restaurant a short walk away.

Then she messaged Charlotte with her location.

"Park in the exhibition venue," she advised. *"It's not a long walk. Call me when you arrive and I'll come and help carry the bags."*

Slumping onto the bed, Olivia stared out over the darkening view, watching more lights twinkle into brightness as she breathed deeply and decompressed. What a weird and unplanned day it had been. From start to finish, it seemed the exhibition had thrown her a succession of curveballs.

She wished that she could call Danilo, but today he was working in the coastal city of Viareggio, installing wooden stairs and carved banisters in a millionaire's seaside home. Olivia visualized him doing his magic with fine mahogany in the sumptuous mansion. He'd be immersed in his project. She couldn't even call him to break the news about what had happened.

But she could call Jean-Pierre!

The day had been so crazy that Olivia had completely forgotten about the developing situation at the winery. What had happened, and why hadn't he called back? Scenarios flooded through her mind, none of them good. What if Gabriella had seen her assistant following, and fired him instantly?

Filled with a whole new set of concerns, she dialed Jean-Pierre's number.

"Salve, Olivia!" he answered. She thought he sounded slightly guilty.

"Jean-Pierre. I hope you've had a good day." Yet again, Olivia had to try her best to stay calm even though she felt like howling inside. There was no need to burden her assistant with the terrible events that had taken place at the show.

"It has been so busy. I am only cleaning up now. We were a waiter short in the restaurant, so Gabriella invited me to help out during lunch service, when I had space in between the tasting room tourists. It was fun, but crazy! She was actually very friendly toward me."

Olivia's eyes widened. Was Gabriella intending to poach her promising young sommelier? She wouldn't put it past her.

"And earlier on, when she headed out of the restaurant?" she prodded.

"Oh, yes. I was able to follow her while successfully camouflaged."

"How did you camouflage yourself?" Olivia asked curiously.

"I broke a few small branches off the olive tree in the parking lot and held them in front of me. That way, I hoped, if Gabriella looked around she would simply think I was a shrub."

"Good thinking. I guess she didn't look around?" Olivia asked.

"No. She went up to the beehive and took many photos. Then she made a phone call. Then she returned to the restaurant. I was able to take a shortcut and came in through the back courtyard, so she never knew I was gone at all."

What had Gabriella been up to? Olivia wondered. Her actions had been mildly suspicious, but without further information, she would have to wait and see what, if anything, unfolded.

"Can you send me a report on today's sales?" she asked.

"Of course. We had ten percent more tasting guests than the same Saturday last year, and our sales are higher by the same amount," Jean-Pierre told her proudly. "You will find it interesting, when you see the list, how our white wine sales spiked. I noticed it myself. People are looking forward to spring!"

Olivia was delighted that he'd developed an interest in the numbers and statistics whose patterns were so vital for the winery's success. She hadn't even realized how important they were until Marcello had explained how he analyzed them daily, weekly, and monthly, to identify trends and any potential problems.

"Have a good evening," she told her assistant. "Thank you for the update."

At that moment, she saw she had another incoming call and quickly disconnected.

The caller was Charlotte.

"I'm driving into the basement now," her friend announced.

"I'm on my way," Olivia said, scrambling off the bed and hurrying out of the hotel. She appreciated how much easier the downhill walk was. It felt like only a minute before she met Charlotte wheeling two bags to the basement's exit.

"Here's your gear. Pirate is fine. She seemed excited at being without parental supervision for the night. Who knows what she'll be up to?" Charlotte laughed loudly. "And Erba already put herself to bed in her Wendy house. I gave them both enough food and water to last until tomorrow night. Your unicorn is installed in the barn and seems very happy there. So we can think of this as an unexpected adventure."

"Thank you," Olivia said gratefully.

"What are our plans for the evening?" Charlotte was clearly on a mission to distract her friend from her woes, and Olivia felt grateful for her cheery support.

"I thought we could shower, change, have a drink in the bar, and then head out for dinner."

"Sounds fantastic. You go first."

Olivia had a speedy shower in the sumptuously equipped bathroom and changed into the fresh top that Charlotte had brought. After refreshing her makeup she felt energized, as if the day's exhaustion had been washed away as well.

Charlotte was the world champion at lightning showers. By the time Olivia had scanned through the report that Jean-Pierre had sent, they were ready to head down to the bar.

The small bar was a haven of polished wood and gleaming leather furniture, and had antique wine bottles displayed in cases mounted on the walls. Olivia looked at them admiringly, deciding she would try to source a similar type to display her own antique bottle, when it was back from being restored.

"It's started drizzling," Charlotte observed as they headed to the bar counter, where there were two empty stools. "And the wind has picked up. That means it's red wine weather, for sure."

"I agree," Olivia said.

They ordered two large glasses of sangiovese, and a big bottle of San Pellegrino sparkling water to hydrate themselves after their long, tiring day.

While Charlotte checked messages on her phone, Olivia tuned into the conversation taking place in Italian behind her.

"How was your day at the festival?" the first man asked.

"Long. I had forgotten how much I dislike expos," the second replied. "They are chaotic, stressful, and expensive."

The first man laughed. "Agreed. My feet are sore, and my back is aching."

Olivia found herself nodding in sympathy as the barman placed their drinks in front of them. She took a grateful gulp of her wine before returning her focus to the conversation.

"Never mind sore feet. Worse still, we may have empty pockets. We have no idea if this show will go ahead tomorrow. If it is canceled, what are our chances of getting any money back?"

The first man thumped the table, making Olivia jump. "Exactly. With the organizer dead, who is going to refund us? It will be a disaster that will take months to sort out. But I am sure, by tomorrow morning, they will have arrested the killer and the show will go on."

Olivia took another swallow of her wine, listening intently.

"You think?" the second man asked.

"I am sure."

"Who?"

"That American winemaker. They say that the organizer refused to accommodate her in the competition judging. So she chased after her with a bottle of wine and begged her to include it. Naturally, her request was refused, but she forced the judge to take the wine all the same."

"Really?" the second man asked.

Really? Olivia mouthed, horrified that her actions had been interpreted this way.

"Absolutely. Eyewitnesses, including my friend Fugo from Siena Associated Wines, saw this. A short while later, Cadenza was found dead, hit over the head with that selfsame bottle? It is open-and-shut, in my opinion."

Olivia listened in mounting distress. People had noticed her pursuing the group of judges and had leaped to the wrong conclusion.

This was just one pair of exhibitors out of hundreds. Similar conversations must be playing out all over Siena, as everyone channeled their inner detectives and came up with one name.

Hers.

Her innocent actions couldn't have landed her in bigger trouble if she'd tried.

CHAPTER SEVENTEEN

"There's a problem behind us." Leaning toward Charlotte, Olivia hissed the warning.

"I've been watching your face. Are those men talking about you?"

"Yes, they are."

"From their tone of voice and that word 'Americano,' I suspected it. We'd better go."

They drained their wineglasses, and Olivia chugged back the rest of the water. Urgently though they had to leave, there was no need to waste perfectly good drinks.

"Let's go see if there's a secluded table in the restaurant where we can hide out," Olivia muttered, as they sidled out of the bar trying not to make eye contact with any of the patrons. "If not, it's to-go pizza on our laps in the hotel room."

They hustled down the cobbled street to the restaurant. As they strode along in the misty rain, hunger and anxiety warred inside Olivia. Would there be a suitable table? She didn't want to unwittingly cause a scene by being recognized. Even though none of what happened had been her fault, she was feeling mortified, as if she were the pariah of the festival.

Peeking hopefully into the warmly lit restaurant, Olivia saw it was still only partway full. Better yet, she spied a secluded table for two in a small annex.

"May we sit over there?" she asked the waiter who greeted them at the door. Fortunately, he nodded and escorted them to it immediately.

The restaurant's welcoming interior featured attractive window arches painted in ocher, and bright tapestries on the walls displaying local highlights. As they passed the artworks, Olivia gazed admiringly at the depictions of the Piazza del Campo and Torre del Mangia, which brought back such great memories of their day in central Siena.

Thinking back to that happy, carefree outing made Olivia even more determined to extricate herself from the awful situation she'd ended up in.

Breathing in the delicious aroma of baking cheese and fresh seafood, overlaid with the fragrance of wine, she sat down with her back to the room.

"We need to plan," she stated emphatically.

"Who could have killed Cadenza? I don't understand it," Charlotte said.

Olivia nodded. "It's boggling my mind, too."

The waiter brought menus, which they perused hungrily.

"This food looks amazing," Olivia said, glad to change the topic to a happier one for a moment.

"We'd better order quickly before this place gets too full. I'm going to have the crab linguine with chili and parsley. And a glass of sangiovese. And I think we need to share the house special salad, with parmesan and pancetta." Clearly just as starving as Olivia, Charlotte was devouring the menu with her eyes.

"I'll go for the creamy lemon and shrimp risotto, and the same wine."

With their orders placed, they returned to the important discussion of the crime.

"I just can't believe the timing of it," Olivia lamented. "Why did I have to find her body? And why was my wine used as a weapon?"

Quickly, Olivia checked behind her, worried that someone might have overheard her words. She didn't want to fuel the fires of gossip any further. Luckily, the closest table was still empty.

Charlotte nodded sympathetically. "It's a dire situation."

"Everyone at the show suspects me. I spent the whole day trying to build a reputation as a winemaker. All I've done is make people think I'm a criminal."

"People have short memories," Charlotte soothed.

"The longer this hangs over me, the harder it will be to erase those memories. And that police detective didn't look like he was the best investigator. He was one of those real muscle-bound, handsome guys."

"He was?" Sipping her wine, Charlotte brightened.

Olivia sighed. Her friend's fetish for well-built law enforcement officers was proving to be a complicating factor.

"Time is not on our side," she reminded her.

"What do you think we should do?" Charlotte asked. "We could write a media release, giving our version. Perhaps that reporter would publish it, the one who visited your stall today?"

Olivia shook her head. "She won't publish anything so controversial, I'm sure. Not when the general public wants to see me locked away. There's only one solution. We are going to have to find out who the killer is."

"Us?" Charlotte said, sounding alarmed.

At that moment the food arrived. Stressed as she was, Olivia took a moment to admire the spread. The sumptuous mixed-leaf salad, generously laden with crisp pancetta, green peas, and slivers of parmesan, looked mouthwatering. And her risotto was fragrant and delicious. Olivia could tell a liberal splash of white wine and a generous dollop of cream had been used in its preparation.

When the waiter had left, Charlotte spoke, sounding cautious.

"How are we going to investigate? We don't know a thing about this woman."

"When the show opens tomorrow, that can be our starting point," Olivia said.

"When? More like 'if.' They might well cancel the second day after what's happened. Especially since she was the organizer, and all. But let's assume it's open. What then?"

Olivia considered their plan of action while spearing some of her crisp, green salad leaves. "We will need to do some background research. The fact that it happened straight after the awards were given out is surely significant. Probably, someone wasn't happy with the outcome of the judging."

"You think?" Charlotte twirled pasta around her fork, staring down at it happily. "I have different ideas. She was a real femme fatale. Her hair must have taken an hour to tong up into those curls. I reckon it was a jealous lover who did her in. Probably she rejected him cruelly and he snapped."

"Why would anyone so nasty have a jealous lover?" Olivia asked incredulously.

"You know how they say bad women attract good men," Charlotte said, shrugging modestly at her ability to back up her own statement.

"And if it wasn't that?" Olivia pressed, needing to get past this ludicrous theory.

"If it wasn't a crime of passion, I think that someone killed her to get hold of your ice wine! You saw how in demand it was. It wouldn't surprise me if someone resorted to those measures."

Olivia snorted. Charlotte's theories were getting more and more bizarre. She needed to guide the conversation back toward common sense.

"I think it's more likely to be someone who didn't win a prize. The timing points to it, and you saw how rudely she treated the competitors."

Charlotte rolled her eyes. "You're not using nearly enough imagination here."

"We have to stick to the facts," Olivia said regretfully.

"But the fact is your ice wine was super-successful and might have caused jealousy."

"I think we must look at the competition first, and keep a lookout for anyone angry with Cadenza. Then we can definitely explore the jealousy motive."

Charlotte sighed. "It's better to have too many theories than none at all. We will have a busy day tomorrow pursuing all of them."

"I'm going to need your help, because so many people at the show know my face and suspect me," Olivia said, taking another mouthful of the deliciously tangy, creamy risotto. "They might not be willing to open up to me."

It wasn't going to be easy, she acknowledged. But at least she'd be spending the day in productive research, and obeying the police by not leaving Siena. Her main worry was that time was tight. After tomorrow, the exhibitors and visitors would go their separate ways. It would be impossible to track all of them down.

Even as she scooped up the last, delicious mouthful of the risotto, Olivia felt her stomach knot with tension.

She had one day to solve this. One short day. If she hadn't found the killer and cleared her name by the time the show closed tomorrow, she never would, and she'd end up in a world of trouble.

Imagine if she had to accept James's offer after all, Olivia thought, with a thrill of fear. What if selling out to him was the only way she could still cling to her hopes and dreams of a career in wine?

A moment later, she was appalled with herself for being so defeatist. How could she entertain such a thought? She could never abandon her ideals. There would be no need to, Olivia told herself firmly. Tomorrow, no matter what it took, she was going to find the killer and clear her name.

CHAPTER EIGHTEEN

Early the next morning, Olivia headed purposefully out of the hotel and walked down the cobbled lane. She'd had a troubled night and felt sleep-deprived, but even so she was determined to tackle the day with everything she had.

The cold, gusty morning felt inhospitable and threatening. Olivia wished for a ray of sunshine to make her feel better, but the dawn was blanketed by clouds and she wrapped her jacket around her tightly, shivering as she strode.

Nearing the hall, she was encouraged to see that lights were on. There was activity inside. Fortunately, even at this early hour, there was an attendant at the main entrance. The young man was perched on a bar stool, eating a cornetto and drinking a massive cappuccino. Olivia suspected that under Cadenza's rule, neither of these activities would have been allowed.

"*Buon giorno*," she greeted him. "Do you know if the show is going ahead today?"

The attendant shook his head. "So many people have been asking. At this stage, we think probably not. The police are inside at this moment, with the assistant organizer and the admin team. They might take many more hours to comb the scene."

Olivia's shoulders slumped. All her plans crumbled around her as she stared morosely inside. Perhaps she could put plan B into action, and hover near the main entrance. Other exhibitors might come by to see if the show would go ahead, and that way she could at least question a few people.

But in apologetic tones, the attendant said, "Please can you keep the doorway clear, signora. The police have requested it."

Turning away, Olivia trudged back up the paved path, her stomach churning. Her troubled night and frantic plans had all been for nothing, and she wasn't even going to be allowed to stand nearby.

As she headed onto the sidewalk, she heard a faint cry from behind her.

"Signora! Signora!"

Olivia spun around. The attendant was waving frantically to her. She rushed back, breathless with expectation.

"We have just heard good news. The police say the show can go ahead. We will start an hour later in order that people can prepare. So the doors will open at ten a.m."

"Oh, thank you," Olivia said, feeling so relieved she could have hugged him.

They now had an entire day to clear her name and to find out what had really happened to the unlikable Cadenza Cachero.

*

Just a few minutes after Olivia had called Charlotte with the good news, she was relieved to see her friend rushing toward the show entrance.

"I was already up and dressed," she said breathlessly. "As I left the hotel I decided to bring this along for you." She passed a carrier bag to Olivia.

Opening the bag, Olivia found a smart, navy fedora.

"I bought it at the kiosk near the lobby. You need to look different from yesterday to prevent too many people from noticing you." She winked at Olivia.

"That's a very clever idea. Thank you," Olivia said gratefully, as she pushed it onto her head.

"If it had been a real gift, I'd have chosen a prettier color. They had gorgeous pink and turquoise ones. But its role is to help you blend into the background," Charlotte said wisely.

Streams of exhibitors were already arriving, all eager to get into the show and spruce up their stall ready for opening time. Swept along in the pushing, barging throng, Olivia felt sorry for the poor officials, vainly trying to hustle the crowd into single file so they could check tags.

"So, what do we do first?" Charlotte asked, ricocheting sideways as a large, stressed-looking man jostled her.

"First and foremost, we investigate the competition results." Olivia swerved to avoid a woman hurrying the other way with a tray of snacks. "We need to know who entered, and who won. That will give us a starting point."

"I still think we should explore that judge's romantic life first, and then quiz the people who wanted your ice wine. But I agree, there's no

104

harm in looking into the competition results to start with," Charlotte added hastily.

"I was entry number forty, so it was a big competition. Where would we find the results?" Olivia wondered.

"I guess in the admin offices."

Olivia grimaced at the thought of going past the backstage area again, even though she knew that the scene must have been long since cleared.

"I reckon we just walk innocently in and ask to see the score sheets," Charlotte advised. "While we're looking, we can photograph them, and then we'll have a complete record."

"What if they pick up we're American? Everyone suspects me." Remembering the gossip she'd overhead yesterday, Olivia couldn't help feeling as if there were a target painted on her forehead. She pushed the fedora more firmly onto her head.

"Turn your tag around so they can't see your name, and speak to them in Italian. You'll manage. Yes, you might have a slight foreign accent but it is an international show and I'm sure they won't pick up where you're from."

Taking a deep breath, Olivia headed to the stage. Around her, the stalls were bustling with activity. She heard the thump of crates being set down and the clink of glassware, but didn't dare to look in anyone's direction in case they made eye contact with her and started shouting.

They climbed the stairs and headed backstage, to find that the police had set up a row of lights on metal stands. The backstage area was brilliantly lit and the shadowy gloom had been banished.

This time, Olivia headed all the way to the door at the far end of the backstage area. It was half open, and stepping through, she headed down another short corridor. At its end was a cramped office. Inside, two harassed-looking women were on the phone. A third phone was ringing nonstop.

"Yes, the show is on today. Thank you," the first one said. She ended her call and grabbed the next one. "Yes, the show is on today. Thank you."

She replaced the receiver, looking sick of her job. Quickly, before anyone else could ask the same question, Olivia stepped forward.

"*Buon giorno*. Are the competition results from yesterday available?" Olivia asked in her best Italian.

"On the wall." The attendant gestured with her phone, which had started ringing again. She answered with an impatient sigh. "Yes, the show is on today. Thank you."

Glad that this had gone seamlessly, Olivia stepped over to the wall, where printed pages were taped in place.

There were four categories, she saw. Best New Wine, Best Overall Wine, Best Low to Mid-Range Priced Wine, and Best High-End Wine.

With a sniff of outrage, Olivia wondered why she hadn't been able to enter one, or both, of the first two categories. According to the description there seemed to have been no good reason at all. The horrible judge-organizer had been prejudiced. No wonder the other judges had been so angry.

Putting aside her personal gripe, Olivia focused on discreetly photographing the lists while she glanced through them. There were four gold, silver, and bronze winners, and eight Highly Commended ribbon earners in the list.

"*Grazie*," she said, quickly heading out. Neither of the two women replied. They were too busy answering phones and saying, "The show is on today. Thank you."

They headed out of the cramped, overly warm office.

"Now what do we do?" Charlotte asked.

That was a good point. Where should she start? Thinking logically, Olivia decided there was no reason for a winner to have murdered Cadenza. They would have been happy with their silver or gold award. So perhaps the first and most important job was to rule out the few people who had no discernible motive at all.

Olivia ran her gaze down the list. Helena from Montepulciano Cellars had won silver in the Best Overall Wine, and the unlikable Signor Rocco Sorrento had won gold in Best High-End Wine. She sighed, disappointed by Rocco's gold. Personally, she'd found him obnoxious and would have been eager to investigate him further. Still, she had to let the evidence make the call.

"I think we need to speak to the other two judges," Olivia said. "Alexander and Aldi would have spent the day with Cadenza. They would have seen all the confrontations and personal dynamics with the competitors. I'm sure they can give us a lead on where to start."

But, as they descended the staircase and returned to the bustling exhibition hall, Olivia found herself walking toward a familiar face. For a change, it belonged to somebody that she was thrilled and delighted to see.

CHAPTER NINETEEN

Happy tears prickled Olivia's eyes as she hurried up to her tall, handsome boss, and hugged Marcello as hard as she could.

"*Salve!* I was looking for you!" he exclaimed, his arms wrapping tight around her. How wonderful it was to be with him again, in his calm, soothing presence and strong embrace.

"I'm so glad to see you," she said. "I didn't know if you would be here and didn't see Castello di Verrazzano's name on the exhibitor list."

He released her reluctantly. Olivia saw Charlotte had discreetly withdrawn and was pretending to look at a nearby stall. Clearly, she thought that Olivia needed some alone time with him.

"Castello di Verrazzano is part of the Organic Winegrowers' Alliance. We are sharing a stall at the north end of the hall with other fully organic wineries, to promote these products to other winemakers and to the end consumer," Marcello explained.

"I hope it's going well," Olivia said.

"It is. But we heard yesterday about an even bigger success." Marcello smiled. "Many people were commenting on the quality of the ice wine that this small, new vineyard produced. I am so proud of you."

"Thank you." Olivia was glowing with delight at the praise. At the same time, though, she wanted Marcello to know that her job at La Leggenda was still her biggest priority.

"Everything's fine at the winery. Sales were good yesterday, particularly our white wines, and the bees are settling in well," she reassured him.

Marcello nodded. "I received photos of the new hive yesterday from Gabriella."

So that was why she'd been taking shots of the bees. Olivia was relieved that the restaurateur hadn't had more sinister motives.

Marcello continued. "She was anxious for me to know that keeping the bees at La Leggenda had been her idea. And she was very surprised when I said you had already told me so."

"It was a brilliant idea and I'm so glad she thought of it." Olivia smiled, eager to credit her rival, especially when she'd wrongly suspected her of sabotage.

To her surprise, Marcello's smile disappeared and he seemed troubled as he spoke. "Gabriella called again late last night to tell me something more serious. She said that a friend of hers had just shared the shocking news that you were involved in the show organizer's death. We were told about that tragedy after we left the show, and today everyone has been speaking of it. I am horrified that some people suspect you, and I know it cannot be true."

Olivia felt appalled. The well-connected Gabriella had been trying to throw her under the bus after all! At least she hadn't changed her ways, she thought, frustrated.

Quickly, she filled in her boss on the real story.

"My wine couldn't be included in the competition. Cadenza wouldn't allow a new category, but that didn't worry me, as it was selling so well. But I could see she was prejudiced against me, so I gave her a bottle of my wine as a gift, just before the results were announced. People saw me handing it to her. When that bottle was found smashed, they drew the wrong conclusions."

Marcello nodded. His face hardened.

"It is bad luck that, once again, you have been caught up in a dire situation through no fault of your own. Regarding the competition, between you and me, this is not the first time I have heard about prejudice and irregular results."

"Really?" Olivia asked. Was Marcello implying this might have provided a motive for Cadenza's murder? Intrigued, she waited for him to continue.

"It is one of the reasons we stopped entering the competition under Cadenza's management. Having won medals many times in the past, La Leggenda was suddenly not placed at all when she took over. When I mentioned this to other exhibitors, I was told of rumors."

"Rumors?" Olivia asked curiously, fascinated by Marcello's account.

He nodded. "The rumors were that having three judges was simply for show, and to attract paying entries. She could overrule any decision made and she had her favorites lined up before the competition began. Although I tried to confirm whether this was true, I was never able to do so. Therefore, I never spoke of it. It was just hearsay, as was the talk that in the past, money has changed hands to ensure a gold medal award. That, to me, was unspeakable."

"Oh!" Olivia was stunned by this bombshell. The judging had been unfair. If it hadn't been for Cadenza's prejudice, she could have entered legitimately and perhaps even won a Highly Commended.

Even though she'd sold out all her wine, Olivia couldn't help feeling angry that this nasty woman might have prevented her from earning an important accolade.

"It is one of the reasons we decided to stop exhibiting here," Marcello admitted. "Though it reaches good markets, it became extremely expensive, and the sudden discrepancy in our judging results made me reluctant to invest the money."

"The woman at the bottling shop also mentioned it had changed in the last few years," Olivia said, and Marcello nodded solemnly.

Olivia felt so grateful that she'd bumped into him. His wise, knowledgeable presence was like a soothing balm. Marcello always had valuable insights.

She wished she could leave the festival with him, find a coffee shop, and have a good catch-up. They'd probably solve this crime within an hour if they put their heads together. But it wasn't going to be possible. Marcello must be chaotically busy, and she couldn't keep him any longer.

"Please don't worry about me," Olivia emphasized in a firm voice. "I'm going to make sure that by the end of today, the perpetrator is arrested."

Marcello's lips twitched. "I have the utmost confidence in you. I'm sure I don't need to tell you to be careful," he said, giving her the ghost of a wink.

Feeling on top of the world after this fortunate encounter, Olivia headed over to rejoin Charlotte. Marcello's insights had provided so much food for thought and Olivia was thrilled that he'd given her a new direction to explore.

If the judging had been so blatantly prejudiced, there would have been other angry people, she realized. Other winemakers had invested far more in the show than she had. Perhaps they had been more disappointed, too. A low score would be a slap in the face, and could even be a costly disaster. Such a person could easily have lost control, confronted the judge, and in a wild moment, killed her.

Which of the winemakers had done that? She needed to find out, as soon as possible, by unlocking the secrets that the score sheets held.

"Did you get any interesting information from Marcello?" Charlotte asked hopefully as Olivia approached.

"Yes. He confirmed the judging was unfair and in fact, hinted that there had been corruption."

"That's appalling!" Charlotte declared in passionate tones.

"So, I think we need to start by looking at who didn't win. We need to examine who came stone last, or whose scores dropped suddenly this year. Then we will find the people who could have been so angry that they took action."

Charlotte nodded. "Brilliant idea. Let's get out of the main thoroughfare and have a close look at these results."

Heading to the side of the hall, they retreated into a quieter corner and peered down at the screen shots.

"Now this is useful! They've also listed the placings from the three previous years," Charlotte said. "That means we can see if anyone mysteriously fell out of favor with the unpredictable head judge."

Scanning through the lists and doing frantic mental arithmetic, Olivia realized she and Charlotte were practically breathing down each other's neck. And then Charlotte announced, in tones of quiet satisfaction, "I've found someone."

"Who? Who?" Olivia said excitedly.

"Sergio from Buonconvento Vineyards. Look at the Best Overall Wine category. Three years ago, gold. Two years ago, gold. Last year, silver. This year, nowhere."

"That's significant," Olivia agreed, excitement surging inside her. "We need to go and speak to him. Perhaps it wasn't due to the quality of the wine at all but rather due to personal issues with the judge. That could rightfully have made him angry."

Still tucked away in their quiet corner, she looked up the location of his stall.

"I think we should approach him one at a time," Olivia advised. "That will give us two chances, in case he's defensive or clams up."

Charlotte nodded in agreement. "That's a wise idea. I'll hang back."

Olivia headed purposefully across the hall. She felt breathless with excitement that this crime might be solved while the day was still young. That would put a stop to the damaging rumors that she feared were eroding her reputation, minute by minute.

As she marched across the floor, keeping her head down so that all people would notice was her unremarkable hat, Olivia jumped as she heard a familiar voice from behind one of the stalls she passed.

"Espresso, please, Artoro. Double, with sugar, and a glass of water on the side."

It was Barrazzi. Worried, Olivia stopped to listen in to the detective's contribution to solving the crime, which at this point seemed to involve nothing more than ordering his second in command to bring strong coffee.

Straining her ears, Olivia picked up that Barrazzi was actually in conversation with somebody else.

With Fugo, in fact. She recognized his voice.

"It was terrible what I witnessed yesterday," Fugo said, clearly having thought of some extra embellishments to his story during the night. "There I was at my stall, innocently selling wine, when there was a commotion outside. That woman, Signora Glass, was pushing through the crowd. She looked murderous. She was shouting for the judge. 'Come here! Come and justify your decision,' she yelled."

Olivia felt as if her eyes were going to pop out of her head with sheer outrage. What a bald-faced lie! How could Fugo make up such destructive falsehoods? What did he hope to gain by slandering her so badly she ended up in jail? And, worse still, what would the detective think of this bombshell?

Olivia didn't dare to breathe as she eavesdropped on this incriminating conversation.

CHAPTER TWENTY

Straining her ears, Olivia listened as the detective's questioning continued.

"Do you know who else heard the exchange between Signora Glass and Signora Cachero?" Barrazzi asked Fugo.

At least he was confirming whether there had been other witnesses, she thought, relieved.

Fugo paused for a moment.

"Everyone must have heard, surely?" he asked, sounding unsure. "But anyway, it was her actions. The way she forced that wine into Cadenza's hand!"

"And was the judge alone?"

Again, Fugo hesitated. "Well, she was with her judging panel. There were three of them. Also a couple of assistants were with the group. So there were witnesses to her actions," he added enthusiastically.

"That is significant," Barrazzi agreed.

Then, to Olivia's frustration, the show music got turned on, far too loud. The thumping, catchy notes of rock star Gianna Nannini boomed through the hall and effectively drowned out further conversation.

With her ears throbbing, Olivia continued on her way. She had heard enough, she decided, feeling anxious. Fugo was out to get her, and Barrazzi seemed more interested in his daily dose of caffeine than in properly confirming a witness's version.

She was going to have to stay well away from the police. If they saw what she was doing, they might believe that she was trying to influence people.

Finally, as the music was adjusted to a more manageable level, she reached Sergio's stall.

It was a symphony of elegance, with dark leather couches at the back and a polished wooden mini bar counter along the front. Gleaming crystal glasses were set out at perfectly spaced intervals.

Sergio himself was at the back of his stall, arranging a lavish pile of crackers on a large porcelain dish.

He turned to carry the elegant arrangement to the bar and noticed Olivia. She knew immediately he'd heard all the rumors. He got such a fright upon seeing her that the plate tipped and the crackers cascaded onto the plush burgundy rug below.

"What are you doing here?" he asked in tones of outrage. "Go away! You do nothing but cause trouble. Look what you have done now."

"Signor, I'm so sorry. Can I help you clear up? I was hoping that I could quickly confirm something with you about the judging yesterday," Olivia began, feeling frustrated that her interview was getting off to such a bad start.

"The judging? I have nothing whatsoever to say about that to you. Nothing. You cannot come into my stall and nor can you ask me any questions," he shouted angrily. "No doubt you are looking for people to blame. Go away."

While making shooing motions at her, he accidentally trampled on the crackers, crushing them into the rug's thick pile. Staring down at the mess he'd made, he began shouting in dismay.

Olivia retreated, feeling discouraged. So early in the day, and she was already encountering massive obstacles.

Heading around the corner, she almost bumped into Charlotte.

"Well?" her friend asked excitedly.

Olivia sighed. "He wouldn't say a word to me. I wasn't able to ask him any questions or connect with him at all. He was extremely defensive. And to make matters worse, he dropped a pile of crackers onto the carpet when he saw me, and then stood on them."

Charlotte let out a snort of laughter and Olivia smiled reluctantly.

"I know. Funny, yet not funny. I'm not sure you'll be able to get through to him. He's very upset and prickly now, and also in a panic about the mess. Perhaps we should leave him and come back later?"

"No, I think now's the time, while he's vulnerable and distracted," Charlotte decided. "I have a plan. Give me a minute to get organized, and I'll go and speak to him. If you can find somewhere to hide out, you can watch and listen. Then both of us will hear if he reveals anything."

Olivia thought Charlotte was being far too optimistic and didn't hold out much hope for her success. Even so, she loitered near the stall's side wall, where she couldn't be seen but could hear Sergio lamenting, "*Mio Dio*, this mess! Five minutes till opening time and my rug is ruined."

Only five minutes? Glancing around anxiously, Olivia couldn't see any sign of Charlotte. Time was running out, and Sergio would soon be too busy to answer questions. With a stab of worry, Olivia wondered if something had gone wrong.

At that moment, a cheerful cry resounded from the other direction and Olivia spun around.

"Hello, hello."

Olivia clapped a hand over her mouth, wide-eyed in disbelief, as Charlotte marched past her hiding place and headed into Sergio's stall.

The stylish scarf that had been knotted around her friend's neck was now wrapped around her head in a workmanlike way, hiding her red hair completely. She'd gotten—from who knew where—a broom and an empty bucket.

"Stall cleaning services. We heard you had an accident, good sir. I am here to help," Charlotte announced in a plummy and wildly fake British accent.

"Oh, *grazie, grazie*," Sergio was so desperate that he bought Charlotte's faux persona completely.

Olivia found a small gap in the panels where she could peer through and see the scene playing out. She watched, enthralled.

"I'm so glad I could travel from London to work at this event. I'm part of Cleaners Without Borders. No doubt you've heard of us." Charlotte confirmed her fake identity chattily as she wielded the broom with efficient expertise. Olivia felt numb with admiration that she'd painted the picture of herself as a Brit. Never would Sergio suspect that this helpful angel in disguise was the suspicious Americano's best friend.

"Now we just have to get these crumbs into the bucket. Tsk," Charlotte tutted. "If only they gave us better equipment, but luckily at Cleaners Without Borders, we're ready for any challenge." She knelt down and began scooping the broken crackers into the pail by hand.

"Let me help you." Sergio knelt down, too.

"So, you've had a good show so far? I saw there were wine awards yesterday. Did you participate in that? Your stall looks excellent. I am sure you must have won a prize," Charlotte said conversationally.

"I wish I hadn't," Sergio spat angrily.

"What, you wish you hadn't won? Why's that?" Charlotte pretended to misunderstand him cleverly.

"No, no. I wish I had not taken part. That event was rigged! The judge was never going to place my wine highly."

"Is that so? You can't be serious. Are you saying that she—er, or he, of course, as I have no idea who the judge was," Charlotte hastily saved herself, "was prejudiced?"

Sergio sighed. "Exactly, yes."

"Good grief! Great Scott!" Having trotted out her only two Britishisms, Charlotte returned to her questioning. "Why do you think you were discriminated against?"

Sergio angrily flung a handful of crumbs into the bucket. "Because I downscaled the size of my stall this year," he admitted.

"You did? It looks jolly big to me. Jolly big!" Rocking back on her haunches, Charlotte stared around.

"In previous years, I took thirty percent more space. This year, I found out that I was going to be short-staffed so I changed the booking. The organizer, Cadenza, sent me an angry email saying I must change it back again, but how could I? One of my winery assistants is on maternity leave, another is attending a family wedding in Milan. And my wife refuses to attend this expo. After helping me the first year she said it is now written into our marriage contract that she will never work here again."

"I can see how difficult that must have been." Charlotte sounded as if she was desperately holding back a laugh.

"I could not cope with a big stall alone. We had to have only one sales point. The pressure was immense. I couldn't even take a bathroom break."

"Seriously?" Charlotte asked.

"Exactly. I did not have the chance to leave my stall from nine a.m. until five p.m."

"You must have been bursting."

"It was unpleasant," Sergio agreed.

"So you literally didn't leave your stall?" Charlotte asked carefully as Olivia leaned in closer. This was important information. Critical, in fact.

"How could I? I know what people are like. If I left my stall, people would walk off with my wine," Sergio lamented.

"What about the competition results?"

"I only saw them after the show had closed. I assumed I would have won a prize and that they would have kept it for me. Everyone was making a huge fuss about Cadenza being murdered, and police were restricting entry, so I couldn't get to the office. Eventually, one of the organizers came out. I explained my situation and she very kindly brought me a copy of the results. When I saw I had come nowhere. I was shocked," he admitted.

The loudspeaker boomed. This time it was a male voice, announcing that the show was open.

"I think that's the last of the crumbs," Charlotte said.

"Thank you, thank you."

"Have a good day," she called, hurrying away.

Behind the stall, Olivia dovetailed with her as Charlotte quickly unwound the scarf from her hair.

"Charlotte! Where did you even get that gear from?" Olivia asked incredulously, stifling a shriek of laughter at the rogue behavior of her friend.

"From a broom cupboard. I found it by mistake yesterday when searching for the ladies' restrooms. We can head back there now and I'll replace it."

"And Cleaners Without Borders?" Olivia asked, and this time she couldn't suppress a guffaw.

Charlotte shrugged modestly. "Well, I had to say something. That leaped to mind so I went with it. Anyway, we got the information we needed. He was very willing to speak."

Olivia nodded, patting down her friend's hair which had frizzed up after contact with the scarf.

"Your questioning was excellent and Sergio didn't suspect a thing. But sadly he has an alibi. He didn't leave the stall and only found out about the results after the death. So he's off the list. That's a pity," Olivia said regretfully.

Charlotte grimaced. "Imagine if we'd collared the right person before the show even opened. Still, at least it means our list is shorter now."

Opening the door of the broom cupboard, which was on the way into the ladies' room, she shoved the equipment back inside.

They returned to the hall. The crowds were thronging in, and it seemed even busier than yesterday. Perhaps it was because of the murder, Olivia thought. People might have come along to see where it happened.

As they wove their way through the thickening press of visitors, a nasty idea occurred to Olivia.

"Charlotte, I've thought of something awful. But we should probably check it out. Given Cadenza's irregular behavior, what if the killer was one of the judges?"

116

Charlotte spun to face Olivia, her eyes wide.

"You're right. We need to investigate that angle urgently. Look, there's our stall up ahead. They never took it down. Let's get out of the way there, and talk about this."

Grabbing Olivia's arm, she drew her into the flimsy shelter of their now-empty stall. It hadn't been dismantled but its structure provided a convenient nook to escape the seething crowds.

"I'd been focusing on the results and how Cadenza's unfairness would have affected people who didn't win. But imagine you're a judge. A leading expert in wine. You have an ego and you have an educated opinion. And it's overridden and ignored," Olivia explained.

She was starting to feel more and more excited about her theory. Charlotte nodded vigorously, her eyes shining.

"It's enough to make anyone feel murderous. And they would have had every opportunity," she agreed.

"Exactly. The judges would have been on stage with Cadenza when the results were announced. Perhaps she taunted them afterward, or rubbed it in that they hadn't had a say."

"One of them could have started arguing with her and it led to a physical fight. Maybe they did it in a moment of anger. Like an explosion of frustration." Charlotte gestured wildly to illustrate the outburst, almost knocking Olivia's hat off. "Sorry."

"We need to find the judges. I'm sure they'll both be here today. They're VIPs, so they must have other appearances to make at the show. We just need to find out where they'll be." Feeling determined, Olivia straightened her hat.

"Let's check the show program and see if they feature today," Charlotte decided. "I've got it on my phone."

She rummaged in her purse and started scrolling, while Olivia craned her neck to see what the line-up was. But, at that moment, they were interrupted by an angry throat-clearing.

CHAPTER TWENTY ONE

Glancing up, Olivia saw an irate-looking woman facing her. The blond-haired show visitor looked vaguely familiar and Olivia thought she might have seen her the previous day.

"So you're here?" The woman pointed an accusing finger at Olivia and Charlotte. In angry, Australian-accented tones she continued. "I didn't think you would be, but just in case, I came prepared. I brought this back. I heard what happened yesterday and I don't want it any more. It's tainted now. I'm not interested in shoddy wine made by a murderer. I want to return it and I demand a refund."

To Olivia's shock, she reached into her shoulder purse and produced a bottle of the ice wine.

Olivia and Charlotte glanced at each other, aghast. Olivia felt herself turn crimson with shame. What a nightmare scenario. After being wrongfully accused, she was now going to suffer the humiliation of having to refund this woman and take her wine back.

"Er, sure," Charlotte said uncertainly. She clearly realized her price hiking might have landed them in trouble because now they had no idea what this unhappy customer had paid for her wine. "Do you have the invoice?"

The woman hesitated. "I—I think I do. I put it into my wallet. But in any case, you should know the price!" she retaliated, and now it was Charlotte's turn to flush red.

Suddenly, Olivia decided that she was letting her friend down badly. Charlotte's hustler mentality and price hiking had meant she'd had a brilliant day yesterday. Now it was her turn to show some backbone and ingenuity.

She folded her arms slowly and gave the woman a considering stare.

"If you can't find the invoice, you'll have to let us know what time you bought the wine," she said firmly. "Did you buy morning, midday, or afternoon?"

"How do you mean?" The woman glared at her.

"Morning, midday, or afternoon?" Olivia repeated patiently.

"I bought it in the morning. Here's the invoice," she said triumphantly, handing over the small, crumpled page.

"Ah. Yes, you bought while it was at the extremely low price of fifteen euros." Staring at the invoice, Olivia tapped her chin thoughtfully.

"I did?" The woman looked surprised.

"You may not be aware but there was so much demand for this wine that the price shot up through the day due to natural market forces. The morning price was extremely cheap. The afternoon price became much more expensive. There are still people wanting a bottle and they are willing to pay a fortune. So, yes, I'll gladly buy it back from you at fifteen euros. I can walk through this show and in five minutes, I'll have resold it for ninety. Especially after this whole murder business which of course is just unfounded accusations from jealous rival winemakers. All it's doing is adding to the rarity value. Wine with a story!" Bravely, Olivia wagged her finger at the woman, who took a step back. Out of the corner of her eye, she saw Charlotte's admiring smile and felt proud.

"I'm not sure I want a refund anymore," the woman stated.

"Give me the wine. I demand that we refund you. Hand it over—we need it!"

Olivia took a menacing step toward the unhappy customer.

"No!" the woman cried. Clinging tightly to her wine, she turned and hurried away into the jostling throng.

Charlotte turned to Olivia. "That was brilliant. Sheer genius. I'm amazed at what you said there."

"Well, I learned from the best." Olivia grinned, feeling triumphant that she hadn't had to take back the bottle for unfair reasons.

"If anyone else wants a refund, we know what to do. All the same, we'd better get moving and not spend any more time at our stall. Let's see where the judges will be."

They peered down at the timetable of events on Charlotte's phone.

"Sunday, eleven-thirty a.m. Food and wine pairing tutorial with wine experts Alexander Schwarz and Aldi Tito, and leading chef Patrice Dupont. In the Annex room."

"So they're both here today." Olivia felt hopeful.

"The Annex room is just inside the main entrance. It's eleven now, so let's head over there. They're bound to be on site already preparing for the class, but with any luck none of the guests will have arrived yet," Charlotte decided.

As they headed across the hall, Olivia's mind was filled with ideas about what she should say. This was a critical interview, and she would need to ask the questions this time around, as both the judges had met her personally and complimented her wine.

She hoped Alexander wasn't guilty. The winemaker and author was her friend. She held him in very high esteem. Olivia wished she could skip past him and leave him out of the questioning altogether, but that wasn't possible. If she did, she might just be giving the real killer a free pass.

Alexander could have committed this crime, and in fact would have had a compelling reason to do so.

At that moment, Charlotte tapped her on the shoulder.

"Police!" she hissed.

Olivia stopped in her tracks. Up ahead was the uniformed officer she'd seen yesterday. To her alarm, she saw he was keeping the crowds away from the side of Sergio's stall, while Barrazzi and Artoro were questioning the vintner.

Today, the gym-toned Barrazzi was wearing a tight, black golf shirt and beige pants that Olivia guessed had shrunk in the wash, so closely did they cling to his muscular backside. Being in plainclothes, the only evidence he was a police officer was the thick, webbing belt around his waist on which two pairs of handcuffs and a walkie-talkie were attached.

"Darn it. We'd better go around the outside," Olivia said.

But it was as if Charlotte hadn't heard her. She seemed rooted to the spot as she stared at the detective.

"Charlotte," Olivia repeated. This time it was her turn to tap her friend insistently on the shoulder.

Still nothing. It was like tapping a statue. Olivia felt she would have had more success in persuading *The Love of Wine* to come along with her.

Sighing, she decided to take the alternate route. After all, she was the one who needed to fly under the police's radar. It was problematic that this radar was exerting a strong attraction on her friend.

As she headed down the row of stalls, Olivia heard someone call out her name.

With a rush of happiness, she turned, delighted to recognize Danilo's voice. How wonderful he'd managed to get here today, she thought happily. She couldn't wait to update him on the amazing success of her wine launch, as well as the catastrophe that had followed.

Her happiness at seeing her beau ebbed, and in fact vanished entirely, as she saw that his dark-haired niece was following him.

Oh, no, Olivia thought. This couldn't be more terrible timing. If her last meeting with Francesca had been awkward, this one was likely to be a hundred times worse.

"Hey!" She hurried over to Danilo, who gave her a big hug and an affectionate kiss. "Hello, Francesca!" Olivia made sure to greet her extra warmly, and hugged her too. Francesca looked stunning, in a short-skirted, crushed-velvet dress paired with long boots. How Olivia wished this head-turning young woman looked happier to see her.

"What a lovely hat you are wearing," Danilo complimented her.

"Thank you." Olivia smiled, glad that the hastily bought item looked good, even though it was only part of a necessary disguise.

Francesca looked less convinced and stared at Olivia more critically.

"The style suits you, but not the color. You need to buy the same model, but in turquoise. Or even pink."

If only, Olivia thought, nodding in rueful agreement.

"We saw your stall was empty and I was worried something had gone wrong. I was actually heading out of the show, to find a quiet place where I could call you. Is everything okay?" Danilo asked, sounding concerned.

"Well, there's good news and bad," Olivia said, trying to lighten the mood. It didn't help. Francesca was staring at her with combined doubt and distrust.

Danilo pounced on the positive angle, clearly hoping to dispel the uneasy tension that had descended now that Francesca was frowning.

"What's the good news?" he asked anxiously.

"The good news is that we sold out of wine yesterday. We did really well and had a super-successful day. That's why we're all closed up now. No more stock."

"That is amazing!" Danilo's face lit up. "I told you that you would be able to work your magic at this festival, and you have. To have sold out is simply incredible. Your wine must have been in such demand. You are the success story of Festa del Vino—a small producer that proved them all wrong."

"It sold way beyond what we expected," Olivia admitted, feeling a thrill of pride that she'd managed to live up to her amazing boyfriend's high opinion of her.

"And the bad news?" Francesca demanded, her dark eyes blazing.

There was no easy way to say this. Olivia decided to get it off her chest as quick as she could. "The bad news—well, the show organizer was found dead at the end of the show. Unfortunately, I was the one to stumble upon her body when I went looking for her."

She saw shock in both their faces at this terrible news. Danilo grasped her hand and held it supportively as Olivia continued. "Although nobody has yet confirmed how it happened, there's a possibility she may have been hit over the head with a bottle of my wine, which I gifted her before the judging. My wine wasn't eligible for a prize. That has caused some petty-minded and jealous people to believe I was involved and I know there are rumors circulating," Olivia concluded in firm tones. Let Francesca decide which team she was on!

Francesca gave Olivia an iron-hard stare, and in an equally firm voice she delivered her bombshell. "Is that why you were made to clear your stall and leave the show? Do the police suspect you of being the killer?"

CHAPTER TWENTY TWO

Danilo swung around to stare at his niece, looking aghast.

Olivia was panicking inwardly. She had all the respect in the world for Francesca's courage to speak her mind, and her ability to put two and two together. It was just a pity that in this case, she was adding up wrong.

Now, Danilo had turned to gaze at her anxiously, and Olivia realized this incident might prove to be an insurmountable obstacle to her friendship with Francesca. Already, the young woman doubted her commitment to Italy. Now, Francesca, like most of the Festa del Vino exhibitors, probably thought she was a criminal.

How could she fix this, and get this intelligent young woman on her side? There didn't seem to be an easy way, Olivia thought frantically.

"They don't yet know who was involved. And I genuinely sold out of wine. I wasn't told to close up," she tried to reassure her.

Francesca glared at her in disbelief.

Thankfully, Charlotte broke the stressful moment by grabbing Olivia's arm.

"Hello, Danilo, lovely to see you again. Sorry, I have to interrupt. We have an important meeting to attend and time is ticking by."

Charlotte spoke in urgent and worried tones, as if she'd totally forgotten she had caused the delay in the first place, by ogling Detective Barrazzi in his form-fitting pants.

Much as Olivia wanted to sort things out with Francesca, she knew solving the crime was the biggest priority. They had to go and interview the judges before the wine and food tutorial got under way.

"It was so kind of you both to come here today. Are you staying for a while longer? Please, let's meet up for a coffee later if you don't have to head off anywhere," she said quickly. Perhaps by then she would have managed to solve the crime and be able to present Francesca with the proof she needed to reassure her.

"I will find you later," Danilo promised.

Turning, Olivia hustled toward the entrance with her friend. Now that Danilo and Francesca had heard the damaging rumors, her mission felt even more imperative. Dodging through the press of incoming visitors, they swerved left into the Annex room just before they reached the main doors.

Olivia rushed into the room and then stopped in her tracks, inhaling the delicious smell of cooking. This must be a hands-on tutorial, where guests experienced wine and food combined.

She stared at the white-clothed tables, which were decked out with small platters containing a variety of delicious-looking, canape-sized portions of starters, entrees, and desserts. There was even a cheese board, Olivia noted, her mouth watering. She'd been so focused on finding the killer there hadn't been time for breakfast.

Behind the tables there was a small gas hot-plate where the chef was at work, browning delicious-looking meatballs and arranging more food into bowls. Alexander and Aldi were clustered hungrily near him, looking eager to sample the creations.

An officious-looking helper rushed over.

"Signoras, signoras. Please wait outside. Booked guests may only enter when the event begins."

"We're not booked guests," Charlotte declared with a grin. "We were just hoping to have a quick word with these very good friends of Olivia."

Upon hearing her loud, confident voice, Alexander turned. His face warmed instantly and he rushed over to her.

"Ah, Olivia. How good to see you after a stressful and tragic day yesterday. Congratulations on your new wine creation. It was outstanding. I am sorry that it did not qualify to be judged. It would easily have earned a Highly Commended, and although the standard was very high this year, perhaps even a medal in the Best New Wine category."

"I agree," Aldi called from behind the food table, where he had speared a meatball on a toothpick.

"After what happened, one should not criticize, I know. But it was clear to me during the judging that our head judge was looking only for traditional wines. We both argued that yours should be eligible but she said it was a 'fancy' wine and refused," Alexander explained. "She told me that they usually weed out the wines that do not conform, as the competition favors the classics. Those vintners are told they cannot take part. Although the entry fee does not get refunded, I believe," Alexander said wryly.

So others had been banned from the competition? That was important information, Olivia thought.

"I was surprised, and very disappointed, when she overruled our opinions," Aldi said.

"As was I. I was planning to write to her afterward, voicing my unhappiness, and saying that I would not judge there again." Alexander nodded.

"But no need for that now," Aldi agreed in somber tones.

Olivia felt comforted by their sympathetic words, and by the fact they had fought for her wine. But she needed to move onto the purpose for her visit, and these comments paved the way for her to introduce it.

"I was traumatized after what happened to Cadenza. Did you know that I found her body?" she asked.

Alexander looked shocked. "I had no idea. The police contacted me last night and asked if I was going to be here today, as they needed to interview me. But they gave no details. That must have been so upsetting for you," he sympathized.

"Did the police not interview you after the show?" Olivia asked, hoping that this subtle question would reveal if he had an alibi.

"Straight after the results were announced, I left the show," Alexander explained. "I had an appointment with friends who own a farm outside Siena. They were having a small wine and music event, which they invited me to attend as the guest of honor. Afraid of being late, I must have appeared rather rude as I rushed away," he said regretfully.

"That sounds like a wonderful event. What time did it start?" Charlotte asked innocently and Olivia knew that her friend was hoping to confirm this alibi.

"At five-thirty p.m. I ran out of the hall, caught a cab, and told the driver I would pay him double if he got me there in time," Alexander laughed. "He did! As I climbed into the cab, Cadenza called me, angrily asking why I was not staying to circulate at the show and congratulate the winners. She cut off the call abruptly, saying there was somebody waiting to see her. Now, I wish I had been able to stay. I will never know who that person was, or whether they were the killer. Perhaps, if I had been there, I could have prevented this tragedy."

Olivia was intrigued by this information.

Alexander was off the hook, and the killer could well have interrupted their conversation. If only Alexandra had thought to ask the mystery visitor's name before ending the call.

"I feel bad also," Aldi observed. "I had to leave straight after we signed off the paperwork backstage. I was late for my interview with the journalist from the *Siena News*, who was covering the festival. We had arranged to meet at a nearby coffee shop where it was quieter. I also headed out at a run."

"Did you get an angry phone call?" Charlotte asked.

Aldi shook his head. "At the coffee shop, I messaged Cadenza, to ask if I should return to the hall after my interview. She never read the message, and I fear by then the worst had happened."

Olivia nodded somberly.

"I am expecting that the police will question me today, too. I hope that they do not interrupt this event," Aldi continued.

So both of the judges were off the list, and had solid alibis that could be confirmed by witnesses.

"I hope your pairing is a great success," Olivia said. Noticing the first guests were hovering in the doorway, she headed out. Looking at their expectant faces, she wished she could stay for the event. It promised to be a treat of note.

As they returned to the expo hall, Olivia focused on the fact that Cadenza had done everything her own way and hadn't seemed to care who she disrespected.

Her session with the judges had given her a new, important lead.

What about the other vintners who had been kicked out of the competition? Could one of them have confronted Cadenza after the results were announced?

It was time to find out who these disappointed, angry, and perhaps even murderous people were.

CHAPTER TWENTY THREE

"Where do we find the names of those banned competitors?" Charlotte muttered into Olivia's ear as they filed into the crowded hall again. Olivia was glad that her friend was on the same page as she was. Hopefully, this line of thought would lead them to somebody with a strong motive.

"I guess we go back to the show office," Olivia suggested.

"And they will give us this list of disallowed entries, why?" Charlotte challenged.

Olivia felt steam coming out of her ears as she fretted over a plausible explanation.

"I have a reason!" she exclaimed. "Let's go."

Feeling eager, she made a bee-line for the offices—although given the crowds, it was a zigzag line, she decided, that might have been made by a drunken bee.

When they reached the offices, they found only one harassed attendant there. Olivia smiled warmly at her as she replaced the phone after taking what must have been the hundredth call of the day.

"Us again," she declared, before realizing in horror she should have spoken Italian as she had on her first visit. Luckily, the frazzled organizer was too busy to notice.

"What do you want?" she snapped.

Quickly, before the phone rang with call one hundred and one, Olivia explained.

"I understand some competition entries were rejected as they didn't fit the categories. Do you have a list of them? I'd like to get together with the winemakers to see if we can lobby for a new category next year."

She sensed Charlotte reeling in admiration at her clever story, which the woman accepted instantly.

"In that file you will find all the entries." She pointed to a large, lever-arch folder on the other desk. "The rejected ones are at the back."

Her phone started ringing.

Olivia paged through the folder. There was her entry, right at the front, with the wonderful comments from the judges written neatly in the relevant fields, and then a scrawled "NOT ELIGIBLE— DISQUALIFIED" in red ink at the top.

Despite that ugly scribble, Olivia discreetly photographed the page. She wanted to be able to reread, in their actual writing, the praise that these experts had given her wine.

Then she quickly paged to the back of the folder. Sure enough, there were two entries with "REJECTED" slashing across the page in that same firm, crimson hand.

Olivia cringed in sympathy. That entry fee had been steep. Surely they should at least have been refunded? Photographing the pages, she felt encouraged that two new suspects had been added to the list.

The first suspect, she didn't know. His name was Enrico and he was from Enrico's Impresa Wineries.

The second, she was shocked that she knew already. Gasping as she read the name, Olivia saw that Fugo's wine had been disqualified.

"What is it?" Charlotte hissed, peering over her shoulder.

Rereading the name, Olivia felt a sense of disbelief. He'd seemed like a good and capable winemaker. At any rate, his stall had looked awesome. Now, looking down at this incriminating evidence, Olivia was starting to wonder exactly why Fugo had insisted to the police that she was guilty.

They retreated outside as the harassed helper was taking her hundred-and-second call.

"So, who's going to question who?"

"I want to talk to Fugo," Olivia said. "He tried his best to make the police believe it was me. Hopefully, if I turn up at his stall, he'll be shocked, and then the truth might come out."

"And if he panics or clams up and refuses to say a word, Cleaners Without Borders can come by and empty his trash." Charlotte grinned.

"Exactly," Olivia confirmed.

"Right. I'll find Enrico's stall, and you can go ahead and interview your close friend Fugo." She grimaced cheerfully. "Shall we meet back at the entrance when we're done?"

Olivia nodded, and then set off into the crowds. She felt very conscious of the shortness of the day. Though it was not yet noon, it already felt as if they were running out of time.

Fugo was at his stall, obsequiously pouring tasting-sized portions for two waiting visitors. Without really looking, he greeted her with a warm smile.

"May I offer you my wine tasting experience?" he purred. Then his expression changed to one of horror as he realized who he was speaking to.

"I—I—you look very different in that hat," he stammered. "What do you want?" He flushed crimson, clearly guilty about what he'd told the police.

"Actually, I'd love to taste your wine," Olivia said sweetly.

"No! Surely not?" Now he was glowering at her, and his tone was sharp.

"It is a wine show," Olivia reminded him with her friendliest smile. "And since I don't have any more stock to sell I want to enjoy the experience."

Fugo tilted his head, still regarding her with deep suspicion.

"What wine do you want to try?" he asked.

Olivia thought frantically. She couldn't remember the name of the wine that he'd had kicked out of the competition.

"I hear you produced a very unusual wine this year," she tried hopefully.

Now Fugo's expression softened slightly.

"You mean our Koshu wine?"

"Yes, that's the one." Relieved to recognize the name, Olivia asked, "It sounds most intriguing. Is it a new type of grape?"

Fugo's suspicious frown disappeared. His face lit up with enthusiasm. It seemed his love for his creation had overridden his misgivings, because he spoke passionately. "It is new to Tuscany, and we are very proud of it. Koshu wine is originally from Japan, and is in fact popular there today. Although classed as white, the Koshu grapes are particularly beautiful, with a gorgeous rose-pink tinge to them. But while they are excellent table grapes, it takes serious skill to make wine from them. The wine produced is low in alcohol, subtle and aromatic with citrus and jasmine overtones. So, a very modern wine. We battled for years to make it, and finally succeeded in producing a batch last year. It is selling very well so far."

"How fascinating," Olivia said, captivated by the wine's story. "Did you enter it in the competition?"

"Yes. However, our entry was declined. I am not sure why as I have been too busy to go and investigate. Perhaps we entered it too late, or else they did not have a category to suit it. It has always been rather a gamble to compete at this show as the organizer is—I mean, was—very whimsical." He shook his head sadly while pouring her the tasting portion. "It does not matter, as we were notified at lunch time yesterday that it is the gold winner in Best New Wine, in the Campione Awards. They are much more prestigious as they cover the whole of Italy. I am sure it is not the only award this wine will win," he said proudly.

"So you were busy here the whole day?" While confirming his alibi, Olivia swirled, smelled, and tasted the pale-straw-colored Koshu. It was fabulous—delicate and fresh. Olivia could pick up a hint of peach in the clean bouquet and taste, as well as the soft yet lively citrus and jasmine that Fugo had mentioned.

"Yes. I worked non-stop with my two team members. We had short breaks on rotation. I took half an hour to rest my legs at lunch time and apart from that, I didn't sit down until I got into the car after the show," he said, with a tired sigh. Picking up on his words, the young attendant at his stall, who had been packing wine, gave a rueful nod.

"I told you to take a break when the awards were announced," the young man chided his boss.

Fugo sighed irritably. "If you remember, I was trapped in my own stall by the German couple who spent nearly an hour tasting and discussing my wines, and then left without buying any. They only went away after that woman started shouting over the loudspeaker that there had been a problem and someone had died."

The attendant nodded. "True. Those Germans were very demanding and it would have been impossible for you to leave. Maybe they will come back today and place a large order," he added hopefully.

Fugo turned to Olivia again, making a face. "Between you and me, Olivia, it is wearying to be so sickeningly charming and polite to all these people. It is not who I am!" Fugo confided in low tones, rolling his eyes.

Olivia suddenly found she liked Fugo a whole lot better. Despite the fact he'd tried to get her arrested, his honesty over his fake-obsequious persona had redeemed him somewhat, and she guessed her interest in his wine had done the same for him. Imagine if, after the crime was solved, they could become friends.

At any rate, Fugo could be struck off the suspect list as he had an alibi, confirmed by his assistant.

"I can't wait to enjoy this bottle. Best of success with your next Koshu harvest." She smiled as she paid for the wine. She stashed the bottle in her new purse where it fit easily.

Then she headed off to find Charlotte, but Charlotte was already heading toward the stall, looking anxious.

"Olivia, I think we have somebody with a strong motive here. Please come along."

Intrigued, Olivia followed her friend. But, as they headed through the crowds, distracted by the possibility of collaring a suspect, Olivia didn't notice that someone else was pursuing her.

"Hey! Slow down. Yes, you! I'm speaking to you."

Finally, Olivia picked up the familiar and unwelcome voice behind her.

It was James.

She spun around to see him swaggering purposefully toward her.

"I was surprised not to hear from you yesterday," James said. Today, he was looking sharp. He wore medium-heeled cowboy boots and jeans that showed his brown, skinny knees through their still-trendy, if slightly last season, rips. A pair of orange-tinted sunglasses was pushed up onto his head.

"James, I've considered your offer and—" Olivia began. But her obnoxious ex-boss seemed hell-bent on clinching the deal there and then.

"I put together some terms and conditions last night. I'll need exclusivity, of course—from your side, not mine, and we should probably include a restraint of trade agreement. And a confidentiality and non-disclosure contract, too. We want to keep our trade secrets, secret. Haha!" he chortled.

"Right now I actually have an urgent predicament to—" she tried again. However, once more, James was an unstoppable force. He grasped her arm, his fingers welded there.

"Let's get out of here. It's far too noisy for such an important discussion. Know any good bistros nearby? Is it too early for wine?"

"James, no!" Angrily, Olivia wrenched her arm away. Enough was enough, she decided. Before she could stop herself, her mouth ran way ahead of her brain.

"Now is not the time!" she screamed, stamping her foot to emphasize the point. "Yesterday, the show organizer was murdered. I'm now a suspect in this whole debacle and every person here thinks I did it, apart from you, because you don't speak Italian. This could affect everything! My winemaking career. My industry reputation. My visa renewal." Olivia could hear her own voice squeaky with horror at the thought of this being declined. "I have to clear my name today. It's my only chance, even though it might get me into more trouble or even put me in danger. After all, someone who'd bash a show organizer over the head with a bottle of ice wine might easily attack a small newcomer winemaker!"

James looked horrified. His mouth dropped open in astonishment and his eyes were bugging out of his head in surprise. Unstoppable, Olivia continued.

"So no, James, right now I don't have time to listen to your proposal. I'm busy trying to save myself. And in any case, the answer is no. No, no, no. I can't sell out and manufacture bulk wine. You'll corrupt any wine you get your hands on, because your vision for personal wealth is based on the unsustainable Valley Wines model. I have to be true to my own vision and my own integrity. Stop trying to pressure me into being something I am not!"

James took a step back, as if her words were scorching him. He'd gone purple under his tan. Most probably, he was now furious and this would end up in a massive public fight. It could result in both of them being kicked out of the show, Olivia thought in horror, wishing that she'd considered her reckless outburst more carefully.

But to her relief, James didn't seem ready to argue back. Rather, he looked deeply affronted, in fact outraged, by her words.

"Well!" He snorted.

Drawing himself to his full height in his medium-heeled cowboy boots, and giving her an irate glare, he turned and marched away.

Olivia sagged with relief. Then, pulling herself together, she headed over to where Charlotte was frantically beckoning.

If her encounter with James had gone differently, it could have prevented her from catching a killer. And the man at the stall in front of her, brand name Enrico's Impresa, might just be that guilty person.

This was Enrico himself, according to his tag.

"He was ranting and raving to the previous customer about having been kicked out of the competition," Charlotte stage-whispered. "They were speaking in Italian, but I got the gist of it because he kept saying 'competizione' and waving his arms, and making like he was tearing out his hair, so I thought I'd better call you. I don't know if he speaks English."

Feeling intrigued and hopeful that this suspect was so visibly distressed about the competition, Olivia headed to the counter.

CHAPTER TWENTY FOUR

"*Buon giorno*," Olivia greeted the flustered-looking vintner who was wearing a branded shirt that sported a large golden EI on the pocket—the initials of his brand, she guessed. "Are you Enrico? I would love to try your wine," she said in English.

"I am Enrico," he replied in strongly accented English. "I am occupying my friend's space at this show, after he had to attend a wine festival in France. I have three highly adventurous, avant-garde creations here today. You can taste all. They would have been award-winning inventions, except the prejudiced judge was saving all the medals for her friends, so my entries were banned."

Inventions? Olivia felt puzzled. That wasn't a word that she would have chosen to describe a wine. What did Enrico have in those dark bottles with the rather ugly labels? she wondered, feeling confused. She guessed he'd been accepted into the festival because he was a substitution. He definitely seemed like the typical small, home winemaker that Cadenza had done her best to keep out.

"I'm sorry to hear that your wines were thrown out," she sympathized. "How did that make you feel?"

"I was furious! Furious! Taste for yourself their excellence and quality."

All Olivia's suspicions were triggered by Enrico's admission of anger. The problem was that it didn't seem possible to continue with the questioning, without sampling the wines. Reluctantly, Olivia accepted her fate as the forceful Enrico placed a tasting glass in front of her and Charlotte.

"My first. The Ginger of Tuscany."

"Wine infused with ginger?" Olivia questioned, but Enrico shook his head. "No. This is ginger ale, infused with my own homemade red wine. Highly modern and designed to appeal to the unpredictable millennial market who adore their soft drinks. It is a fascinating blend. Note the slight sparkle from the ginger ale."

Olivia stifled a cough as she choked down the tart, gingery, and indeed unpleasantly fizzy mixture that tasted of sour wine.

"Inventive!" she exclaimed loudly, to drown out the sound of Charlotte spluttering next to her.

"Onto my second." Pleased to have an enthusiastic captive audience, Enrico proceeded apace. "This magnifico creation is what I call Brandy Soaked Biscotti."

"And why do you call it that?" Olivia asked nervously. She had a feeling that the answer was going to be all too literal, and she was right.

"It is a blend of red wine, brandy, and all the ingredients for biscotti. Nuts, berries, raisins. And of course some pureed chunks of the cookies themselves."

Olivia stared wide-eyed at the rather grainy mixture that he was now pouring into the tasting glass. It reeked of brandy. As he lifted the bottle, a raisin dropped out and splashed down into the glass.

"So this is also made from your wine?" she asked conversationally, to delay the moment when she had to sip.

"Oh, no. I had a very small harvest this year. This is bulk, five-liter wine from the grocery store. Any five-liter pack of red will do. The brandy creates a uniform taste. My talent here was not so much in making the wine but rather in marrying the ingredients. A match made in heaven, I am sure you will agree."

Olivia sipped the tasting portion. The raisin floated between her lips, but she pushed it back into the glass with her tongue. Then, swallowing the minuscule sip she'd taken, she inhaled deeply. She needed air. She didn't think she'd ever be able to look at biscotti the same way again.

"Now, when you have finished this, I will pour you my third and final creation. Made with white grapes and a few other secret ingredients, it is called Nonna's Loving Hands."

As Olivia recoiled, Charlotte began choking and couldn't stop. Coughing and spluttering into the wad of Kleenex she'd grabbed from her bag, she wheezed out an apology. Olivia guessed she'd gasped suddenly and inhaled a cranberry.

"I'm sure it is lovely but it can't beat the Ginger of Tuscany. I'd like to buy a bottle of that," Olivia said, deciding it was probably the least awful of the three. Making a purchase would be the quickest way to halt this tasting session and start the hunt for Enrico's alibi.

"Forty euros. The tasting fee is waived since you have made a purchase," Enrico told her kindly.

Behind her, she heard Charlotte choke again. Olivia couldn't blame her. Forty euros? That was daylight robbery! And if she hadn't bought, they would have incurred a tasting fee for being practically forced to sample these wines?

Concealing her outrage, she handed the money over. Perhaps Fugo should come and take lessons from Enrico, she thought with a flare of inappropriate humor.

"I still can't get over that you were banned from the competition," she said, knowing that she might just have purchased wine from the killer and needing to get to the serious reason for her visit. How could she encourage him to blurt out the full story?

Enrico nodded sadly. "To you, a fellow wine lover, I can confess the truth. I was so angry, so bitterly disappointed, that I acted recklessly. I did something that I have had cause to deeply regret."

Olivia's head was spinning, and not just from the high dosage of brandy in her tasting sip. Was this going to be the moment they'd been waiting for—when a killer admitted to his crime?

"Why is that, Enrico?" she asked gently, hoping that the words she was waiting for would pour out.

Enrico sighed deeply. "I headed to the organizer's office just after lunch to find out what time the judging was. They told me that my entry had not been accepted. I shouted and screamed as I tried to plead my cause but that nasty organizer was stubborn and unaccommodating. So then, I did something I later wished I had not."

"What was that?" Olivia whispered. How had he done it? she wondered. Had he lain in wait?

"I stormed out of the show and in fact, I left Siena. I closed up my stall for the day," he said. "I went to visit a friend in San Donato, and we spent the afternoon drinking sangiovese in the local bistro, and enjoying a few games of *scacchi*. During the afternoon, I received an angry text from the organizer when she realized I was gone. She said that I would incur a fine for having left early. I hope that now she has passed away, I will not have to pay it."

"Oh," Olivia said. This wasn't what she'd expected at all. "So it was a bad decision financially?" she tried, battling to understand the reason for his deep regret.

"Exactly," Enrico sighed, looking forlorn. "I let my pride get the better of my business sense. I should have stayed at the show. They say it was very busy yesterday afternoon. I missed out on many sales. And now, I might have to pay a fine, too," he said sadly.

Olivia and Charlotte exchanged equally sad glances. This promising suspect had fizzled out entirely. Instead of admitting his guilt, he'd confessed to bunking the show and playing chess with a friend.

"It was only when I arrived here this morning that I heard that she had been killed." Enrico gave a satisfied nod as if, in his opinion, she'd had it coming.

"Isn't it strange how the wheel turns? Thank you for the wine," Olivia said, placing the bottle in her purse, which was now beginning to feel heavy.

They left the stall and trudged away, with Charlotte sighing morosely.

"I feel crushed," she shared.

"Me, too," Olivia said.

"Now you've got a bottle of overpriced, unpalatable wine as a reward for your hard work. What are you going to do with it? Throw it away?"

Olivia shook her head. "As I was paying, I realized it will be a great treat for Erba. She loves bad wine and hasn't had the chance to drink much of it recently, with me working at a good winery and all! And I know she likes ginger because I left a box of ginger chocolates on the kitchen counter, and she stuck her head through the window and stole three of them right out of the tray."

Charlotte nodded wisely. "That's the perfect solution then. She'll be pleased to find two of her favorite things, wrapped up in one bottle that should never have seen the light of day."

"We need to regroup and relook at our list," Olivia decided, feeling frustrated. Time was ticking by. It was already after twelve noon. In a few short hours, the show would close and she would lose her chance forever.

"Heads up!" Charlotte said in a strange tone that sounded happy, yet sad.

Raising her head from the gloomy contemplation of her feet, Olivia stared in alarm.

Detective Barrazzi was striding toward them, with a purposeful set to his firm jaw.

CHAPTER TWENTY FIVE

"Why are you not answering your phone?" Detective Barrazzi asked Olivia, staring at her through narrowed eyes, as if this was a clear admission of her guilt.

"Phone?" It was at the bottom of her purse, squashed under two bottles of wine, her jacket, and her wallet. Olivia delved for it, and stared in mystification at the three missed calls.

"I'm sorry. It's so noisy here, I didn't hear it ring."

Dropping a strong hand to his hip, Barrazzi jingled the handcuffs meaningfully. Olivia heard Charlotte draw in a sharp breath. Glancing at her friend, she noticed Charlotte was looking strangely flushed.

"I wanted to speak to you urgently. We have new information that has come to light regarding this case," Barrazzi told her.

From the way he was looking at her, Olivia was pretty sure that the new information wasn't that a suspect had been arrested. Her heart plummeted as she wondered if the news was that a suspect was about to be arrested.

"What information?" She knew Barrazzi was assessing her reaction to his words. She hoped she didn't seem guilty.

"Forensics has informed us that the bottle was not, in fact, used as a weapon."

"Oh!" Olivia felt a prickle of relief. Surely this let her off the hook? But from Barrazzi's expression, it didn't seem so. Her relief turned into trepidation.

"Why did it get smashed then?" she wondered aloud.

"I wonder what the reason for that could be," Barrazzi agreed, looking at her closely.

"Could it have been because of fingerprints?" Olivia guessed.

Barrazzi made an impatient face. "The shards of glass are still being tested, but the pieces are small, and the bottle has clearly been handled by a number of people. We may get partial prints at best, or none at all," he admitted.

Why was he still looking at her in that strange way? Olivia wondered.

After a pause, Barrazzi continued. "We believe it might have been smashed out of anger, or to make a violent point. We are therefore investigating your actions prior to this event even more closely. Do you know anything about why that bottle was broken?"

Barrazzi's voice was stern. Clearly, given the difficulties with fingerprint evidence, the detective was trying to force a confession from her. Olivia shook her head vehemently.

"What weapon did you use to strike her?" he asked suddenly, and Olivia gasped.

"I didn't use anything! I wasn't there at the time and have no idea what happened," she protested.

"A couple of key witnesses have come forward to describe a scene that played out between you and the victim, before the competition results were announced," he continued.

Olivia swallowed hard. This highly inaccurate and incriminating version had been accepted by the police!

"Why can't you ask the other judges what they thought? They can confirm I gifted the wine to Cadenza in a spirit of friendship," she pleaded in a hoarse voice.

Barrazzi folded his arms. She thought she saw Charlotte's knees buckle.

"I cannot ask the other judges because they are still busy in the food and wine pairing seminar," he said. From his tone of voice, Olivia guessed that not even a police detective on an urgent mission would dare to interrupt such a sacrosanct occasion.

Thinking back to the timetable, Olivia remembered that the wine pairing ran for an hour and a half. That meant it would be finished soon, and hopefully then Barrazzi would get the more accurate judges' take on her wine's handover.

Without that important testimony, Olivia dreaded that Barrazzi would arrest her anyway. But it seemed that, at this stage, he wasn't ready to.

"Answer your phone if I call you again," he said sternly.

"I'll keep it in my pocket," Olivia agreed humbly. She let out a sigh of relief as the detective strode off. Charlotte sighed too, and then fanned herself.

"There's no time to lose. He won't let me go again," Olivia said, looking anxiously at her friend.

"We'd better split up," Charlotte decided. "Otherwise, we're wasting time. Double dipping, if you like. There's a third person on the competition list that I'm keen to investigate, just to tick that box. It was a guy I noticed who was highly commended the last few years, and then this year he was in the middle. I don't know if that would be reason enough to be murderous but it seems worth questioning him. Let's message when we're ready to meet up."

Olivia stared at her departing friend, feeling despondent. She was beginning to lose faith in her brilliant theory. How was she supposed to know which of the remaining competitors, with their varied but average results, might have gotten upset enough to take drastic action?

As she peered down at the photos of the printed pages, a warm hand clasped her shoulder.

To her delight, Danilo was back, and this time he wasn't with his niece.

"Francesca is job shadowing at a salon in Siena this afternoon," he explained. "Come. Let's go and sit down. You look exhausted and in need of a coffee."

"Oh, I'm so glad you found me." Filled with relief and joy, Olivia hugged Danilo for the second time that day. He'd caught her at a low point and saved her from sinking into despair over this troublesome case. Now, with the help of caffeine and company, she might gain a new perspective.

They headed to the show's roped-off catering area. There, Danilo ordered two giant-sized cappuccinos while Olivia snagged one of the last unoccupied tables. Sitting down and placing her heavy purse on the floor, she watched the magnificent sight of her handsome beau approaching, laden down with strong coffee.

"How is your day going? You look very worried," Danilo said, sounding anxious as he sat next to her.

"I'm terrified that I might be arrested at any moment," Olivia admitted. "But I'm doing my best to figure this out, all the same. You see, Danilo, to me it's obvious that the perpetrator must have been one of the competition entrants, as it happened soon after the awards were given out. So Charlotte and I are going through the list and trying to eliminate suspects."

"You are investigating yourself?" Danilo gazed at her admiringly. "How are you going about it? What have you discovered so far?"

Olivia sighed. "We've identified a few surprise competition results that could have made people angry, and a couple of competitors whose entries were rejected and who would have forfeited the expensive entry fee."

Danilo nodded wisely. "That sounds like a sensible place to start," he agreed.

"The problem is that they all have alibis and can account for their time after the results were announced," she explained, feeling discouraged all over again. "We even checked the judges' alibis because Cadenza treated them badly, too. They were really just there to make up the numbers, and she was able to override their opinions."

"A sensible move to investigate them, too. It would have been insulting for that to happen," Danilo said supportively.

Olivia drank down her cappuccino, hoping that the caffeine would have an effect, and power her brain to find a breakthrough.

"I'm at a loss now. Do you want to have a look through the list of entries and see if anything stands out?" she said.

Danilo shook his head. "Olivia, if you have checked it, I am sure you've done a thorough job. But maybe it was nothing to do with the competition. It could simply have been that the killer chose that moment to go in search of Cadenza. Perhaps, toward the end of the show, exhibitors were relaxing and focusing less on their sales."

Olivia nodded.

"So we're back to looking at the whole pool of exhibitors then."

"Not only exhibitors but everyone who worked at the show. A huge show like this would have many associated service people. Setup, stage, sound. If she treated everyone badly, somebody could have a strong motive. It sounds, from what you say, as if she is a person who takes others' money unfairly. Perhaps she was a bad payer?" Danilo hazarded.

Draining her cappuccino, Olivia felt grateful that she'd had this meeting with her wonderful boyfriend, and been able to discuss this issue so constructively with him.

"You're right. And you've given me a great idea," she said, brimming with confidence all over again.

Danilo's face warmed. "I'm glad to have been able to help. Will you be okay, Olivia? I can stay and investigate with you if you like."

Olivia was sorely tempted to ask him to do just that, but it wouldn't be fair. She knew how much work he was hoping to do in his garden today. Plus, she didn't want to get him into trouble with the Siena police.

"It's amazing of you to offer. You are so supportive! But I think I'll manage with Charlotte's help. Thanks to you, I know exactly who I'm going to question next. Without a doubt, this person will know those crucial details."

CHAPTER TWENTY SIX

Olivia marched to the show entrance, her determination flooding back. This interview could be a game-changer. If she was lucky, it would yield information that would crack this case.

To Olivia's relief, the attendant who had been checking passes the day before was still at her station. The young, curvaceous woman seemed tired and disgruntled. Her face told Olivia she was sick of the show, even though when she saw her approach she straightened up hurriedly.

"May I ask you a favor?" Olivia queried politely.

The woman nodded, looking curious, if not cooperative.

"I am looking for the assistant organizer. After Cadenza's tragic demise yesterday I am not sure who the right person would be. I need to speak to someone who was involved with the show."

The woman stood taller. Proudly, she tapped a finger on her name tag which Olivia now saw read *Josefina Amato, Assistente.*

"That would be me," she said.

"Would it be possible to ask you a few questions?" Olivia said, stepping back as a group of visitors approached the vine swathed entrance. Carefully, Josefina checked their tags. Olivia hoped she would agree. The show was still very busy. This poor overworked attendant would be within her rights to refuse.

But to her surprise, the woman picked up a walkie-talkie and spoke briefly into it.

"One of the other assistants is on her way to relieve me," she said. "I can take my hour's break. Shall we go to the café around the corner?"

Eagerly, Olivia followed the woman out of the hall and onto the streets of Siena. After the bright, artificial glare of the show it felt strange to be outside in the slightly overcast natural light.

Josefina led her purposefully along the main street. Olivia felt charmed to be treading over the ancient, smooth cobblestones on the sidewalk, and happy to see throngs of tourists, whose colorful jackets stood out against the backdrop of silvery-gray stone buildings.

How she wished she could spend the afternoon shopping on this scenic street, and not pursuing a killer.

Josefina turned into a small bistro, where she welcomed the owner with a friendly hug.

"The usual for me, please," she said.

"I'll have a sparkling water, thanks," Olivia said in careful Italian, as she paid for the drinks order.

They sat down at one of the tiny tables. From her face, Olivia could see that this young woman was relieved to be out of the show environment.

"Thank you so much for agreeing to chat," Olivia said.

Josefina shrugged. "You helped me yesterday. I appreciated that you stood up for me in front of my boss. She was not an easy woman. Most times, I didn't enjoy my job."

The waiter set a San Pellegrino Aranciata in front of Josefina and a San Pellegrino sparkling water in front of Olivia. Josefina took a grateful gulp of the fizzy orange, making the ice clink invitingly.

"Was the show well organized?" Olivia asked, deciding to lead into her line of questioning gradually.

Josefina made a face. "It was not. It should have been, but Cadenza made things difficult when they could have been easy. She never praised or thanked us, even when we worked many hours of overtime. Also, she was a very slow payer, and not efficient at handling queries. There were always many complaints from creditors that they had been paid late or not at all."

"Really?" Olivia was excited to hear this information. Danilo's instinct had been right. It seemed that Cadenza did, indeed, have a love for money, and a reluctance to part with it.

"Cadenza did not like to pay when she could get a job for free," Josefina confirmed sadly, sipping at her drink. "Every year she would force me to ask my friends to come and work. She would call the colleges in Siena and request unpaid student help. That was becoming more and more difficult, because students need money and are paid for every other job they do."

"Why was that? Surely there was a budget? Did the show not do well?" Olivia remembered the price of her stand. Her eyes watered at the memory of paying over that steep amount.

"The show did very well. I do not know why she did not like to pay. It was just how she was. What could I do? I did not want to lose my job by interfering," Josefina admitted.

The cogs in Olivia's brain were starting to spin and she had an idea.

"Do you have a business card? I would like to stay in touch so that I can book in again with whoever takes over the festival."

"Sure." Josefina handed over a card.

Olivia glanced down at it and saw to her triumph that it contained the information she needed.

"It's been great talking to you. Let me leave you to enjoy your break." She thanked Josefina and headed out of the bistro.

Hurrying back to the show, Olivia hoped she could find Charlotte quickly. Their next job would be an urgent, and most probably risky, mission.

*

After waiting near the entrance for five long, impatient minutes, during which she messaged Charlotte twice and tried to call her three times, Olivia finally saw her friend appear, rushing through the crowds.

"I'm sorry. It was so busy at that stall, it took a while for me to be able to speak to the owner and then he wouldn't stop talking and made me do a full wine tasting. He was very friendly. He has an alibi as he was hosting a Sangiovese Appreciation tutorial in that side room at the time Cadenza was killed. He had a group of twenty guests. He said, in confidence, that he was expecting to get a low mark in the competition this year, as he refused to do the tutorial for free and insisted on payment upfront. He didn't care and was rather amused by it."

Olivia nodded, impressed by how the evidence was coming together.

"Your research confirms what I have just discovered." Proudly, she showed her friend the business card. "These are the show offices where Cadenza worked from. They're right here in Siena and must be nearby. Her assistant said she was disorganized and hated to pay her bills."

Charlotte's eyes lit up. "If that's the case, angry creditors could have come by at the end of the day. Perhaps they asked her for payment and she refused. That could so easily have caused a fight. I think we may have the answer. Right here."

"Well, not here, exactly. There." Olivia pointed to the address on the business card. "There is where the records will be and we can find out who was owed money."

"How far is it? Do we need to get a cab, or can we walk?"

Olivia pulled up a map on her phone and consulted it.

"I think we should get a cab," she said. "It's probably half an hour's walk away."

"We don't have half an hour," Charlotte agreed.

They headed down to the main street, where Olivia was relieved to find a row of taxicabs already waiting to pick up departing show visitors.

Climbing in the closest one, they spent the short ride planning their strategy in low voices.

"What are we going to say to get us inside?" Olivia asked.

"One of us needs to distract whoever is there, and the other one must sneak in," Charlotte decided. "Presumably they'll have a skeleton staff on duty so it should be easy once we're in."

"Ask to use the restroom?"

"Or maybe ask if we can see the show plans. We can say someone at the festival sent us here and we are very keen to exhibit next year," Charlotte said.

"That's a good idea. Both of us go in, and then one creates a distraction," Olivia planned.

"While the other searches."

"We're on track!"

The cab turned a corner and pulled up outside a small, simple-looking yet stylish and scenic stone building. It was sandwiched in between a row of others, with trees outside and a park opposite. Olivia could imagine how pleasant it must be for the assistant to work there every day, organizing a wine festival. What an idyllic life. Although she had a feeling that Cadenza's personality would have thrown a wrench into the works as far as job satisfaction went.

Feeling nervous and expectant, she climbed out of the cab and walked alongside Charlotte to the entrance door.

She raised the knocker and tapped three times.

"The blinds are down," Charlotte said, strolling over to peer through the sash window.

Olivia frowned. Surely somebody would be attending to the show office on the day of the festival? Or were they strictly weekday-only? she wondered, starting to feel panicky. This detour from the festival had wasted precious time, and now they were facing a locked door.

"Probably, the person who was supposed to be here bunked off after they heard what had happened," Charlotte decided. "Perhaps they knew all the shenanigans that had been going on, and decided to get out of Dodge while they could."

"We'll have to go back," Olivia said regretfully.

"We can go in a minute. There's one thing I want to try first." Charlotte rummaged in her purse.

Olivia sighed. Short of climbing through the firmly closed window, she didn't see a way in at all. It would be better to get back. Gloomily, she stared at the road, wondering how soon a cab would pass by.

Then, behind her, she heard the door opening.

Olivia spun around, her heart racing. Someone had been inside after all. Their luck had changed. Now, would their carefully discussed plan succeed?

CHAPTER TWENTY SEVEN

To Olivia's confusion, nobody else was at the door. Only Charlotte, with a satisfied expression on her face as she removed a bent bobby pin from the lock.

"Wait, what?" Olivia exclaimed in shock. "You—you picked that lock?"

Charlotte nodded modestly. "It's nothing, really," she said.

"Nothing? You just picked a lock! You afforded us illegal entry into a place we really need to be. How did you even do it? I thought I knew you. I'm starting to realize I don't know you at all. What other ninja skills do you possess?" Olivia's head was spinning. She needed a reality check. She was beginning to think she needed more coffee.

"I learned how when I was looking for videos for Bagheera to watch, to keep him entertained. You get those bird and mouse videos, they're really cool. I left him with it, but by the time I came back that video was finished and there was a lady showing you how to make a lock pick."

"Go on?" Olivia said, still feeling shocked.

"I got interested, and watched more of them. There were a few really cold days this winter when it wasn't pleasant to go out, and luckily I had a whole pack of bobby pins. It passed the time perfectly. I learned the basics, and from there on I became self-taught. I'm naturally talented too, I believe."

"Well!" Olivia said.

Facing the open doorway, she looked around.

This was technically not at all legal. But, on the other hand, what if the door had just been unlocked all along? She hadn't seen Charlotte do anything!

Olivia told herself she didn't have a choice. If they didn't search this office, a killer might get away with a crime.

Taking a deep breath, and trying not to feel bad about what they were doing, she stepped inside. The hallway was very dark. Olivia closed the door, Charlotte snapped on the light, and they looked around.

There were doors on the left and the right. Straight ahead led to a kitchenette and dining area.

Olivia pushed open the door on the right. Clearly, this was Cadenza's office. It contained a glass-topped desk which looked empty and bare; a bright red leather chair that might have been designed by Ferrari; and shelves lined with pricey-looking objects d'art. A large wine rack along the back wall held an array of noble and distinctive bottles.

Glancing around, Olivia noted an absence of anything vaguely work related, apart from the wine. There wasn't a paper in sight.

"I'm guessing the grunt work is done by someone else, somewhere else," Charlotte agreed, rolling her eyes.

They walked out and pushed open the door on the left.

As Olivia stepped inside, a musty smell rushed out—the smell of hundreds of cardboard files and folders, stacked on metal racks. Clearly, this office with its two scuffed chairs and two cluttered, small desks was where the real work took place.

"Accounts, accounts," Charlotte muttered, prowling around the desks and peering down at the papers that littered them. "It's this side!" She stabbed her finger decisively down.

Olivia hurried to join her. Sure enough, there was a pile of invoices and associated paperwork. Quickly, she leafed through.

"Did she pay anyone?" Olivia asked incredulously. The top four documents were all final demands.

"Doesn't look like it. Lighting, sound, and music, a stack of advertising. And this is a massive invoice."

Olivia stared down in awe at the number of zeros it contained.

"No wonder. It's for all the setup and infrastructure. All the stalls, all the booths, all the furniture. She rehired it out to the exhibitors and never paid the original supplier! Listen.

"Signora, we cannot accept any longer that you are ducking and diving and refusing to pay! Unless we receive payment in full we are going to hand you over to debt collectors and get you blacklisted! You now owe us for two years of service, after promising to pay us on Thursday! I am furious and feel you have tricked me. Settle this immediately or you will be sorry!"

This invoice had been emailed on Friday, Olivia saw from the date at the top of the message. The next day, Cadenza had been killed. Excitement surged inside her. There was every possibility that these creditors had come looking for her. In fact, it was a certainty.

Quickly, she photographed the invoice and the angry, slashing signature of Signor Mose Bellini, the company owner.

"We need to go and speak to Signor Mose. I'm sure he will be at the show," Olivia said. "It's closing time in a couple of hours. He will be taking down all his equipment."

She and Charlotte headed back down the narrow corridor. But, as they neared the entrance, a loud banging froze them in their tracks. Someone was knocking impatiently on the now-unlocked door.

As they skidded to a stop, something even worse happened.

A familiar and authoritative voice called out, "Police! Open up immediately!"

Turning to stare at Charlotte, Olivia saw her horror reflected in her friend's eyes. This was a catastrophe. The timing couldn't have been worse.

"What shall we do?" Charlotte breathed.

"We have to hide. They can't find us here."

"Especially you! You'll be arrested for sure. Let's split up. You take the restroom, I'll go in here," Charlotte whispered, and dived back into the cluttered admin office.

Hyperventilating as a second, louder, knock rattled the door, Olivia ran toward the restroom. Any moment the police would try the door and find it unlocked, thanks to Charlotte's skilled picking.

The tiny restroom was on the right, but it didn't seem like a sensible hiding place. The door wouldn't close fully unless it was locked, and if she turned the lock from Vacant to Occupied she suspected that even the narcissistic Detective Barrazzi would realize there was somebody inside.

She headed past, with her heart jumping in her throat, to the kitchenette they'd glanced at earlier.

This was even worse. There was nowhere to hide. Nowhere! The tiny bar fridge would barely have provided cover for a mouse, and the row of shelves under the counter were packed full of ancient files. Olivia wished she could downsize herself and crawl into the magnificent-looking coffee machine that dominated the counter.

The restroom it would have to be.

She hurtled back and dived inside, shoving her foot against the door to keep it closed, and trying her best not to breathe.

At that moment, the front door crashed open.

"Unlocked," she heard Barrazzi say in disappointed tones. She guessed he'd been looking forward to testing his strength against it.

Perhaps he'd wanted to show off by busting the door open with a wrench of his muscular arm or a well-placed karate kick.

Officious footsteps tramped inside. Definitely more than one set. But she would have known that anyway. Barrazzi hadn't been talking to himself.

"Interesting that it is open," she heard Artoro agree.

Olivia shivered at his words. Her rash decision to enter the building was coming back to bite her now.

Behind them, another man cleared his throat, and Olivia's legs started quivering. Three of them! Three. This small space felt overcrowded and dangerous. There was simply no way the police wouldn't find them. No. Way.

"This must be the organizer's office," she heard Artoro observe.

So they'd all crowded into Cadenza's domain first. She could imagine them staring around, looking perplexed. They wouldn't spend much time in there. There was nothing to see.

"There is nothing to see here," she heard Barrazzi announce, as if he was channeling her. "This woman keeps her office too tidy," he added, in suspicious tones.

Despite her terror, Olivia found herself nodding. She and the well-built inspector agreed on one thing at least.

She glanced at the restroom window. Olivia had been known to squeeze her way out of restroom windows to avoid the police. She had a successful track record in that regard. But this was a tiny sash window. Even a cat would have struggled to get through, and Olivia reluctantly acknowledged she was much bigger than a cat.

She held her breath as she heard the tramping footsteps passing by. Two sets. So one of the officers had stayed behind and was probably checking the admin office. She wondered where Charlotte was hiding, and guessed she'd squirreled herself away under the desk at the back of the room. There was a good chance that they wouldn't find her. After all, they were looking for evidence, not people. That fact gave her a flicker of hope.

"Nobody here. Let us help Artoro comb through the other office for evidence," Barrazzi said, sounding disappointed again.

The two pairs of footsteps headed back the way they had come. Clamping her lips together, Olivia saw dark spots were starting to float across her eyes. Her breath-holding didn't help, because as they passed the door, the footsteps stopped again.

"This must be the restroom. Check it," Barrazzi said in a loud, commanding voice.

The dark spots were replaced by Olivia's entire life flashing across her eyes as she froze, petrified.

This was the end. In a heartbeat the door would be shoved open, the police would discover her, and she'd be carted straight off to prison. Thanks to her suspicious presence in this most embarrassing of locations, she would be instantly arrested.

No way would her visa be approved now, Olivia realized in despair as she watched the handle turn and counted down her last remaining moments of freedom.

CHAPTER TWENTY EIGHT

As the restroom door began to move, pushing Olivia's shaking foot out of the way, Charlotte shrieked loudly from the admin office.

"What on earth are you doing here?"

"There is somebody hiding!" Barrazzi shouted.

He released the handle with a rattle, and the footsteps pounded away from her, running to the office.

Over the drumming sound of her heart, Olivia heard Charlotte cry out. "Oh, it's you. You gave me such a scare. I didn't even hear you come in. I was on the floor behind the desk looking for a—er—looking for a euro coin that fell out of my pocket. It's bad luck to leave money that's been dropped, don't you know?"

"You? You are the friend of the Americano, our main suspect!" Barrazzi announced.

Olivia's stomach plummeted with dread.

She guessed Charlotte must have kept quiet or at best, nodded, as Barrazzi then spoke again.

"Signora, are you here alone?"

That was his first, and Olivia had to admit, relevant question. She felt a surge of gratitude as Charlotte held her nerve, replying in outraged tones, "Alone? Well, I *was* alone until the three of you came trooping in. Now I'm starting to feel this place is way too crowded."

"What were you doing in this office in the first place?" Barrazzi asked in tones of deep suspicion.

"I came to talk to somebody in charge. We want to pre-book for next year," Charlotte said innocently. "Nobody at the show could help. They were all running around like headless chickens. Olivia's still there, trying to sort it out. I decided someone might be here or at least I could pick up a booking form. But all I've found are these unpaid invoices," she added in meaningful tones.

"I do not believe you. I was watching you and your friend today. You were circulating among the show and asking questions. You did not show any intention of pre-booking. Rather, you were speaking to people who were involved with the show, and you were trying to find reasons for them to be guilty of the crime. We spoke to a number of them afterward, and they told us what had occurred."

"It's just morbid curiosity," Charlotte explained, and Olivia could imagine how she'd wave her hand dismissively as she spoke—if the police weren't grasping her wrist, of course. "Morbid curiosity is a thing, don't you know? It's what makes ordinary, innocent people like me desperate to find answers and closure after a terrible event has taken place."

"Or to try and deflect the blame away from the real killer," Barrazzi explained.

Olivia heard her friend's voice change to a low purr.

"You're in really good shape, Officer," she said. Olivia could imagine her undressing Barrazzi with her eyes. "You could give our American police some lessons. About health and wellness, physical strength. They're all obsessed with donuts!"

Barrazzi sighed. In a slightly mollified voice, he continued. "We must bring you into the police station immediately, for further questioning."

"Okay," Charlotte said, sounding eager. "That's no problem. No problem at all. Delighted to assist. Do you have coffee there? Can I choose which of you three rides in the back with me?"

Olivia felt her stomach clench. Despite her friend's cheerful words, she was being taken into police custody. She would end up being rigorously questioned in a spartan interview room if she was lucky. If she wasn't so lucky, they would lock her in a holding cell.

"Oh, Charlotte," she mouthed the words in horror.

The tramp of footsteps receded, accompanied by murmured voices. Olivia couldn't make out the words. A moment later, the front door opened and then slammed shut again.

Finally daring to gasp for air, she waited where she was in case any of them came back, but the offices remained silent.

Olivia was safe. To save her, Charlotte had sacrificed herself.

She'd never intended her friend's vacation to have such a horrific outcome. Selflessly, she'd caused a diversion so that Olivia could remain in hiding.

This unfair arrest could have a dire outcome for her loyal friend. Never mind the stress and trauma, this could result in serious trouble with the law. What if this meant she could never return to Italy again?

The pressure was on. Olivia needed to question Mose Bellini and hopefully prove his guilt.

Ten minutes later, feeling determined, she climbed out of the cab and headed back into the festival hall, showing her tag to the attendant with a smile.

She was just about the only person entering the show. The flood of visitors had dwindled to a mere trickle. Everyone had clearly enjoyed a mellow afternoon of quality wine tasting—assuming they'd managed to avoid sampling Enrico's creations—and they were now heading out. Happy people were smiling and laughing, clutching heavy-looking bags. Presumably, none of them had tasted Nonna's Loving Hands. Olivia thanked her lucky stars she'd been able to avoid it!

Over the background music, the faint sound of clattering and hammering came from various directions. It sounded as if structures outside of the hall itself were already being dismantled. Her suspicions focused sharply. This was where the perpetrator might be, bad-temperedly bashing away at the show's infrastructure.

But where would he be? There seemed to be several teams at work. How would she find this individual when all she had was a furious, scrawled signature above his name?

"Do you know where Signor Mose is?" she asked two men hurrying past, carrying a ladder.

They looked perplexed. The man in front replied, "We have only just arrived, and are working in the back storage room. He is not there."

Well, that ruled out one of the teams, Olivia thought, noting in which direction they headed off. He had to be somewhere else. That left about four banging, crashing hotspots to search, and time was running short if the dismantling was already in progress.

She headed to the closest one, which was the nearby Annex room. Inside, a small team was packing away the tables and chairs.

"*Ciao!*" She greeted the three men with a friendly smile. "Where is Signor Mose?"

Unerringly, one of the crew pointed across the expo floor. "He has just gone over there."

As Olivia headed swiftly in that direction, she realized a disturbing fact. She was heading directly toward the stage area. The louder banging confirmed her fears.

Mose must be managing the breakdown of the very place where the murder had occurred. That was creepy. Goosebumps prickled up and down her spine. This location didn't bode well. What if his violence erupted again?

A piece of red-and-white barrier tape strung across the corridor signaled to her that the area was now cordoned off. Well, it wasn't as if it was actual crime scene tape, Olivia thought, threading herself underneath it.

The banging was now deafening. A posse of hammers and mallets were at work to get this massive structure packed away in record time. Rounding the corner, she met the surprised gazes of five mallet wielders, all working in different areas of the tall stage. Two were perched on stepladders.

In the center, standing with his arms folded and clearly taking a supervisory role, was the man Olivia instinctively knew she was looking for.

Tall, broad, and bulky, the bearded man had a red scarf knotted around his plump neck, and looked to be in a terrible mood, glowering from beneath his dark brows.

His frown intensified as he swiveled between his teams, clearly dissatisfied with the speed they were working, although not quite dissatisfied enough to climb onto a ladder and offer to help.

Rather, he was barking out commands in rapid Italian to his crew.

"Go faster! Grab that corner piece before it falls!" he yelled at one toiling man. Then, swiveling around, he directed his criticism to the other side of the stage.

"What are you doing? Do not just drop those supports! Anything dented cannot be reused. Do you know how expensive aluminum is? Climb down the ladder, you lazy idiot, and place them carefully on the ground!"

Cautiously, Olivia approached him.

"*Buon giorno*," she said in a friendly way, hoping to open this tricky conversation on a good footing.

It was not to be. He swung around and lanced her with a piercing glare.

"No members of the public allowed during breakdown. Leave at once!" he commanded. Clearly, he identified her as a tourist and had switched to strongly accented English.

"Actually, I was hoping to speak to you," Olivia said. "Are you Signor Mose?" she asked, just to confirm before continuing.

"I am," he replied.

Olivia wished she could ease into this with small talk, but what with the pressure of time and the incessant banging, she decided it would be better to get to the point.

"I understand you weren't happy with Cadenza's management of the festival, and that you have unpaid bills owing." She had to raise her voice to be heard. Nobody dared stop hammering for a moment, not even to let her have a conversation.

He glared at her. "Yes. I am very unhappy. Delaying payment in a festival this size is extremely irregular. I was, and am, angry about it. Ridiculously unprofessional." As if needing to vent, he swung around again and jabbed his finger at a luckless crew member teetering on a ladder.

"Hammer carefully! Those bolts can easily be warped. If they are, I will deduct it from your wages." He swiveled back to Olivia again. "That is all? You came to ask me that? Yes, I am unhappy. No, I do not have more time for you. Go away!"

"You must know that Cadenza died yesterday? People are saying she was murdered," Olivia called out.

Mose shrugged expressively. "So be it," he said in a hard voice. "I hope her successor will take invoices more seriously."

Gaping at him in astonishment at his callous words, Olivia couldn't suppress a flare of excitement. This sour and unsympathetic man could easily have lashed out at Cadenza in fury. His lack of human empathy was only intensifying her suspicion.

"Were you at the show yesterday?" Olivia wished everyone would stop hammering. The noise was distracting. It certainly wasn't helping her test this unfriendly man's alibi.

He gestured impatiently at her.

"Was I here? Of course I was here. When you supply equipment to a show, you are wedded to it for the duration. Things go wrong. Bolts shift out of place. People break structures. You have to stand by every minute of the day, ready to repair and replace."

"Did anything need replacing just after the competition results were announced yesterday?"

Mose frowned at her. "That was near the end of the show. I went out to get a bite of food."

"Oh?" There was a perfectly good catering area within the festival. Olivia herself had sat down there. "Where did you go?"

Mose shrugged, looking down. "Outside. I needed to take a break from the show."

"To which bistro?" Olivia pressed further.

"What are you saying?" The clanging had intensified. A stubborn piece of metal was clearly resisting the takedown. Even though Mose had said he couldn't hear her, he was also still not looking directly at her. Was he hiding something?

"TO WHICH BISTRO?" Feeling frustrated, Olivia wondered if real detectives ever had these problems. Most probably, Barrazzi would have ordered everyone to cease hammering. And they would have ceased. All she could do, though, was yell over the racket.

"I DON'T REMEMBER!" Mose shouted back, clearly as frustrated as her.

Well, she wasn't going to give up. This could prove to be a pivotal moment in her investigation. If she pushed through now, it might just trigger a breaking point in her suspect.

Olivia stepped closer to him. She was going to pin him down over this darned bistro. If he really had gone out, he would have remembered which direction. And surely, what he'd eaten! Olivia couldn't imagine not remembering what she'd eaten the day before. She hoped that didn't make her a greedy person. But if food was the critical factor in solving this mystery, so much the better, she decided, facing up to him boldly.

Now, at last, he met her gaze with an angry growl. "Get out of here. This is a construction area."

Deconstruction, actually, but Olivia wasn't going to argue semantics with him.

"Which way did you go?" she pressed.

Clearly, Mose had reached the end of his tether—or perhaps, the limit of his ability to withstand her inexorable pressure.

"Will you get out?" he snarled.

His hand dropped reflexively to his waist, and Olivia stared at him in shock.

Attached to his belt, she saw a large Maglite flashlight. It was big, heavy, and solid. Olivia's eyes widened as he grasped what must be the murder weapon.

"Why are you asking these questions?" he bellowed. "You will stop them, and leave. Now."

He wrenched the Maglite off his belt and brandished the heavy item threateningly at her.

CHAPTER TWENTY NINE

Olivia realized too late she'd gotten herself into a sticky situation. She had to act immediately to save herself. Mose had killed once, and might do so again. Worse still, everyone was hammering so intensely that they might not see or hear him attack.

Perhaps he would explain to the police that a falling piece of equipment had struck her at the wrong time.

Olivia stumbled back as fast as she could, desperate to get out of reach of the lethal weapon. She nearly jumped out of her shoes as she collided with another big, solid person behind her.

"Eeek!" Olivia exclaimed, turning to find Detective Barrazzi, who had clearly just arrived on the scene.

As if by magic, all the hammering stopped. A solid silence descended.

Was he here to arrest her? In panic, Olivia wondered if Charlotte had broken under questioning and confessed how they'd gained access to the show offices.

After a suitable pause, Barrazzi spoke in a loud, confident voice. To Olivia's astonishment, his words were not directed at her.

"I saw how you threatened this signora," he reprimanded Mose.

"What of it?" the contractor blustered.

Barrazzi placed his hands on his hips. "We raided the show offices and saw the unpaid invoices, and the angry letter you wrote. This provides a compelling motive. We are arresting you on suspicion of the crime. Your threats will add to the evidence."

Barrazzi didn't exactly click his fingers, but he might as well have. Two uniformed officers materialized; they must have been waiting in the semi-dismantled wings. They bracketed the astounded contractor, and the next moment, handcuffs clicked around his wrists.

Olivia fought to keep her expression calm, although she was equally stunned by the outcome. She felt dizzy with relief that the evidence had led the police in the right direction at last.

Then Barrazzi turned to her and Olivia found herself feeling nervous all over again.

"Perhaps you will accompany us back to the police headquarters?" Barrazzi invited Olivia.

It didn't sound like a request, but more of a command.

Hesitantly, she followed the group of officers. As they passed through the expo, they caused a sensation. Mose was bellowing in anger.

"Let go of me! This is wrongful! You are arresting an innocent man and keeping me from my work!"

As he crossed the festival floor, his protests became even louder, and panic filled his voice.

"All right, I confess, I did pass by the stage just after the winner announcements. But I left immediately!"

Heads turned in concern as they hustled him by. Olivia kept her head down and trailed a few paces behind. Despite his protests, she was convinced of his guilt, but didn't want anyone to think she was being arrested, too.

By the time they reached the exit gate, Mose had added yet more detail to his impassioned cries.

"Please understand. When I arrived backstage, Signora Cachero was concluding paperwork with the judges. I wanted to speak to her alone! So I went out to get a coffee. Why are you picking on me, and not questioning the other man who was lurking behind the stage entrance when I left?"

Olivia rolled her eyes. Now Mose was fabricating a mystery suspect. That smacked of desperation to her.

Heading outside to the police van, Mose began struggling as well as yelling, but it didn't make an iota of difference. Barrazzi bundled him in the back of the van and the uniformed officers got in alongside him.

Then he opened the passenger door for Olivia.

"We need to take a statement from you. One of the team will do it at the police station while we process this man's arrest," he said.

Olivia climbed in. She hoped that in the confines of the police van, Mose would calm down, because otherwise it was going to be an uncomfortably loud ride. Luckily, once he was out of earshot of the general public, he subsided into an angry silence.

Barrazzi sped to the police station, weaving the van expertly at high speed through the slower traffic. Olivia was surprised by how close the police station was. If she'd known the direction, she could have walked and met him there.

He screeched to a stop in the designated parking area behind the building, which Olivia took a moment to gawk at admiringly before they hustled inside. This was Italy, after all. Even police headquarters were located in old, stone buildings that exuded beauty and grace.

"Go to interview room number one," the detective directed Olivia. He gestured in a harassed way to a half-open door, and then returned his attention to processing his suspect, who had started shouting all over again.

Olivia slipped through the door and found herself in a small, well-lit room that was sparsely furnished with two plain chairs and a small table. She walked around and perched on the chair facing the door, listening anxiously as the yelling outside subsided. Footsteps tramped—some of them. Others stamped and struggled. Then all the noise subsided and, from somewhere, she smelled the fragrant tinge of good coffee.

It wasn't coming her way, though. The uniformed officer appeared in the doorway, carrying a tape recorder and notepad but otherwise disappointingly empty-handed.

He sat down facing her and cleared his throat.

"Signora, please. Can you kindly relate what occurred when you spoke to Signor Mose. You can start with your full name, and your role at the show."

Pleased that her testimony as an honest citizen and show attendee would contribute to this case being solved, Olivia took a deep breath and began.

"Well, my name's Olivia Glass, and I was an exhibitor at Festa del Vino. I also happened to discover the organizer's body. Then I became curious after discovering that certain bills at the festival were unpaid, so I decided to find the contractor and ask him, to satisfy my morbid curiosity about the death."

Taking a leaf from Charlotte's book, Olivia hoped this explanation ticked all the boxes. She surely didn't have to give detail on how she'd discovered all those unpaid bills?

"Continue, signora," the officer said.

"I found Mose with his crew, dismantling the stage. I asked a few innocent questions, but to my surprise he was angry and aggressive. He became unreasonably furious when I asked where he had been at the time the crime was committed. After stating he had left the show, he seemed unable to recall where he had gone. Then he started to threaten me," Olivia elaborated. "He seemed ready to strike me with a Maglite flashlight when fortunately Detective Barrazzi intervened."

She paused to be considerate of the officer, who was struggling to keep up, frowning in concentration as he handwrote his notes.

"Thank you, signora," he said. "Please sign here."

Olivia signed her name to the page.

The officer gave her a stressed smile. "Now we are done. Thank you. You may leave."

He stood up, gathered his equipment together, and rushed out of the interview room. Olivia wondered if his next stop would be the angry Mose, or if Barrazzi was handling that issue.

At any rate, she could now leave—but with a jolt, she remembered Charlotte. Her friend must still be here somewhere.

Olivia felt a pang of concern as she remembered the Italians' casual attitude toward administration. It wasn't a national strong point. If all the detectives were clustered around the enraged Mose, it could well be that poor Charlotte was languishing in a holding cell, alone and forgotten.

She had to find her, Olivia resolved. Otherwise she might end up spending the night locked away! Standing up, she left the interview room, alarmed to see that nobody was at the front desk. It was temporarily unmanned. Where was everyone?

As she stared around, anxiety filling her, Olivia heard the faint sound of voices. She decided it would be best to follow the sound and ask. She was almost sure that the person she heard laughing was Detective Barrazzi. Perhaps he was laughing at Mose's flimsy version of events.

Olivia had been in jail herself in the past. She remembered how stressful it was to be locked away behind steel bars in an uncomfortable cell, anxiously hoping that the police would believe her innocence and let her out. Her poor friend didn't deserve to be treated this way, Olivia thought, feeling determined to get this sorted out as quickly as she could.

She headed down the corridor, past another interview room that was dark and closed. Even so, she peeked inside, just to check, but it was empty. The voices ahead were louder now. She heard Barrazzi laugh again, and the scent of coffee was stronger. Olivia could hear where the sound was emanating from. It was the last door on the right hand side. The coffee smell was confusing. Perhaps this was the break room?

They must have finished processing Mose and snuck off for a coffee before questioning him, Olivia thought, amused. Well, it was time for them to end their break and release her friend.

But, as she approached the door, her mouth fell open in astonishment. She heard *another* laugh she recognized.

With confusion surging inside her, Olivia peeked around the door.

CHAPTER THIRTY

Olivia's astounded gaze rested on Charlotte. She was sitting between the two police detectives, Barrazzi and Artoro, on a comfortable-looking plaid couch in the small but well-furnished room.

A tray of fragrant-smelling coffee steamed in front of them, accompanied by a mostly finished plate of delicious-looking biscotti that were rich with cherries, Olivia noted. Small chunks of chocolate scattered over the plate indicated something even more delicious had been guzzled completely.

Olivia hadn't even been offered a glass of water the time she was taken into police custody! It had been a miserable and fearful few hours that she thought might have scarred her permanently. She'd worried that her poor friend would endure the same. Clearly, she'd not needed to fret for a moment. Here was Charlotte, with drinks and snacks aplenty, being spoiled rotten by these two starry-eyed officers, who'd invited her into their recreation room.

The two detectives were fascinated by something Charlotte was showing them on her phone.

"So comical!" Barrazzi chortled, clapping his hands as he stared at it, and her, admiringly.

"That is epic. Is epic the right word?" Artoro asked, gazing adoringly at Charlotte and looking delighted when she nodded.

"Your English is excellent," she praised.

At that moment, they all noticed Olivia. It was clear from the officers' expressions that she was raining heavily on their parade. Fed-up frowns greeted her and the atmosphere cooled noticeably. Luckily, Charlotte was thrilled. Jumping to her feet, she ran across the carpeted floor and hugged her.

"Olivia! How amazing to see you! I was just showing my new friends that hilarious video of Erba drinking the ice wine from the coffee cup." She turned back to the two men. "Erba is Olivia's goat. She lives on her farm."

"Your goat?" Barrazzi looked at her, now with a trace of warmth. "What an animal. Very funny."

He, too, rose to his feet. Then his walkie-talkie crackled and he seemed to mentally shake himself. In a moment, the stern detective that she was familiar with was back.

"Our suspect has been processed," he told Artoro. "We can go and question him."

Artoro got up from the couch reluctantly.

Barrazzi turned back to Charlotte. "Thank you for your assistance with our investigation, and apologies that we had to question you further. You have been of such help."

"It was wonderful to meet you," Artoro added eagerly.

Charlotte beamed. "It's been fascinating spending time with you. I have so much respect for you guys. Seriously, so much respect. You are absolutely amazing. Amazing, is all I can say. Thank you for all you do to keep this amazing society, and country, safer," she enthused.

"We'd better go," Olivia said, having finally had enough of this sycophancy. Guiding Charlotte gently but firmly out of the door, Olivia had the feeling that if she released her grasp for as much as a moment, Charlotte would dart back to the break room, jump onto the couch, and refuse to leave.

She kept a close eye on her as they headed to the exit. It was only when they were safely out of the building that Olivia allowed herself to relax.

"I can't believe it," she spluttered. "How did you manage to charm them so completely?" She literally didn't know whether to laugh or cry.

"Oh, I didn't really try at all. It happened naturally. I think it might have been due to that wish I made before we climbed up the Torre del Mangia," Charlotte confided.

"You wished—*what*?"

Charlotte sighed. "It was after we saw that rather good-looking carabernieri on his beat. I had his toned form in mind. And I wished that during my brief vacay, I could have a spark of romantic attraction between myself and a handsome detective. And so it proved to be!" She tossed her red hair back in a pleased way.

Olivia felt as if she needed to keep up with current events because her friend was racing ahead.

"Wait a minute. Romance? Not flirtation, but actual romance? Charlotte, are you sure?"

"Of course I'm sure. There was an instant connection between us." Charlotte gave her an enigmatic smile that put Olivia in mind of the *Mona Lisa*.

"But—isn't he a bit of a narcissist?" Olivia had to be honest with her friend. "Good-looking and all, but I'm not certain he's romance material."

Charlotte gave her a pitying glance. "Olivia, I'm not talking about that gym bunny Barrazzi. Give me some credit. I saw him for exactly what he was right away. He only joined us to assert his managerial masculinity." Clearly pleased with her choice of words, she gestured expansively.

"Oh!" Light dawned for Olivia.

"Exactly! Artoro and I had a lovely heart to heart before he arrived. Artoro adores cats. I mean, could it be more perfect? And he's very intelligent and driven. He should really be in charge at the precinct, except the area commissioner is Barrazzi's uncle. Corruption, so sad. But luckily, Barrazzi is moving to Imperia, on the Italian Riviera, this summer. So then Artoro will command the Siena investigation team," Charlotte announced.

As she hustled along next to her friend, Olivia felt lightheaded with shock, and also hope. Imagine if this connection went further, and her friend found reasons to spend more time in Italy? How amazing would that be?

"It seems that our walk up the tower worked out well," she said.

"So far, so good," Charlotte said with a meaningful wink. "By the way, where are we going?"

"Back to the show. It's an easy walk. And then I guess we can head home, because a suspect has been arrested. The angry unpaid-invoice man, Mose, is in custody now."

"Barrazzi and Artoro told me all about how that went down," Charlotte said. "It was so brave of you to confront him."

"I didn't know he'd threaten me with an actual weapon," Olivia admitted. "He seemed like a violent person, though. He caused a big scene when he was arrested."

"Oh, yes," Charlotte said. "Artoro and I heard him being taken through to the holding cell,. He was yelling out a whole story. He shouted that he was innocent, that he'd gone looking for Cadenza but he'd left before speaking to her. He was screaming out that they must arrest the wild-looking stranger with frizzy hair who'd been hiding near the stage entrance."

"I'm surprised he didn't start describing Bigfoot," Olivia snorted.

"He did sound impassioned. I actually wondered if his story was true, until I heard he'd threatened you also. Then it all made sense. Of course he went backstage and attacked her."

As they hurried toward the show entrance, Olivia wondered why she felt a clench of panic that they had failed, and were too late. There was no need for her to worry anymore, with Mose now locked away.

But when she walked into the hall, she found herself reviewing Mose's words again, obsessively trying to work out what he'd meant.

Had it all been a creative lie? What if he'd been telling the truth, and somebody had been hiding? With the show about to close, Olivia knew she had only moments left to find out.

"Quick!" she said to Charlotte. "We need to go back to the stage, now!"

"Why?" Charlotte yelped excitedly, but Olivia was already on the run. Thanking her lucky stars that the crowds had thinned out enough for her to be able to sprint, she hurtled toward the stage.

Pounding up the stairs, she rounded the corner and burst into the backstage area.

The structure had been dismantled now. The walls were gone, and only the skeleton of the platform itself remained. Breathing hard, Olivia paced over to the far side of the stage, where Cadenza had fallen. The patter of feet and a loud puffing from behind her told her that Charlotte had caught up.

Olivia stared down at the steel edge of the stage. The white tape that covered it had been peeled away during breakdown. There, in the steel, she could see a small but visible dent. Closing her eyes, she could visualize where Cadenza had lain. Her right temple had rested exactly where the dent was.

There must have been a struggle for her to have fallen so badly. Without any doubt, the fall itself had killed her.

Why the struggle, though?

"What are you thinking?" Charlotte asked anxiously.

"I'm thinking she fell and hit her head. There's the dent to prove it. But why did she fall?"

"Mose could have pushed her," Charlotte theorized.

"Why was the bottle smashed, then?"

"Perhaps she was holding it. If someone had been hiding, wouldn't the judges have seen him?"

"Not if they rushed away in a hurry. Which they both did."

"True."

166

Olivia sighed. "As much as I dislike Mose, what if he was telling the truth, and somebody else really was waiting? The way Cadenza treated people, she must have had a few enemies. And something that Mose shouted stuck in my mind."

"His comment about the crazy man's hair?" Charlotte asked. "That was a strange detail. It made me feel I was missing something, too. I guess the police will get to the bottom of it, though."

"What if it's too late?" Olivia asked, thinking again of how big this festival was, and how many thousands had streamed through the doors. Tracing one person who had mussed hair and a motive for attacking Cadenza would be impossible.

If Mose was released, that meant suspicion would fall back on Olivia again. Even if she wasn't accused, the rumors would persist and could destroy her.

"Mussed hair," she repeated, feeling flustered, as if the answer was lurking just out of reach.

"Mussed hair, and a motive for attacking Cadenza. Look, why don't we go back to my original theories? I agree with you, a rejected lover was pushing it. But I still can't get past the idea that it had something to do with your ice wine. With the bottle being smashed and all," Charlotte insisted.

"There was no reason for anyone to attack Cadenza for my ice wine," Olivia protested. "Everyone who wanted a bottle bought one, even though some paid a steeper price."

Charlotte shook her head. "Not everyone. There were those two customers who came by after you sold out."

Olivia stared at her friend in growing consternation.

Suddenly, she remembered clearly the wild-haired man who had seemed desperate to obtain her wine. She'd sold out as he was asking her about it.

"Where is he?" they said to each other in unison.

Together, they turned and sprinted down the semi-deconstructed corridor, back into the now-echoing hall.

It already looked alarmingly empty. Guests were flocking out of the exit. Even the exhibitors were packing up and leaving. People were queuing at the service gate, ready to commandeer the wheeled carts which seemed to be scarce resources. Nobody wanted to be the last to go. Everyone wanted to head home for a well-earned glass of wine and their Sunday evening dinner.

"Where is he? Where is he?" Olivia shouted as they bustled their way along the emptying aisles.

"Try down this aisle. Shall we go left or right?"

Nerves clenched at Olivia's stomach. Such a small and innocent decision could prove to be a massive disaster if they chose wrong, and in that time he left the show.

"Right," she decided.

More puzzle pieces slotted into place as Olivia replayed the events of yesterday. "I remember his name now. Giacomo."

Turning right had taken them to a dead end. The stall at the bottom of the row was already empty and abandoned.

"Giacomo? That's it. What if he's left already? How can we track him down?" Charlotte gasped, sounding desperate.

"Perhaps we can—oh, look! There he is!"

CHAPTER THIRTY ONE

Olivia skidded to a stop. A moment later, Charlotte collided with her and she staggered forward. Only Charlotte's bear hug stopped her from overbalancing completely. Luckily, Giacomo was so focused on his mission that he didn't notice the minor commotion behind him.

The wild-haired man was standing near the olive oil stall, facing the woman who'd asked Olivia if she could return her ice wine for a refund earlier in the day.

"Please, signora. I must have the ice wine you bought. I need to buy it from you!"

She turned to him, exasperated.

"For the fourth time today, Mr. Giacomo, the answer is no. I do not intend to sell this wine. I am keeping it as an investment after having been assured it will be very valuable one day."

"You're the last person still at the show who has a bottle of it. I HAVE to have this wine." With a crazed look in his eyes, he tugged hard at her arm. Olivia caught her breath as she watched. Giacomo seemed like a man obsessed.

Irritably, the woman wrenched away.

"You're more annoying than a bluebottle fly! Now buzz off," she told him with a dismissive toss of her head.

Giacomo stamped his foot, looking furious. "You will sell it to me! I'll give you back the empty bottle to keep."

"I will not! Get out of my way. I need to buy my olive oil and go home." Now the woman sounded genuinely upset.

Giacomo grabbed hold of her plastic carrier bag and raised his other hand threateningly. He was going to hurt her, Olivia realized, with a thrill of panic. He didn't care who he harmed in his quest to obtain her wine. She had to intervene now.

"Stop!" Olivia shouted. She stepped forward and grasped his wrist, her heart hammering.

Giacomo whirled round and looked at her in astonishment. So did the ice wine woman, who looked even less pleased to see her.

"I told you before, I do not want a refund on my wine," she seethed to Olivia, tugging her bag out of Giacomo's grasp. "I am quite happy with it and no longer want to return it. Will you all stop harassing me?" Her angry glare encompassed Charlotte, Olivia, and Giacomo.

Olivia suddenly recalled her short conversation with Rocco at the start of the show. He'd come around to their stall and been surprised that his "friend" Giacomo was not there. So Giacomo had been supposed to exhibit and then something had gone wrong.

Olivia was certain that this deranged man's circumstances must have motivated his actions.

"You were determined to get your hands on my ice wine. So much so that when you heard I'd given Cadenza a bottle, you immediately headed to the stage, and lurked nearby until you saw she was alone. You tried to take it from her by force, just the same as you're doing now to this poor lady."

"Who made a very wise investment in our wine," Charlotte added loyally.

Olivia continued, feeling breathless, and not liking the look in Giacomo's eyes at all. He seemed unhinged.

"You got into a struggle with her, during which the bottle was smashed, and Cadenza fell and hit her head on the stage, so hard that she left a dent there." Olivia pointed a finger at the appalled-looking man.

The ice wine woman gasped in astonishment. So did the attendant at the olive oil stall, and a few others nearby. Their loud confrontation was starting to attract a crowd. At least that meant there would be witnesses if Giacomo blurted out the truth—but would he?

"I did no such thing. In fact, I don't know what you are talking about," he insisted stubbornly.

Olivia pointed her finger at him accusingly. It was time to bluff, and hope that she could force a confession from this guilty man.

"I thought you would probably lie. Luckily, I have proof. You may not know it, but there was an eyewitness to your struggle and I have this person's name."

Giacomo's jaw dropped in horror.

He seemed about to speak in his defense, but then, abruptly, he turned. He shouldered the ice wine woman aside and pushed his way roughly through the crowd. Breaking into a run, he headed for the exit.

"Stop him!" Olivia called, horrified that he might escape.

"Stop that man!" someone else called.

"Stop him!" the attendant at the olive oil stall called out, sounding stressed.

They all set off in pursuit. Olivia was at the back of the group, and frustrated by how slowly everyone was moving. The olive oil attendant was in the front, and the problem was that she was wearing high heels. Worse still, whenever Giacomo hurtled past people, they gathered curiously in his wake. Everyone following had to push through the onlookers.

Charlotte, however, had a plan.

"After two days here, I know this place inside out," she yelled to Olivia. "I'm taking a shortcut!"

She darted to the left and disappeared down one of the aisles.

Giacomo's lead was rapidly increasing. Where were the police? Olivia thought desperately, before remembering they were probably all cloistered in the interview room with the wrong suspect.

The fleeing man was almost at the exit. But at that moment, Charlotte erupted from a side corridor like a mini-tornado. She hurtled toward him and didn't even slow down as she cannoned into his left side.

It was like watching a game of human bowling, Olivia thought in amazement. Charlotte skidded to a stop, and Giacomo spun off. He sprawled to the floor and rolled wildly before scrambling to his knees and then to his feet. He was breathing heavily.

Finally, Olivia caught up and pushed her way to the front of the group. She was panting almost as hard as Giacomo.

Charlotte dusted off her hands in satisfaction, and went back to the side corridor to fetch her scarf, which had fallen off just before she'd successfully tackled him.

"Why did you attempt to flee?" Olivia asked sternly, deciding to get to the main point of the issue in record time, in case he decided to run again. But now, more curious onlookers were bunched at the exit and she saw to her relief that his way was blocked.

Giacomo realized he was cornered. And, clearly, he'd bought Olivia's story about the witness.

"It is not fair. You beat me to it. I was supposed to be the maker of Tuscany's first ice wine," he explained in agonized tones. "That was the offering I was going to bring to the show this year, after all my sangiovese grapes froze on the vine. But my wine didn't work out! I think the grapes defrosted too soon. When I checked it during winter, I found the wine was sour and undrinkable!"

Olivia couldn't help feeling a flare of sympathy. Ice wine was difficult to make and she was sure it was only because her batch had been so small, and the weather so unseasonably cold on the day she'd harvested, that she'd been successful.

Then her sympathy evaporated as Giacomo continued with a personal attack on her.

"You! How did you get it right, an ignorant and untalented winemaker who is not even local, but a brash Americano? How could this be possible? I had to have a bottle so that I could taste how you had done it. And you would not even sell me one, but selfishly refused!"

"I'd run out," Olivia said, stung by his words. How dare he be so rude?

"I needed your recipe, to see what you had done, so that I could do it better than you next year, and destroy you. I had to get a bottle at any cost, whatever it took. Cadenza refused to give me hers, and laughed insultingly at me, saying I was a loser and a pathetic amateur. I tried to take it from her but she resisted, and the bottle was smashed when she fell. Now I have failed, twice. I cannot reproduce your recipe so I am going to make sure you won't be here next year to take my victory from me!"

Giacomo's face contorted into a snarl, and to Olivia's alarm, he raised his hands so that they looked like claws. His gleaming eyes were fixed on her and the next moment, he charged toward her.

"Help!" Olivia yelled.

He pounded toward her. Pinned in place by the now-screaming crowd, Olivia realized exactly how an antelope felt as it waited for a lion to attack.

CHAPTER THIRTY TWO

Giacomo's angry cries screeched in Olivia's ears. His gaze pierced hers. He was a moment away from reaching her, his clawing hands aiming for her neck.

And then, with a clatter of medium-heeled cowboy boots, the cavalry arrived.

Charging forward from the show entrance, James leaped in front of him. In a startlingly athletic maneuver, he grasped Giacomo's arm, doubled his own body over, and sent Giacomo shooting over his head.

Giacomo landed on his back with a thud and lay there, gasping like a stranded fish.

Olivia stared at James in astonishment. James looked even more surprised than she did. Luckily, he recovered himself quickly.

"I knew taking that beach judo class in Copacabana would pay off," he said, smirking at the crowd and preening as he took in the amazed cries and admiring glances.

"Quick, arrest this man," Olivia squeaked, pointing at the winded Giacomo. Her voice was unsteady thanks to the adrenaline surging inside her. "He publicly confessed to the crime. Arrest him, now!"

There, at last, was show security. A burly man pushed his way into the hall and to Olivia's relief, Detective Barrazzi was hot on his heels. Someone must have called the police when Giacomo started to run.

"Wait! Don't arrest me," Giacomo begged, as Barrazzi and the show security officer grabbed his arms. "Arrest her!" He jerked his head in Olivia's direction. "She committed the real crime, fraudulently making a Tuscan ice wine and robbing me of my livelihood, when she's actually an Americano."

"Shut up and come along," Detective Barrazzi growled. "You can talk when we have processed your arrest. We'll be back to take witness statements shortly. Nobody who saw this incident is to leave the show until then."

As the two men led the struggling vintner away, his cries became fainter. Watching as they left the hall, Olivia felt dizzy with relief when they were out of earshot, and then out of sight. What a nerve-shredding experience that had been. Giacomo had almost gotten away with murder, and had been within a hair's breadth of attacking her.

Someone tapped her on the shoulder and she jumped, still fizzing with adrenaline. Turning, she saw to her surprise it was Fugo.

"I must apologize to you, signora," he announced. "I saw you approach Cadenza yesterday and I drew the wrong conclusions. I gave a damaging testimony to the detective and am sorry I acted in such a passionate way, without thought. I was wrong, and what I said was harmful. I am sorry for my words." He slapped himself upside the head angrily. Behind her, Charlotte giggled.

"It's no problem at all," Olivia said, touched by his genuine apology. "I went wrong along the way, too. Thank you for trying to help."

"I hope we shall see you here next year." Fugo smiled.

"I must apologize for suspecting you, also," someone else said behind him. "Olivia, you made a great ice wine. You will be an asset to our wonderful province's offering."

"It will be nice to see more small wineries like yours included at this show again. After all, boutique vineyards and talented new winemakers are the lifeblood of our industry, and will add interest and character to the festival." These unlikely words were spoken by Helena of Montepulciano Vineyards. Olivia felt astounded by her turnaround. At the start of the festival, she'd been complaining about lowering the tone!

Murmurs of agreement resonated around the crowd and Olivia felt ten feet tall with relief and pride. Thank goodness the right person had been arrested, and that she'd managed to save her name and be accepted by the Siena winemaking fraternity.

"Thank you," she said humbly, before remembering there was an even more important person she needed to thank.

Turning back to James, she found he was very busy. Circulating among the crowd, he was accepting back slaps and handshakes from the admiring winemakers. He had a fistful of business cards in his hand and was distributing them like confetti.

As soon as Olivia was able to get his attention, she smiled gratefully at her ex-boss.

"That was amazing! You saved me, James, and I can't thank you enough."

"It was nothing. You mentioned earlier you were in danger, so when I saw you running, I kept an eye out for you. I'm glad the beach judo class was such a good investment. It was expensive, but hey, I had the money to burn," he said, flexing his skinny arms in satisfaction.

"I was rude to you when we last spoke. I'm sorry about that. I was stressed, and should have taken the time to explain my reasons for refusing your offer," Olivia said.

"Taken the time? Have I taught you nothing about elevator pitches and concise copy? Were your years at JCreative wasted completely?" James asked, raising his eyebrows. "You explained yourself just fine. And, in fact, after mulling over your words, I realized you were right."

"What?" Olivia said, startled. James had never said anything like that to her before.

"You were right. I was trying to superimpose an unsuitable and perhaps redundant business model onto an existing one that works better. You see, during my very productive time at this festival, I was able to tap into the buzzwords that I believe the wine buying market of tomorrow will be seeking."

"What are they?" Olivia asked curiously.

"They are," James counted on his fingers, "authenticity. Locality. Value for money. Boutique. And lastly, organic—or at any rate, produced by the tireless personal toil of healthful vineyard workers with honest perspiration and minimal spraying involved."

With all four fingers and his thumb outstretched, James stared down at his hand, looking pleased.

"Those all sound good, and definitely reflect the spirit of winemaking in the area." Olivia felt pleased to be able to concur.

"Exactly. A spirit that needs to be nourished, just like a grapevine plant. So, with this in mind, I have adopted a new strategy."

"What's that?" Olivia asked, hoping it would be something she could get behind, and which wouldn't trigger another confrontation.

"I am looking for vineyards to invest in. With my resources and newly acquired local wisdom I believe the sky's the limit. I will bow to their time-honored production techniques, while channeling funds to optimize their growth."

A smile spread over Olivia's face. "That's a great idea," she said, with genuine enthusiasm.

"Thanks to my timely use of beach judo, I've been able to do a massive amount of speed networking in the last short while, and already have several hot leads. Take one of my cards. I'll be spending a lot more time in the area now, assessing wineries of all shapes and sizes, and who knows? When you're ready to open to visitors, perhaps I'll even look at investing in yours!"

Shoving a shiny platinum business card into Olivia's hand, James crinkled his face in a conspiratorial wink before rejoining the throng.

"Aren't you glad you're not working for him any longer?" Charlotte muttered into Olivia's ear. She'd been standing nearby and had clearly picked up every word of James's loud and confident voice.

"It's one of the top five items on my 'all-time gratitude' list," Olivia agreed. "But even so, he bravely saved me from a potentially lethal attack. Perhaps he's a better friend than boss. Maybe we should go out for a glass of wine one day, and chat on an equal footing."

The thought of doing that boggled her mind, but this was a day for pushing the boundaries.

Remembering who her wonderful *new* boss was, Olivia guessed that Marcello would still be at the festival, packing up his stall. Seeing she couldn't yet leave the hall, she decided to update him on the good news, so that his mind could be put at rest.

"I'll be back in a few minutes," she told Charlotte.

Rounding the corner, she was pleased to see the Organic Winegrowers' Alliance was still doing business with a trickle of customers. Marcello was standing in the corner, conversing with two men who Olivia saw from their tags were exhibitors. Clearly, he was explaining the value, and challenges, of going organic. His face always lit up when he spoke about his passion.

Luckily the conversation seemed to be wrapping up with handshakes and smiles all round. The men turned away, deep in discussion with each other as they left, and Olivia approached, hoping she could grab Marcello before anyone else came along.

His face lit up even more when he saw her.

"How has your investigation been going?" he asked hopefully.

"I caught the killer at the last possible moment. It was a crazy local vintner who got into a tussle with Cadenza. Over my ice wine, in fact."

With his face alight, Marcello stepped forward and hugged her.

"I cannot tell you how relieved I am. You did not deserve to be caught up in such a terrible situation, or for our Siena winemaking friends to think badly of you for unfair reasons. I have been so worried. Now, I feel thankful that this is behind us and grateful you are safe."

Olivia felt warmed by his kind words.

"Can I buy a bottle of the Castello di Verrazzano rose, please?" she asked. While Marcello rang it up, she confided in him, "I'm looking forward to you returning to La Leggenda. Your mentorship ends next week, doesn't it?"

"Yes and no," Marcello said, smiling wryly.

"What do you mean by that?" Olivia asked.

Marcello sighed. "Our organic alliance has been an unprecedented success. It has opened many more doors. Although my mentorship at Castello di Verrazzano is ending soon, I have had numerous offers of networking and collaboration from places further afield. Top winemakers in France, Chile, even Australia are eager to exchange ideas. So, before very long, I will be traveling again. What we are able to learn now will pave the way for greater success this year. I have been able to accept these opportunities because I know that the winery will be in the very best hands in my absence." He smiled.

So Marcello would be traveling again? It sounded as if he might be away periodically through spring and summer—and whenever he was gone, she would be in charge. Olivia felt stunned to be awarded this responsibility, and humbled by Marcello's wonderful words of praise.

"I've been trying my hardest," she mumbled. Quickly, she stowed the wine in her purse.

"I understand from others at La Leggenda that you have been doing an excellent job," Marcello reassured her.

"Oh!" Jolted by the unexpected compliment, Olivia flushed even redder. She had? Who would have been generous enough to say so? she wondered.

As if reading her mind, Marcello continued.

"Ever since you were put in charge, I have received good feedback from Nadia and Antonio. They have told me things have run smoothly, problems have been handled with thought and care, and our customers have been well looked after. Then, this afternoon, I received another compliment." There was a smile in his voice as he delivered the astounding news. "Gabriella spoke favorably of you."

Olivia was relieved she'd put that wine away, otherwise she'd certainly have dropped it in her utter shock at the words. Gabriella? Speaking well? Of her?

"She called me to say she was still feeling stunned that you credited her for the idea of keeping the bees," Marcello said. "She admitted that you have been a very fair manager. In fact, she laughed as she said she would probably not have been so fair! She said that apart from your habit of getting caught up in murders, she has decided you are not such a bad person to work with after all. And that so far, you've managed to solve the murders, so that probably shouldn't count against you."

Marcello had a chuckle in his voice as he spoke, and Olivia found herself letting out a snort of laughter too at Gabriella's wry, yet honest, admission.

"I'm so glad to hear that. I hope it's a step toward us getting along better." It was strange how upon hearing that positive comment, the specter of Gabriella's unlikeable presence dissolved. Yes, she was passionate, and outspoken, and had her own strong opinions. But maybe she wasn't the awful person that Olivia had come to think she was.

"I hope so, too," Marcello agreed. "You do not realize it, but you have much in common with her. I hope that you two are able to build on what you share, for the benefit of us all."

"Thank you," Olivia said in a heartfelt voice before turning away.

As she headed back to the show entrance where she saw Barrazzi had just arrived, she had a sudden thought. Seeing as how today was proving to be a positive one for mending bridges, she should try to smooth things over with Francesca. After all, the pretty young woman was her beloved boyfriend's favorite niece. With the crime solved, the sooner she could do damage control, the better.

Quickly, she messaged Danilo. *"I have solved the case. The murderer has been arrested. Would you and Francesca like to come around for dinner tomorrow night? I have a lovely bottle of Castello di Verrazzano rosé and I'm in the mood for cooking."*

Less than a minute after she sent the message, her phone buzzed in reply.

"Well done! I am relieved for you and can't wait to hear more," Danilo texted back. *"Francesca and I will be there."*

Olivia took a deep breath.

The deal had been sealed. Now, tomorrow was going to be another make-or-break day.

Could she confront the issues that had arisen between them, and set herself and Francesca on a new path of friendship? she wondered, with a shiver of nerves.

CHAPTER THIRTY THREE

At seven p.m. the following evening, Olivia stood at her front door, watching the blaze of approaching headlights that signaled Danilo's arrival. His pickup swept through the gate. As tires scrunched on gravel, Olivia swallowed down a whole flock of butterflies. This was such an important occasion. Would everything go well? she agonized.

"How many candles on the dining room table, do you think?" Charlotte called. She was putting the finishing touches to the decorations they'd been busy with. The creatively adorned table featured sprigs of rosemary, gold-wrapped Ferrero Rocher chocolates, and silver serviettes.

"How about one on the main table and one on the sideboard?" Olivia called. Her stomach clenched as Danilo climbed out, and tautened even more as Francesca opened the passenger door. At this rate, all the tension was going to give her abs to rival Barrazzi's, Olivia thought, glad she was able to find humor in this nerve-racking moment.

"Done!" Charlotte called.

Olivia watched her two guests walk along the paved path and into the glow of her outside lanterns. She was relieved to see Francesca chatting lightheartedly with Danilo, who was laden down with gifts. He'd bought her a beautiful bunch of flowers, she saw to her delight, and was holding a large carrier bag.

"*Buon giorno*," Olivia greeted them.

"You look gorgeous," Danilo complimented her with a smile. Putting the bag down, he embraced her tightly and kissed her affectionately. Olivia felt her heart speed up in the presence of her romantic boyfriend. She took the bouquet of glorious red and white roses from him, feeling happy and loved.

"Welcome, Francesca. I'm so glad you're here," Olivia said.

They headed inside, where Charlotte was hurrying out of the kitchen.

"Hello, Danilo. Hello, Francesca. Olivia, your goat's out of control. She just tried to climb in through the kitchen window and steal the salad skewers!"

"You have a goat?" Francesca said, sounding enchanted. "I didn't know that. Why didn't you tell me, Danilo? I love goats. Can I meet her?"

"You don't have a choice in that. Here she is," Charlotte said wryly, leading the way into the kitchen, where Erba's orange-and-white face was pressed against the window glass.

"Oh, so cute," Francesca breathed.

Olivia felt encouraged. If Erba proved to be the deciding factor that made the young woman like her better, she would be forever in her goat's debt.

"She enjoys carrots. Would you like to give her some?" Quickly, Olivia rummaged in the fridge and took out a packet of baby carrots, then shook a few into a bowl.

She opened the kitchen door and they watched as Francesca headed outside to meet a frolicking Erba.

It seemed to be love at first sight, Olivia thought, pleased to see how Erba was cutely giving her new friend gentle head-butts, in between staring up at her adoringly.

"Wine?" Charlotte asked, getting the hospitality back on track. The Castello di Verrazzano rosé had been chilling in the fridge. Olivia took it out while Charlotte arranged the glasses.

"This kitchen smells delicious," Danilo said.

"I made chicken cacciatore," Olivia said, lifting the lid to give the pot a stir. Fragrant steam billowed out. She was pleased that the tender chicken pieces, swimming in rich tomato gravy with bell peppers, carrots, olives, mushrooms, and herbs, looked mouthwatering. She was serving the dish with a large bowl of buttery mashed potatoes, already prepared and warming in the oven.

"You have been working hard." Danilo peered hungrily over her shoulder.

"I only got away from La Leggenda after five, so had to rush to finish it. And then I had to submit an additional document for my long-stay visa application. Luckily Charlotte made us the most gorgeous tricolore salad skewers, or we wouldn't be having starters at all."

"Long-stay visa?" Danilo asked, raising his eyebrows.

Olivia nodded proudly. "I submitted the application first thing this morning. Apart from the one document, which was my proof of employment. I had to send that to Marcello to sign as he's still on his mentorship. He had a look through the other documents as well, and assured me that it's all in order, and certain to be approved."

Especially since she was no longer at risk of being arrested, Olivia thought, feeling relieved. Out of the corner of her eye, she saw Francesca had come back inside and was listening curiously.

"That is such good news. How wonderful that you will now have a proper visa instead of just the holiday renewals." Danilo turned to his niece. "We, too, have some good news."

"You do?" Olivia said, wondering what it was. Both of them were smiling like co-conspirators.

"You made the press." Danilo opened up his carrier bag. He took out a bottle of wine, a delicious-looking slab of hazelnut torrone, and a tablet. Excitedly, he powered up the tablet. "Check this out. You are the headline story in today's *Siena News*."

"I am?"

With a flourish, Danilo opened the link.

"The headline reads, 'Italy is My New Home, Says Sensational Newcomer to Festa Del Vino,'" Danilo translated for Charlotte.

"Well, isn't that something!" Charlotte exclaimed.

Feeling breathless with delight, Olivia remembered the speedy interview she'd had with the journalist while at her stall. She'd tried her best to say nice things. How fortunate her efforts had reaped rewards.

"The story talks about Tuscany's first ice wine and what a success it was, and also mentions how your stall supported local schools," Danilo said for Charlotte's benefit, as Olivia read carefully through the Italian text. "It also states at the end, in an editor's note, that you were a great help to the police in identifying the culprit responsible for the organizer's death."

Olivia felt ablaze with happiness. Francesca was beaming at her. Clearly, all her fears about Olivia's commitment to her new country had been put to rest.

"It's a fantastic article," Olivia said. "And it was a profitable show. With the money from sales, I'll be able to buy a lot more vines to plant this coming year. My vineyard will be off to a flying start. But I still have one very serious worry."

She glanced at Francesca and saw the young woman's smile fade.

"What is that, Olivia?" she asked.

"This photo." Sighing, Olivia pointed to the news article. "My hair! I didn't realize how outgrown my roots are. They look terrible. I'm desperate to brighten up my highlights. Would you be able to create me a lovely blond color? I'll pay, of course," Olivia added hurriedly.

Francesca's eyebrows shot up. "Blond?" she said, as if someone had offered her an all-expense-paid, around the world cruise. "I adore doing blond! I was top of my class in our blonding module, and I have just been on a balayage course. I would love to do your hair."

As if already taking ownership of her tresses, she stepped over to Olivia and peered consideringly at her roots. "Hmmm," she said in a thoughtful voice, and Olivia could see she was making mental notes. "What do you like your blond tone to be? Are you a lover of platinum? It seems so from what I see here."

"In the past, I've been really into platinum and all about the cooler shades, but recently I've been looking at the multi-tonal blonds and wondering if I should try something more adventurous," Olivia admitted.

"Yes, I think that would work well for you, and it is very on trend. Multi-tonal will look stunning with your skin tone," Francesca agreed.

Olivia had asked for a hairdo to show good faith but she now felt genuinely excited at getting a new blond look from someone who was the class champion and clearly very knowledgeable. Francesca was beaming in excitement, all her misgivings clearly put to rest. And Danilo looked as happy as could be, to see his favorite niece and his girlfriend finally getting along.

"Come on, let's sit down in the dining room," Charlotte encouraged. "It's getting chilly, and there's a fire burning in the family room. We've set out grissini and dips to snack on before we have our salad skewers."

She ushered everyone through to the dining room, where Danilo and Francesca exclaimed over the pretty, colorful table decorations. Everyone sat down except Danilo, who wandered over to admire the antique wine bottle. It had been delivered back from the label restorer that day. Olivia had already ordered a special display case, but for now, she had set it in pride of place on the sideboard.

"*Mio Dio*," they have done an excellent job," Danilo praised. "This label is unrecognizable. Or, should I say, recognizable at last."

Olivia laughed. "Recognizable but yet mysterious. I'm not sure what it's supposed to be. I thought when I found the bottle that the three blobs represented grapes, but now I can see they're actually three stars set in a triangle shape, among a whole pattern of lines and dots."

"It looks familiar, somehow," Danilo said, cradling it in his hands to look more closely. Olivia loved how the restorer had made the lines clear. Even though she had no idea what it was, she thought her label looked noble and unique. You could even see the winery name—Terra Toscana Vigneto.

It was exciting to be able to piece together more of her farm's history and to know what its trading name had been more than a century ago. But from the way his expression was intensifying, Olivia realized that Danilo was piecing together more than that.

He grabbed her hand. "Come with me, quickly. Bring the bottle."

The bottle?

Being careful not to drop it in her haste, Olivia grasped the neck of the antique glass firmly before accompanying him to the kitchen.

"Look. Look at this!"

He was pointing to her map. Her framed map on the wall, with that tantalizing square gap in its center.

Except, as Olivia's astonished gazed darted from the map, to the bottle, and back again, she felt her spine constrict with goose bumps.

The square label filled the gap in the center of the map. It filled it perfectly. She could see where every line led from one to the other.

"Oh, my word," Olivia breathed. She put the bottle carefully down and assessed the two again. "This is the missing section. It's been hidden in their wine label. So, all along, these people were hoping that down the line, if someone loved the property and kept their wine, they might piece the clues together."

"Exactly!" Danilo gripped her hand, his eyes shining.

"What an amazing coincidence," Francesca exclaimed. "You will have a real, live treasure hunt on your farm now."

"Do you think the three marks on the map are where different things are hidden, or do you have to triangulate and find a central point?" the ever practical Charlotte asked.

"I don't know. I guess we'll find out. It still won't be easy. The map's very small and the farm's very large, so it will require a lot of digging to find the exact points," Olivia said.

Olivia carried her precious bottle back to the dining room and they all sat down again. Suddenly there was a different atmosphere in her dining room. An excited, hopeful vibe filled the cozy, open-plan space.

"I'm planning to come back to Italy again as soon as I can, to visit a new friend I just made," Charlotte was telling Francesca, with an expressive wink. "I'll be able to help Olivia find whatever's hidden, as I know how busy she gets."

"Where are you going to plant your new vines?" Danilo asked her. "Can I help you? Now is the perfect time. There should not be another frost."

"You're right. I don't just need to plant, but also to plan. I have to decide what to grow, and where to locate it, and think about my vision for the farm's future. I'd love your help," Olivia said.

"You have it." Danilo smiled.

As she dipped her crostini into the delicious tapenade, trying to scoop up as much of it as possible, Olivia felt a surge of happiness. She'd imagined such an occasion, in a vague way, ever since she'd bought the farm. Now here it was, playing out in real life, with her boyfriend by her side and friends old and new around the table.

She felt like the luckiest person in the world.

But then her phone began trilling loudly from the kitchen.

"I'd better take this," she said, thinking of her duties at La Leggenda. She was still in charge, and had to be available at all times. Hopefully the call would be quick, and then she could bring the salad skewers back with her.

Grabbing the phone off the counter without looking, she answered, "*Salve!*"

There was a surprised pause on the other end.

"What? What did you say, sweetheart? Did you just call me Sally?"

Olivia grimaced in consternation as she recognized her mother's distinctive tones. As always, Mrs. Glass's timing was impeccable. She'd called at exactly the moment Olivia couldn't speak to her. Even though, in her email yesterday, Olivia had clearly mentioned she'd be hosting a dinner tonight.

"Hello, Mom," Olivia said resignedly, switching back to English.

"Olivia, we have a crisis here. An absolute crisis!" Her mother's tone dropped dramatically, and Olivia's heart sped up.

"What's happened?" she asked anxiously.

"A couple of hours ago, while I was out on my morning walk, we had an unexpected phone call. From the Italian authorities!" her mother announced.

Olivia froze. The thing she'd most dreaded had happened and they'd actually called. What surprising efficiency.

"Your father took the call. Sweetheart, they were phoning to confirm that we are your next of kin. When Andrew asked why, they said they were busy preparing your year-long visa! Along with Italian residency. Residency?"

"Well, yes," Olivia mumbled. She felt relieved beyond words that her father had taken the call.

"I said to Andrew this has to be a joke. Or some kind of mistake. If I'd answered, I'd have told them so. Unfortunately, Andrew didn't mention their huge error to them. But the authorities have messed up, and you need to fix this urgently."

"No. It's not a mistake." Olivia squared her shoulders. If she could assert herself with her ex-boss and get a clear message across to him, she could and would do the same now with her mother. It was time for her mother to face up to the truth and respect Olivia's decisions, she resolved, feeling determined.

"I am staying in Italy," she said, making sure to speak loudly just in case Francesca heard her over the convivial banter in the dining room. "I have told you before, I'm making a new life here. I have a new career. And now I'm getting a brand new visa to make sure it's all properly legal."

"Well! Well! If that's going to be your decision, your father and I will certainly respect it," her mother said, sounding affronted.

"Yes. It's all very exciting. And now, I really must—" Olivia began.

But her mother steamrollered over her words.

"However," she said firmly, "there is no way I can possibly sleep at night without seeing the place for myself. I have to know where you'll be living for the next year, or maybe longer."

Olivia gaped in horror as her mother continued, in smoothly determined tones. "I'm going to go tomorrow and apply for my first-ever passport. And as soon as I get it, angel—the very minute it's in my hands—I'm going to book a flight and come to visit you!"

NOW AVAILABLE!

AGED FOR MALICE
(A Tuscan Vineyard Cozy Mystery—Book 7)

"Very entertaining. I highly recommend this book to the permanent library of any reader that appreciates a very well written mystery, with some twists and an intelligent plot. You will not be disappointed. Excellent way to spend a cold weekend!" --Books and Movie Reviews, Roberto Mattos (regarding *Murder in the Manor*)

AGED FOR MALICE (A TUSCAN VINEYARD COZY MYSTERY) is book #7 in a charming new cozy mystery series by #1 bestselling author Fiona Grace. The series begins with AGED FOR MURDER (Book #1), a free download with over 200 five-star reviews!

Olivia Glass, 34, turns her back on her life as a high-powered executive in Chicago and relocates to Tuscany, determined to start a new, simpler life—and to grow her own vineyard.

Olivia is stunned when she discovers the treasure map may lead to a historic wine cellar, hidden on her estate, filled with priceless wine. It seems like the stuff of dreams—until a dead body puts her at the center of the high-stakes discovery, and turns her heaven into a hell.

Can she clear her name?

And will the priceless find be hers?

Hilarious, packed with travel, food, wine, twists and turns, romance and her newfound animal friend—and centering around a baffling small-town murder that Olivia must solve—the TUSCAN VINEYARD is an un-putdownable mystery series that will keep you laughing late into the night.

Fiona Grace

Fiona Grace is author of the LACEY DOYLE COZY MYSTERY series, comprising nine books (and counting); of the TUSCAN VINEYARD COZY MYSTERY series, comprising six books (and counting); of the DUBIOUS WITCH COZY MYSTERY series, comprising three books (and counting); of the BEACHFRONT BAKERY COZY MYSTERY series, comprising six books (and counting); and of the CATS AND DOGS COZY MYSTERY series, comprising six books.

Fiona would love to hear from you, so please visit www.fionagraceauthor.com to receive free ebooks, hear the latest news, and stay in touch.

BOOKS BY FIONA GRACE

LACEY DOYLE COZY MYSTERY
MURDER IN THE MANOR (Book#1)
DEATH AND A DOG (Book #2)
CRIME IN THE CAFE (Book #3)
VEXED ON A VISIT (Book #4)
KILLED WITH A KISS (Book #5)
PERISHED BY A PAINTING (Book #6)
SILENCED BY A SPELL (Book #7)
FRAMED BY A FORGERY (Book #8)
CATASTROPHE IN A CLOISTER (Book #9)

TUSCAN VINEYARD COZY MYSTERY
AGED FOR MURDER (Book #1)
AGED FOR DEATH (Book #2)
AGED FOR MAYHEM (Book #3)
AGED FOR SEDUCTION (Book #4)
AGED FOR VENGEANCE (Book #5)
AGED FOR ACRIMONY (Book #6)

DUBIOUS WITCH COZY MYSTERY
SKEPTIC IN SALEM: AN EPISODE OF MURDER (Book #1)
SKEPTIC IN SALEM: AN EPISODE OF CRIME (Book #2)
SKEPTIC IN SALEM: AN EPISODE OF DEATH (Book #3)

BEACHFRONT BAKERY COZY MYSTERY
BEACHFRONT BAKERY: A KILLER CUPCAKE (Book #1)
BEACHFRONT BAKERY: A MURDEROUS MACARON (Book #2)
BEACHFRONT BAKERY: A PERILOUS CAKE POP (Book #3)
BEACHFRONT BAKERY: A DEADLY DANISH (Book #4)
BEACHFRONT BAKERY: A TREACHEROUS TART (Book #5)
BEACHFRONT BAKERY: A CALAMITOUS COOKIE (Book #6)

CATS AND DOGS COZY MYSTERY
A VILLA IN SICILY: OLIVE OIL AND MURDER (Book #1)
A VILLA IN SICILY: FIGS AND A CADAVER (Book #2)
A VILLA IN SICILY: VINO AND DEATH (Book #3)

A VILLA IN SICILY: CAPERS AND CALAMITY (Book #4)
A VILLA IN SICILY: ORANGE GROVES AND VENGEANCE
(Book #5)
A VILLA IN SICILY: CANNOLI AND A CASUALTY (Book #6)

Made in United States
North Haven, CT
26 January 2023

31672444R00117